Adam's Ark

Also by Frances Brand

THORNS
A story set against the horrors
of the 1990s Bosnian conflict

Published in 2018

Adam's Ark

Frances Brand

ISBN: 9781916270824

North Hill Publishing

*For the beautiful valley which I hope
will never be so blighted*

••••

*My thanks again to Howard Waters
who has set aside so much time
to create a cover for Adam's Ark*

*His support, encouragement
and suggestions have been invaluable*

*And to all those friends and critics who
have read the manuscript
and helped with the editing and proof-reading*

Chapter one

All day the child watched rain falling, like fine rods of steel, endless from a leaden sky. Each drop increased the torrent of brown water surging through the village. Now in the dim afternoon she watched, wide-eyed with increasing awe, as the flood rushed past her home. The water dragged tangled tree branches and detritus washed down from the hills and she giggled as a wheelie bin went bobbing by.

Alone in the house with only her toy rabbit Benji for comfort she gaped at a scene of chaos. In the bedroom she lugged her wooden toy box to the window to lean out for a better look. Along the road people struggled against the muddy tide, scrambling into boats or tractors, others waved from windows, calling for help.

She felt the first twinge of fear. The flood didn't look that deep but the panic unfolding in the street alarmed her. The rain still fell with menacing determination. It hadn't bothered her, not at first. But the water had risen fast while she waited for her grandmother. But granny hadn't come.

She tried calling but the phone rang unanswered. Then she tried her mother, without much hope -- she'd be in a meeting. TV distracted her but when she looked out again from the kitchen water had crept under the fence at the end of the garden. Next time she checked it stretched half way across the lawn and the seat of her swing was submerged.

The first trickle seeping under the back door brought a shock of fear and she shivered. She'd never been alone so long but when her mother left in a hurry that morning, it hadn't worried her. 'Granny will be here any minute,' she'd said.

But she wasn't. When she looked outside again the water at the front was much deeper and she saw people floundering chest-high in the swirling water. They were all leaving.

She didn't know what to do. She was only seven.

Downstairs the flood had breached the front door and covered the ground floor. She stared at the rising water lapping at the bottom stair.

She ran back to her window and saw a big tractor with a trailer full of people. She opened the window wider and waved to attract them but it was too late. The tractor passed and intent on their own escape nobody heard or saw her. Tears welled up as panic took hold and when another tractor appeared she dashed downstairs into water up to her chest. The full force of a great surge of water rushed over her when she opened the door and she fell under the dirty brown tide, filling her mouth and nose. Choking, she struggled to her feet and through the open door. She made it to the gate and scrambled onto the wall, still above the flood.

But her frantic eyes saw only the rear of the tractor and the waves in its wake. She was too late.

At this level the real menace of the water terrified her. Icy water chilled her feet where she stood on the wall and she realised with sudden horror that this vicious torrent would kill her. Her eyes focused on what seemed to be a sodden fluffy rug in the stream, someone's sheepskin rug. But the tumbling water rolled it over and she screamed when she saw black hooves and a head. She watched the drowned sheep carried away and shuddered as she pictured her own small body dragged under.

Soaked to the skin, the rain running with tears down her face she searched in despair for any sign of rescue. There was nothing, nothing but water everywhere -- no gardens, no road, no pavement.

And now the water was at her knees.

'Can't stay here,' she said out loud, looking back at the house and the open door. It was the only way for her but the thought of wading through the flood made her hesitate.

Staring again at the water she saw something else. Swirling along close to the wall, the torrent brought what seemed at first like one of the mannequins in shop windows, a giant doll, its limbs loosely tossed. But the tide flipped it over beside her and she screamed at the staring eyes, wide to the pitiless rain. For an instant the eyes met hers as if there was life lingering, then the head rolled again into the water. A teenage girl, dark hair plastered in wet strands across the face.

The reality of this horror snapped her into action and she forced herself back up the stairs to safety. She found her phone and called emergency but the automated voice said: 'Please hold' -- and the dialling carried on. She threw down the phone and forced her cold fingers to work on changing into dry clothes.

Wrapped in a quilt she considered the desolation outside. Her mother had impressed on her the need to be positive so she concentrated on shutting out the desperate thoughts of what might happen and focused on survival. Her only chance would be if rescuers came back to search for anyone left behind. She needed a signal. She pulled a sheet from the bed and hung it from the window, the rain whipping it flat against the wall. Then drawing the quilt over her head and hugging Benji close she settled down to wait.

Five miles away Adam Woolton watched the water coursing down the kitchen window. Banks of grey cloud and driving rain obliterated the view. The persistent onslaught fascinated him, pouring down day after day, starting to change their lives.

Turning his back on the weather he went upstairs to finish updating his blog.

It's still raining. It hasn't stopped in four days and then it was only for about three hours. I haven't bothered writing much as there's nothing to say that I didn't say the last time. It's so miserable, this incessant grey. It's not like summer at all. Summer's vanished. Outside it's filthy, with slush and muck everywhere and every time we go out we tread the dirt inside on our boots. The bloody mud has a life of its own, it gets everywhere on clothes and carpets. And it's so cold. That's the thing with stone, cool in summer and warm in winter but with this seeping damp it holds the cold and the whole house is chilled through. It seems to be in every room.

The cloud cover makes darkness come early and with no sun the house is always gloomy. The whole world has turned grey. And now they're saying the floods are worse, out of control. The main road is blocked in the valley and we have to go the long way round to get out.

Of course that was the thing when we found this place, it ticked a box in my head -- as a safe place to be. I can't say it was a conscious decision but I remember thinking at least we wouldn't get flooded.

The increased drumming of the downpour drew him back to the window. Forehead against the pane he felt the cold bite into his skin and his fair curly hair grew damp from condensation. He peered at the rivulets streaming down the glass and skewed his chin to watch water pouring over the sill to hit the flagstones below. All the while heavy, steady rain fell from a leaden sky.

He couldn't help it. Staring at the runneled glass, whatever he was doing he couldn't stop himself from glancing up constantly to watch the falling rain.

'Adam, are you coming down?' It was Sally. 'John and Eve are here. They've walked over.'

In the kitchen his friends stood by the Aga, each on one bare foot as they held the other against the casing. Eve leaned forward for Sally to towel her hair, as their wet socks steamed on the top. He smiled at the scene. 'It was brave to come on foot.'

John nodded: 'It seemed to be easing a bit, it had almost stopped, so we thought we'd walk. Anyway the car needs charging.'

'Sorry we're so early. We nearly didn't come,' mumbled Eve through the towel. 'But we thought we might as well all be miserable together. At least we can have a drink.'

In the porch their wet coats dripped in puddles on the tiles and mud slid from their boots.

Sally eyed the mess and sighed. 'I'll get on with supper,' she said. 'We might as well have it early as there's nothing else to do. Here,' she passed a bottle to Adam, 'get that open.'

She bustled about the kitchen, trying to keep the conversation going as she worked while they wondered where she found her energy. Despite their gloomy faces she showed her usual zest for life.

But her generous smile belied a steely determination which sometimes led to conflict. She and Adam often agreed to differ but on the fundamentals they thought the same way. She'd run a busy office before the children arrived and had a strong urge for control.

'Can I do anything?' Eve asked, feeling guilty.

'It's fine. I'll shout if I need you.' Sally preferred to do it herself, sometimes impatient with the efforts of others.

The pall of cloud which made the interior of the house appear dismal at the best of times plunged it into near-darkness by seven. She moved three candles from the windowsill to the table andAdam struck a match.

'I love candlelight,' said Eve. 'It softens things.'

'What, the harsh realities?' said Adam.

'It's such a gentle light,' John said in his quiet voice.

'Mmm, and handy in a power cut, ' Adam was realistic.

'Are you worried about the electricity?' John said. 'D'you think we might lose it?'

'Don't you?'

'Not yet surely, it's not that bad.'

Adam shrugged. 'Have some wine.'

Candlelight imbued the old farmhouse kitchen with a comforting glow, with shadows dark below the beams and in the corners. On one wall, retained as bare sandstone, a glistening diagonal trail caught their attention.

'What's that?'

'I'm afraid it's a slime trail, snail or slug, snail probably.'

Eve's wrinkled her face in disgust: 'How horrible.'

'Can't keep them out,' said Adam. 'They're everywhere this year.'

Sally half laughed. 'It's their sort of weather and you learn to live with them.'

The Kerrs were the only close friends they'd made since coming to Down Farm. They got on well enough with their other neighbours but he kept them at arm's length. He'd bought the isolated holding to be king of his own castle. It seemed meant to be and they both loved it from the start -- remote and a long way from urban life.

When John and Eve bought a rundown cottage on the other side of the hill the men ran into each other, almost literally, on the road. Something clicked and when they met again he invited them over.

Three miles across the wavering length of Rueberry Down was just far enough for Adam's comfort and the four of them discovered a shared love of privacy and came to rely on each other in a crisis. A few years the younger, Adam helped John with the ongoing renovation of the cottage. It was a big undertaking and when the rain began to fall in earnest the place had only half a roof in place. The Kerrs had no children but John had forged a strong bond with their young sons Tom and Ben. Especially Tom who took to him at once as a welcome change from his often over-serious father. He soon became their 'Uncle John'.

John was easy to like. Adam thought he must've been a good teacher till frustration made him quit. He said the increasing bureaucracy had made life impossible. He was reticent about his career but Adam reflected that most people had something to hide. He had his own no-go areas.

Soft spoken and apparently tranquil he was a sharp contrast to his wife. Eve's nursing background made her frank in her opinions which she voiced readily, asked for or not. She was the bread winner, working shifts at the region's hospital. John was free-lancing, though it wasn't clear at what.

Weekend suppers turned into routine, at least once a month, at one house or the other. Usually at ease together now they found it hard to talk, always reverting to the same subject, the rain, the endless rain.

When it first began to rain more than usual it was a joke, the British weather could do its worst but they would all be safe on the hill. This was something different .

In early June it had been hot, unbearably hot, up at 39 degrees for a few days, parched fields and gardens aching for rain. Then came three days of heavy mist, like February, hanging dank and still on the land, shutting down the light and blocking the ultra violet they needed for the solar panels. The constant rain imposed a cloak of grey over everything so that the view of the valley lost all definition as if permanently out of focus. The grey hills met the menacing grey of the water. It was as if nature paused and held her breath. Not the slightest wisp of wind stirred to chase away the mist draping the heavy leaves of summer with clagging dampness.

It was a waiting time, so still -- and people spoke in quiet voices, conscious of impending crisis. On the second evening Adam said to Sally: 'It must be like this before an earthquake, this weird quiet.'

'Don't say that,' she said. 'This stillness is eerie, it reminds me of the virus year.'

'Which one?'

'The first, the Chinese virus, do you remember? It was spring, coming up to Easter when they brought in the first lockdown, the weather was wonderful but very dry and the valley was so still.'

'Yes,' he said thoughtfully. 'I remember it clearly and I couldn't believe what was happening out there. And there wasn't even a breath of wind.'

'It was before we did the garden and I sat on a pile of stones enjoying the sun.'

He smiled at her. 'It was a lovely spring, a relief after that dreadful winter with those terrible floods. But we talked about April showers, or lack of them, another change in the climate.'

'Yes and the cuckoos came earlier too.'

'There'd been all that talk of spending huge sums on flood defences?'

'Yes, big talk.'

'And that's as far as it went,' he said ruefully. 'God knows what's coming now, the heat wave was weird but this fog is worse, like we're in for something.'

They were. In the night the rain came, unremitting for ten days. Not gentle life-giving, crop-growing showers but a torrential lashing downpour that washed away soil and flattened hay grass and standing corn and turned fields and hillsides into mud. Mud that slid away and left bare rock and brought down trees which blocked roads like dams with flood water held up behind them.

For years, the words climate change were tossed about. Adam grew up hearing scientists and pundits argue about the weather. Was it changing due to human activity, or just repeating the cyclical variations over millennia?

As he understood more he came to believe that humanity had made a difference and the earth, the poor abused earth, was getting warmer. The warmth meant more rain with wetter summers and long wet months in the winter instead of ice and snow.

From his twenties, on duty tours with the Army Reserve he recalled hot places being extra hot and increased flooding at home. Accusations of government and planning mismanagement dominated news headlines. Year by year it was worse, thousands of homes were flooded and people began to realise the weather meant business. The words climate change took on a new significance.

Things began to go get worse in the early years of the century, when it became impossible to ignore the fact that the earth was getting warmer. The oceans rose stealthily year by year, terrible fires engulfed the landscape in the world's hotter climates but the quickening melt of the massive Thwaites glacier in the Antarctic really put the issue into overdrive. Rightfully nick-named the doomsday glacier its store of water threatened to en-gulf some of the world's major cities.

The experts said it was a taste of things to come. But the weather improved and attention switched to the series of pan-demics which wreaked havoc with world economics. Billions were spent on fighting a new enemy and baling out the popula-tion. The water menace and the promised cash for flood defences were forgotten. Until now, when this interminable deluge fell from the sky as if it would never stop.

Eve stared at her glass, glinting ruby in the candle glow, and asked: 'Anyone seen a forecast today? I noticed your barometer is nearly off the bottom.'

She'd stood in the hall admiring the fine carving on the ele-gant oak neck and antique gold lettering with capitals inset with red.

Adam smiled. 'Yes, it's been stuck on stormy for weeks. Old technology but it works. It tells it like it is.'

'Must be worth a fair bit,' John said.

'Probably, it was my grandfather's, beautifully made. I love it.'

'Nobody's allowed to touch it, except him,' Sally broke in. 'He taps it every morning though it hardly moves.'

'The met charts don't change, ' John said. 'I watched earlier, just a massive depression over the Atlantic, covering everywhere except the north of Scotland.'

'I can't remember rain as heavy as this for so long. Listen to it.'

They listened. The repetitive drumming and the sound of dripping were now part of daily life. That and water creeping in as it found weak spots and the louder threatening noise of wind whipping rain almost horizontal against the windows.

Just then the boys came in from feeding the ponies followed by Polly, the gentle black labrador, dripping on the kitchen tiles.

'Get a towel on her quick,' Sally shouted, too late. The dog shook herself, showering the room with muddy water which reached them at the table. Adam swore but they managed to laugh.

Ben hurried to the table. 'Dad, it's scary out there, looks like the water's rising fast.'

'I'll look later when we've finished eating. You two need to have yours.'

'At least it's warm in here,' Eve said, moving to press her bottom against the Aga. 'It's cosy when it's so awful outside.'

Sally nodded: 'We'd really miss the Aga, a cold kitchen and nothing to cook on.'

'I thought you'd got that sorted,' John looked surprised.

Adam grunted: 'Not as much as we hoped, the solar's no good without UV. We're hardly pulling in any power at all. If the mains goes we're stuffed.'

Always the optimist, John tried to make light of it. 'That's a blow,' he said. 'We were planning to move in with you if it gets worse.'

He was joking but Adam said: 'Good idea. They are starting to move people already.'

Eve laughed nervously, not sure if he meant it. She felt warm for the first time since they arrived. 'I reckon you'd soon be fed up with us. Do you really think it's that bad?'

He shrugged. 'Hard to say.'

Sally said: 'We'll manage somehow. We've got plenty of firewood and the camping gear with spare gas.'

'That won't last long,' said Adam.

'What?' John saw frustration in his friend's face.

'We keep saying we'll get a generator.'

'But he hasn't got round to it,' Tom interrupted.

'Quiet you.' Adam took a playful swipe at his son who dodged away.

'Pity,' said John. 'But you'd still need fuel to run it and as the way things are you wouldn't get it.'

Sally found another bottle in the cupboard and handed it to Adam. 'Open this and cheer up a bit. You two had better stay tonight,' she grinned. 'Start practising.' She enjoyed their company and Eve was a good sounding board especially when she disagreed with her husband.

'Thanks Sal. I don't fancy walking back, specially after dark.'

'No, stay put. You know you're welcome.'

'I'll get the coffee,' Adam said, filling the kettle. Glancing at the window he ran his finger through the condensation on the glass, looking for streaming water. The glass was still. He went outside and held up his hands. They were dry. The rain had stopped.

Walking further into the garden he looked to the sky. Away in the west, behind the crest of Ashes Raise a single shaft of sunlight probed the cloud cover. The dark cumulus had gone and in its place were tumbles of grey and softer white. As he watched the now forgiving sky the curtain parted enough to offer a thread of blue.

He hurried inside: 'It's stopped. There's a patch of blue sky. Come and see.'

Ben and Tom led the rush, eager for fresh air. Gazing at the hill they held their breath as suddenly the evening sun broke free and shone its triumphant warmth on the scene.

The sunlight grew stronger and as if one impulse struck them all, they ran to the terrace. The view was nearly five miles along under the Edge and the other way to the rocky peaks of the hills behind. They sat there on sunny evenings, drinking rose wine, to talk and admire that view. Now they gazed in awe at a changed landscape.

Meadows and ripening corn, hedgerows and roads had vanished into a long shimmering lake, dotted with roofs and trees half submerged. The sun glittered on the flood, serene and still after the rain. But the sound of water dominated – water on the move, rushing downhill, seeking the easiest route to join and deepen the flood. Every insignificant ditch and brook had over-flowed and turned the usually gentle streams and a steady river into raging torrents. The lane outside was awash.

Down at the head of the drowned valley the church stood alone on its hillock, water lapping around the ancient stone. The tower looked defiant, its copper weathervane catching the sun. But the surrounding graveyard was gone, its aged, chiselled tombs and moss-marked headstones swallowed up.

'That's some lake,' whispered Ben. 'You won't be singing in there for a while, Tom.' His brother had recently joined the church choir.

'Oh God,' breathed Eve. 'It's awful.'

She'd had doubts about buying a cottage so far from town and the rain worried her more than she let John know. She glanced at him and he read her thought. He drew her to him saying: 'Our old place would be flooded now. Don't worry, we'll be okay.'

Tom looked at them all, with real fear in his face. 'This rain's not natural, it's climate change, got to be, what we get for ignoring it for so long.'

They all turned to look at him. His anguished eyes showing clearly what they all felt.

'I'm afraid you're right, the rain's so menacing,' John said.

'All my life they've argued and done nothing!'

'All your life, you're only fourteen,' Sally said.

'What does that matter? I'm old enough to know what we've done.'

Ben bit his lip as he listened to his brother. 'We'll be all right up here, Dad, won't we?'

'Should be -- but we're stranded till it goes and that could take a long time.'

'The land's saturated, the water's got nowhere to go,' John mused.

'It won't reach us, will it?' Ben asked.

'If it does there's not much chance for everyone else.' Adam studied the drowned valley. 'I've a bad feeling we're going to end up with company we don't want.'

Tom was watching the water and pointed out a rowing boat making its way between two houses. He ran inside for binoculars and through them they saw a motorboat on what should be the main road, its wake washing more water into homes. A helicopter appeared over the village and began to hover and lift people from rooftops.

'The water down there must be up to the second floor,' Adam said, sighing. 'We should do something to help.'

John checked his watch -- gone eight o'clock. 'Less than two hours daylight left.'

With a sudden vision of what lay ahead, Adam knew what he had to do.

'We'd better go see what we can do,' he said in a quiet, miserable voice.

'We'll come with you,' said Tom.

'You won't. There's real danger down there and we don't need you to worry about as well .'

'Call Ron Hutchins,' urged John. 'He'll know what's happening.'

The number rang busy but at last the parish clerk's voice barked: 'Unless it's urgent, piss off.'

Abrupt and intolerant maybe but Ron was the man for a crisis.

'It's Adam Woolton. What can we do?'

'Can you take people in up there?'

He hesitated, hating the thought of strangers in his home but said: 'I suppose so.'

'Good. We were using the village hall but the water's round it already.'

Adam thought quickly: 'We'll ring the Beasleys and Mike Clayton, they'll take some.'

'Do that. Can you pick up from Bankside Bottom?'

'Will do.' He put the phone down. 'John, ring them while I get the truck. Tell them to get to Bankside Bottom with a tractor and trailer. They'll have to back down, they can't turn -- the road'll run into the flood.'

Chapter two

Bankside Bottom was only a dot on the map, a handful of homes, including a converted chapel, where the road began to climb more steeply. Below it the tarmac disappeared into water. As they arrived in the Land Rover with the trailer behind, the rain began again.

A drizzle at first but then the darkening sky threw a heavy drenching downpour over the huddle of miserable souls waiting in the open. With the rain the wind rose to turn the drops to icy shafts. In silence they watched another boat load of frightened, cold people scramble out onto the wet road and a tractor behind carried more.

Adam whispered in something like panic: 'Look at them. What are we going to do with them?'

John said nothing but shook his head in disbelief, then he murmured: 'I never thought it would get this high up the hillside. I've never seen anything like it.'

'It's an island and we're stuck on it,' Adam said, realisation bringing fear for the first time. The two friends watched, unsure what to do or where to begin. Near the water's edge a lone policeman shouted something as he struggled to deal with the crowd around him, demanding answers to so many questions. Adam couldn't hear through the rain and moved closer.

'I think he's asking for volunteers to go in the boat, not sure.' He got to the constable and shouted: 'What d'you need?'

'There's still people stranded. We need someone to go back with the boat. The wind's too strong now, it needs two men.'

'I'll go,' Adam said without thinking.

'I'll come too,' John said.

'No John, he only needs one of us. You start getting some of this lot back to our place.'

'But Adam ---'

'One of us needs to be up there with the girls. They shouldn't be alone with all this. Best if we don't both go -- just in case.'

'But Adam --'

'Please John, I'll go. I'll be all right -- and I'm taller than you -- and this was what they trained me for.'

He climbed into the boat, nodding to the skipper who just said: 'Well done, mate. I'm Ian'

'Adam.'

He looked back at John, miserable at the water's edge, frustration in his face as he turned to gather people to fill the trailer. Clenching his hands on the sides of the boat Adam steadied himself against the thrust as the craft surged through the flood, rearing up to balance the heavy weight of the outboard motor. At water level he saw at close quarters the debris flung around by the wind-whipped current, including tree branches and chunks of metal, some large enough to threaten the boat. A loud thud made him turn to see a dead calf tossed aside in the foaming wake, large, soft brown eyes glazed open.

Seconds later the sleek tan body of a small dog swept by, its rib cage starkly obtrusive. A plastic dustbin hit the boat and then a sheep carcass rushed at them.

Stunned by the sheer force and speed of the water Adam stopped looking at what went by, afraid of what he might see.

'Why's the current so strong?' he shouted.

Ian bawled: 'This wind and the volume of water off the hills.'

The boat cut through the torrent, waves streaming from its bow and overhead he caught the growl of a helicopter and he shouted: 'Chopper up there.'

'They won't manage in this wind. Too dangerous, it's down to us and the other boat.'

With the cloud-darkened daylight fading fast Adam feared their journey would be useless. He peered ahead through the

16

driving rain and wind and wondered how they would find any-one in these conditions. But in the inundated village streets lights burned in some of the houses and Ian switched on the boat's powerful spotlight. Cutting back the engine he cruised up one road and down another, searching for signs of life. It seemed weird to be moving between the houses with the water now higher than the ground floor windows.

'You watch to the right, I'll look left,' said Ian and Adam gazed intently at each house they passed. He heard a shout and felt the boat lurch to the side as they steered towards a large corner house. Two women and a teenage boy waved frantically from a window, faces alight with relief as the boat headed towards them.

'Are we glad to see you!' said the younger woman as Ian ma-noeuvred the rocking boat against the wall. Gauging the distance between the window and the boat, she pulled back. 'D'you think you can do it, mum?' The other woman stepped back into the room, fear sharp in her face.

'You have to do it,' Adam said. 'There's no other way.'

'We thought we'd be all right, just waiting till it goes down. Didn't think it -- '

'Forget it,' Ian said. 'We've got to move. Come on you,' he urged the teenager.

'Best way is get over the sill backwards and let yourself down into the boat. Adam will steady you.'

The boy hesitated but Adam said: 'Come on, you can do it.'

Ian struggled to keep the craft steady in position as the boy managed to move his legs over and get a grip on the sill. He glanced down: 'It's not far, mum. It's okay.' He let go and dropped the few feet. The boat rocked wildly as he landed but Adam grabbed him. 'Sit there. Don't move'

'Now you,' Adam held up his arms to the mother perched on the edge but she was paralysed with fear.

'Mum, you've got to do it!' urged her daughter and from the boat the boy said again: 'It's not far mum. You'll be fine.'

Her legs dangled over the sill but she couldn't make the move to turn. Ian said: 'We can't wait much longer.'

'Hold the boat steady, Ian,' Adam said, holding up his arms again. 'Push her!' he shouted, pulling the legs. The heavy woman screamed and fell into the boat, landing on the wooden seat. She carried on sobbing and moaning as Ian said to the daughter: 'Now you, hurry.'

She did it well and started to calm her mother who seemed unable to stop her dreadful noise.

'Can't you shut her up?' said Ian harshly. 'What's the matter with her?'

'It's grandad,' the boy whispered. 'We had to leave him. Strapped in his wheelchair, in the kitchen. He's very fat, far too heavy.' His pained, guilty eyes met Adam's.

'The stairlift wouldn't work, the motor jammed -- we tried to lift him but it was hopeless. We had to leave him there.'

Through hysterical sobbing the mother broke in: 'He just sat there as the water rose. My dad! We couldn't move him. I watched him drown. There was nothing we could do.'

'You sure he's dead? Shall I go in?' Adam said.

Ian shouted harshly: 'Don't be stupid.'

The woman said between sobs. 'He's down in the water -- there's no way he's alive.'

Ian turned the boat away and Adam stared back at the house as they moved off.

Down another road and an old man in another window with a little sandy dog wrapped in a blanket.

'I won't leave him,' he said as they angled towards him. Ian nodded.

Dropping the yelping bundle into Adam's arms he scrambled into the boat with a nimbleness that surprised them. 'There's been several drowned dogs gone by,' he said.

'What's his name?' Adam asked.

'Bertie. I couldn't leave him there alone.'

'Course not.'

'Are there any more people left here?' Ian asked the little group who shook their heads.

'We'll just keep looking then.'

The old man wore an ancient heavy raincoat but the other three had only fleeces. Beneath the torrential rain they huddled together for protection, ice cold penetrating to their skin.

'We'll check every road before we turn back,' Ian said. 'Anyone we miss has had it. We're the last chance.'

The grim words made sense. Adam, though still alert for any sign of life, thought that in darkness with the rain and howling wind and the water still rising there was little hope of finding any more.

'We must go back down the High Street,' he said. 'We turned off at that corner and we haven't done the top end.'

The boat moved quietly through the water, engine ticking over, the spotlight sweeping ahead and round the next corner its bright arc picked out two men clinging to the apex of a garage roof, water lapping at their feet, eyes shut against the dazzling light. Not daring to let go to wave they were shouting as loud as they could and when the boat slid alongside they dropped into it without a word.

'There may be others,' Ian said. 'But we can only take a couple more.'

Trawling through the back lanes and alleys of the village they saw no further sign of life except a cat up a tree. Adam tried to get it, despite Ian's protests but as he grabbed the branches and reached for the animal it sprang higher and stared at his upturned face in terror. He would have climbed up but Ian had had enough. 'Leave it, Adam. It's a cat for God's sake. It'll have to take its chance.'

'Sorry puss,' Adam whispered, hating to leave it.

They turned into High Street and Ian said: 'That's it then. We'll get this lot back to safety.'

The engine roared and the boat moved ahead faster. 'Not too fast, Ian, we haven't done this stretch.' Adam strained his eyes through the darkness either side but there was nothing. Yellow rectangles of light showed in several houses, left on when owners fled in panic. He searched them in vain for human silhouettes. Then his eye caught something as they passed and he looked back, peering through the gloom. Something pale flapped beneath a lighted window.

'Wait!' He shouted. 'We must go back.'

'You sure?'

'No but we must check.'

Ian brought the boat around in a curve, tilting the occupants who grabbed the sides, steering where Adam pointed, maybe twelve yards from the house.

'Looks like a sheet. Could be a signal.'

'Can you see anyone?'

'Nothing -- but the light's on.'

'Left on when they went, like all the others,' said Ian. 'Let's go.'

Adam shouted, loud as he could against the wind: 'Anybody there?'

No answer.

'It's empty, Adam.'

'But the sheet --'

'You want to go close?'

Adam nodded. 'Just got a feeling, you know.'

He watched in admiration as Ian skilfully brought the boat close to the wall, several feet below the open window. They both called again and listening intently he thought he heard a sound, a faint whimper.

'I'm going in. I've got to be sure.'

He jumped for the sill. The action rocked the boat so it banged against the wall bringing cries of fear from the passengers. It was a long stretch but kicking for impetus his arms pulled him up to the sill.

Chest hurting against the wood he looked down on a bundle of quilt and a child's face, half covered. He climbed in and knelt to move the cover, revealing a little girl. She looked so pale for a moment he feared she was dead but a slight movement reassured him. He touched her cheek and found it warm. In a wave of relief he shuddered at the thought they might have missed her.

'There's a little girl here,' he shouted.

The sound of his voice made her stir and she opened her eyes to stare up at him without fear and say: 'Have you come to save me?'

He nodded and she whispered: 'I dreamed I was in the water and I couldn't breathe.'

'It's all right, you're safe now. There's a boat. Will you come with me?'

As he lifted her, a rabbit toy dangling from one hand, she smiled and threw an arm round his neck, clinging on as if she would never let go.

Chapter three

Head bowed against the rain Adam crouched by Ian at the rear of the boat, shielding the shivering child. After those few words in the house she'd said nothing. He tried whispering small words of comfort, asking her name, how long she had waited but nothing brought a response. She cried for a few minutes but the choked sobs ceased and she huddled in silence.

The others in the boat stared at them. 'Do you know her?' he asked but they shook their heads. The cold numbed them all, even Ian despite his oilskins. Every word hurt.

Wet clothing clung to the skin and Adam's arms were rough with goose bumps. Ahead of them the lights and activity at Bankside Bottom beckoned and he saw John and his own Land Rover.

John rushed to the boat as it touched tarmac and steadied his friend as he climbed out, trying to stay balanced with the clinging child.

'Are you okay? Who's this? Shall I take her?' Adam felt her arms tighten their grip and shook his head.

John said again: 'You okay?'

'Cold and wet.'

'What happened? Was it awful?'

Again he shook his head. 'Leave it. Tell you later.'

Surveying the vehicles and groups of people being directed to different farms and houses along the ridge of the down he turned to John. 'Tell me the worst. How many are we stuck with?'

'Not so bad. I think it's twenty-two. I took them all up to yours. Wondered about having some at ours but with the state of the roof Eve said no.'

Adam nodded: 'She's probably right. Are they coping? It must be chaos.'

'Yes. But they're managing and the boys are great. They were all soaked and perishing cold. Poor Sally, she was frantic when I told her where you'd gone.' He looked at the child and the toy nestled in Adam's coat and the arms tight as ever round his neck. He asked again: 'Who is she?'

'Don't know. She was on her own. Tell you later but my neck's killing me. See if you can get her off me. But gently, don't frighten her.'

The child's fingers were locked together but John forced them open. As the grip loosened Adam took the little hands in his and brought them to her lap then held her closer, twisting his neck to ease the discomfort. 'That's better,' he whispered.

Updating this because I can't sleep. Sally's fast asleep but she must be exhausted after organising all these people. It's rough on her -- and Eve -- on all of us really. I don't know how we're going to manage this, it'll be a nightmare and it can only get worse.

Right now the rain has stopped and the sky's cleared. It's moonlight out there -- the moon's almost full but it'll be gone soon -- there's a bank of black cloud coming up. I've been sitting by the window looking at the valley and I'm sure the water level is higher. The moonlight is glistening on the water, wonderful -- so serene but it's hard to imagine the reality of it. I can see the church tower but there's less of it now, which only means the water has risen further.

It was horrible in the boat -- a lot of dead things in the water, sheep, cattle and a dog. I can't get rid of the image of that old man stuck in the wheelchair as the water rose. Horrible.

God knows how many more people may have been trapped like that. And the silly cat, stuck in the tree, it wouldn't let me get it. I could have saved it. I keep thinking of that. Silly really, when you consider the human cost.

I'd no idea how bad it was. Living up here we didn't realise the extent of it. The radio says most of the east and the south is under water. It's unbelievable but they say we've already had more than the total annual rainfall dumped on us. I found a little girl, all alone in the house, very strange. It was pure chance we found her.

No idea who she is and I didn't have time to go looking for paperwork. But I'm sure there was no one else in the house. Certainly not upstairs. I didn't attempt to go down, water was nearly at the landing. If anyone was downstairs they'll be dead -- like the old man.

She hasn't said a word yet, just hangs onto me. She's here in the bedroom near me, with the boys. They've had to give up their rooms for these 'guests'. I call them that -- it seems kinder than refugees or survivors -- though that's what they are.

But I'm not having anyone else in here, not in my own room. You have to draw a line somewhere. That's definite. Some of them are out in the barn and that didn't go down well. The problems will be endless, hope I can stand it.

I bought this place to get some peace and be away from people and now we've been invaded. I'm stuck with it till the powers that be find somewhere to put them. I just hope it doesn't take too long.

Logging off as the room darkened he looked out to see the sky had changed. Clouds had swept back like a curtain to hide the moon and soon the familiar thud of rain began again.

Up early soon after dawn John found himself face to face with a belligerent couple who burst into the kitchen complaining of back pain and itching. Wisps of straw stuck to their clothes.

'There's no toilet or anything out there,' said the husband.

'Well, no,' said John. 'It's a barn and people don't normally sleep in there -- except the boys for fun.' He smiled to soothe their feelings but his goodwill faded as they scowled.

'What are we supposed to do?''

'You'll have to wait. We have three bathrooms and a down-stairs loo but there's a queue.' Then he added, knowing as soon as he said it, that it wouldn't help: 'If you're desperate you could go out behind the barn and find a spot.'

The wife reacted in fury. 'What d'you mean? I can't go and squat in the field like an animal.'

A man lying on the sitting room floor chipped in: 'You might have to love, we're all in the same boat y'know.' He chuckled at his own joke but quickly shut up, daunted by the contempt on the woman's face.

Her husband said: 'Never mind, Rosanna. We'll soon be away from here.'

'It could be a while,' said John, 'the valley's in a bad way.'

'We can't stay.'

'You'll have to, at least until some better arrangements are made.'

'It's unhealthy,' said the petulant Rosanna.

John's polite patience ebbed away: 'You were bloody miser-able when you arrived last night.'

Rosanna sniffed. 'Well, we don't want to be here.'

The exchange brought everyone fully awake and Adam came down to find them waiting for information.

'Where's the kid?' John asked.

'Still sleeping -- best thing for her. I've told the boys not to leave her till she wakes.' He paused, glancing at the guests. 'Have you said anything?'

John shrugged: 'Like what?'

Adam stared around then hurried into the kitchen to find Sally. John followed and closed the door. 'Listen all of you, this thing's much worse than I realised and I doubt if any of those people out there realise what's really happening.'

He took a breath and went on: 'I saw bad things last night, horrible things and heard about worse. It's going to be horren-dous, dreadful before it's finished. But we four, we've got to pre-tend it's all okay. We need to keep it light, play it down. If they know how bad it really is, they'll be much harder to deal with. Do you understand?'

Sally frowned: 'Aren't you a bit over the top? In a crisis like this people are usually pretty good. It tends to bring out the best in people.'

'I haven't your faith, Sal. This is something that's never happened before. I think when they realise the truth we'll have trouble. Panic changes people.'

They stood in silence, digesting what he'd said.

Eve asked quietly: 'Do you really think it's that bad?'

'Yes.' But he smiled saying: 'It's tough on us but we're stuck with it, all we can do is try to hold it together."

The sound of impatient voices was getting louder out in the hall.

'You'd better get out there,' Sally said.

'What shall I say to them?' he whispered.

'Search me,' she said 'but we need to know who they are and perhaps set up a rota to help with chores.'

'That's a start. Can we find them breakfast?'

'Already in hand,' said Eve, busy with the toaster. 'I hope this will do for everyone.
We've already had five in here to tell us they're vegetarian and two vegans as well. There may be more. They're on black tea.'

He groaned. 'We can't cope with that.'

Sally peered into the hall at the crowd of expectant faces. 'You'd better get out there and say something.'

'Like what?'

'Stand on the stairs,' said Eve. 'That way they'll have to look up.'

They came from the villages, outlying cottages and housing estates along the valley and he guessed similar groups were waiting like this at their neighbours' homes around the hill.

Studying faces he saw only two who seemed familiar, an older couple, though he couldn't place them.

26

But he noticed the man didn't look well.

Warm and rested they appeared very different from the cold bedraggled people dumped at Bankside Bottom and the level of good humour put Adam at ease. He heard the chatter and laughter with relief. The man who'd spoken to Rosanna was still making jokes about the rain which was pouring again. Most smiled at his humour.

He cleared his throat. 'Morning everybody, we're glad to see you looking more cheerful. We're going have to make the best of this situation.'

'Do you know what's happening?'

'To be honest I haven't a clue.'

Rosanna's husband asked: 'Have the authorities been in touch?'

'No. But when I hear anything I'll tell you right away.'

'That's not much help.'

'I know,' Adam said, ignoring the truculence, 'but we need to get organised.'

He stopped again and looked for back-up. 'Anybody any thoughts? My wife suggests a rota to help with chores. Is that agreeable?'

A ripple of consent went round and Sally appeared with a notepad and said something to him.

'The first thing we need is a list of names so we can report that you're safe.'

A pretty brown-haired girl spoke up. 'I can do that. I work for the council.'

'Thanks. Who are you?'

'Amy Lock. This is my boyfriend Jock, we live on the Drake estate.'

Adam found himself shaking hands: 'Good to meet you, pity it's like this.'

'We'll be all right, it can't be for long. It's quite exciting really.'

'Right everyone, give your names to Amy, then get something to eat. And there's another thing I need to say,' Adam hesitated.

'Obviously weren't planning a party so there's only our normal food stock.You'll have to be patient and make do with what we have. I expect they'll arrange something,' he ended vaguely, unsure of his ground.

'I hope so,' John muttered.

Someone said: 'Thanks mate,' and they all clapped.

He smiled. 'Thanks. It'll be hard going. We have to hope it's not for long.'

'We're British, we'll cope,' said the elderly man, the only one sitting down. His frail looks belied the strength of his voice. 'We survived all the virus problems, when we all went round wearing masks. I'm sure we can handle this.' A few voices cheered him and a woman said: 'He'll be talking about the Blitz next.'

Adam approached the man and his wife: 'I know you, don't I?'

'Yes, we used to run the hardware shop in Shrivenor but I had to pack it in. The old ticker let me down.'

'Can't recall your name.'

'Bryston, Phil and Jane.' His breathing was laboured and his wife's anxious glance sparked alarm.

'Are you okay? You look a bit shaky.'

'I'm fine. I'm rationing my tablets, in case I can't get any for a while.'

'Right.' Adam said slowly. 'Take it easy and thanks for your support.'

Laughing, Phil Bryston said: 'I don't envy you, Adam. You'll have your work cut out keeping the lid on this.'

'Who's this?' said his wife, smiling as she looked past Adam. Turning he saw the hesitant figure of the child. As soon as he looked at her she rushed across the floor, threw her little arms round his legs and hid her face.

At a loss what else to do he whispered: 'So you've woken up. How are you this morning?' But she didn't speak.

'I found her left alone.'

'What a sweet child,' said Jane Bryston.

'She just hangs onto me,' he said. 'She hasn't said a word since we got in the boat.'

'I expect she's in shock,' Jane said. 'You'll have to be patient.'

'Keep talking to her,' advised her husband, studying the child. 'All of you -- all of us, just keep including her and she may open up.'

'Such a sweet child,' Jane said again.

Adam grunted but clasped the small hand in his and led her towards the kitchen.

'Come on sweet child, let's get you something to eat.'

But Rosanna's husband was hovering beside him. 'Can I have a private word,' he began.

'What is it?'

'My wife's very delicate, she suffers with her digestion, she's not used to this sort of thing.'

'None of us are.'

'I know but she can't eat certain foods and we only drink skimmed milk so if you could manage to allocate -- '

Adam cut him short. 'We don't have skimmed milk. You'll have to muck in like the others and take what comes. We can't make exceptions unless there's genuine illness.'

'Are you saying it's not genuine.'

'No but this is no time for faddy diets. I don't know when we might get supplies. We'll do our best for you. That's all we can do. Now, I must get on.'

But the man wouldn't let it go, following Adam as he turned away, wittering about milk and toilets and lack of organisation.

Choking back an oath as he swung round Adam said: 'I don't know what you expect. You're lucky to be here but you can leave any time you like.'

The rain kept on all day and the high wind that had blown up the previous night still battered the farm, thrashing the bay tree in its pot near the kitchen door. Sally watched it, wondering how long it could survive the onslaught. To go outside meant gearing up in boots and waterproofs. Rosanna had made it clear she wouldn't return to sleep in the barn. There'd been no word from outside and they took turns to call Ron's number -- the only point of contact.

Everywhere he went the little girl followed, clutching her floppy toy. She clung to his jeans or sweater and sorry as he was for her it soon got on his nerves. Whatever he tried to do she was in his way. In exasperation after lunch he picked her up and stood her on the kitchen table, eye to eye with him.

She stared wide-eyed into his face. Adam spoke softly to her: 'We don't even know your name, little one. Can't you tell us that?'

Her blank face gazed back at him. 'Are you frightened? We're well away from the floods. You're safe here.'

Nothing. A thought struck him: 'Can you hear me?' That brought the slightest, hardly perceptible nod and Sally said: 'Perhaps she's lost her voice. Shock can do that, I read it somewhere.'

On impulse he shook her so she blinked at him, startled.

'Oh don't,' said Eve, rushing forward.

'I'm sorry, it's so frustrating -- I didn't hurt her,' he looked ashamed.

'Leave her with us, Adam, leave it for now. Shaking her won't help.'

The child still watched him and he said in his gentlest voice: 'Didn't mean to frighten you. Are you frightened?' She shook her head and then launched herself into his arms again.

'Look, little whatever your name is, I can't hold you all day. I've got things to do. I'm going to leave you here for a while but I won't be far away.'

He went out saying: 'Call the boys, maybe they can get through to her.'

At last in mid afternoon Ron called. He'd had word that helicopter drops were coming to groups marooned all over the country.

'Who's running it?'

'Joint Helicopter Command's in charge and the government has finally declared a national emergency. You know how they hate doing that. You'll have to keep your group for now.'

'Any idea how long?'

'No. The whole valley's been evacuated, thousands taken into Wales to higher ground. It's never been so deep, there's always been a way round but this time the water's hit too many places.'

Through the window Adam noted the ashen sky and sheets of rain.

'And it's still raining,' he said.

'Yes,' Ron's voice betrayed anxiety. 'I never thought I'd see it like this, not in summer -- not this non-stop deluge.'

'We'll look after them best we can,' Adam said. 'We need a lot of stuff, we've got food for two days at most.'

'You'll have to ration it. I don't know when the drops will begin.'

'That'll go down well.'

'You'll have to be firm, Adam.'

'I know.'

'There are people on the move all over, looking for shelter -- don't be surprised if more turn up.'

'We can't take any more.'

'How many have you got?'

'Twenty-two, plus John and Eve and a little girl I found.'

'You'll have room for plenty more,' Ron laughed.

'Bloody hell, Ron. It's bad enough now.'

'Believe me, there's worse to come.'

Retreating upstairs to think he wondered how much worse it would get and how the authorities would cope. He wasn't optimistic. He logged on to check his work. Since the fuel laws came in he worked mostly from home. It got more and more difficult to get diesel for his old Land Rover and for client visits he used Sally's electric car, though it was still unreliable for long journeys. He resented the unfairness of the fuel ration which made life unnecessarily complicated for the rural population.

With a deep sigh he noted nothing relevant had come in, the rain had put his business life on hold. Not surprising -- most of the sites would be under water. But he updated his blog, wondering how soon the diary would have to be continued on paper.

It's much worse than we thought and the same in the other valley. We can't get off the hill at all, even where the land is higher. Bottom line is we're on an island. The water won't go down in a hurry and not at all if it keeps on raining. I need to get these people away -- we've very little food.

I always keep the freezers full but we'll soon get through that. There's a good stash of tins to fall back on -- I didn't tell Ron that.

If they think we're okay they'll say we're not priority. And I don't fancy eating nothing but baked beans. Though Tom's always saying you can never have too many of them.

Don't know where we're going with this but several are vegetarian and vegan. They're already making a fuss. Once we've used our own stuff we'll have very limited sources of protein to give them so they may be faced with a hard choice.

The little girl still hasn't spoken, she seems healthy enough, eats well -- but she won't speak. All we've had is a nod and a head shake. I don't know what to ----

'Can you come, Adam.' Sally rushed in, face blushing with indignation. 'That awful couple are demanding another meal. Eve told them no more till supper but they keep on. Can you come and sort them out.'

'It'll be a pleasure,' he grinned. 'Give me a minute to log off.'

Got to go, most of the crowd seem pleasant apart from this awful selfish pair. If they don't watch it they could be the next meal. If it gets bad enough they'll be the first to go.

'God, I can't stick this for long,' he muttered to Sally, resentment rising as he saw the state of his home -- people everywhere, fiddling with pads or phones, waiting, gathered round the TVs, or getting in the way. The BBC ran non-stop coverage of the crisis, endless shots from the air showing mile after mile of flooded landscape.

Rosanna's husband accosted him, a fleshy man brimming with self-importance who Adam thought would benefit from a few days starvation.

'Look here, Woolton. We need some food, it's been three hours since lunch and we're hungry.'

'You were told there's nothing more till supper.'

'That's not good enough.'

Adam reached in his pocket for his notebook: 'What's your name?'

'Smith, Marcus Smith. Why?'

'This is the third time you've complained already. I'm noting your attitude. What's your job?'

'I'm an accountant, why?'

'Just wondered.'

'What about this food?'

Adam moved closer, eyeballing him for effect. 'Which part of no don't you understand? There's no food till supper. Look around you.' He raised a threatening arm. 'Have you any idea what's going on here?'

'Of course. We're waiting till the water goes down and it's safe to go home. The authorities will sort it out.'

His intention to underplay the situation went out of his head at the man's attitude. Without thinking he shouted.

'You think so? Look out the window. It's raining. It's gonna keep on raining. You're stuck here and we're stuck with you. We're short of food, we might lose the power and you're worried about fucking tea. Now you've got a choice. You can stay here and muck in or you can go out that door into the rain and drown

33

yourselves for all I care. Is that clear enough?'

'How dare you speak to me like that. We can't live like this.'

'You haven't got it, have you! The water's still rising, it could be weeks. As long as it keeps on raining it won't go away.'

'But we've got a golf tournament next week...'

'Golf! You won't be playing golf in that valley for months, if ever.'

Smith stepped back, wincing with shock. Adam wondered if he'd said too much. Rosanna stood behind her husband, open-mouthed in horror.

'Look, you've got to --' he began, but the sound of banging on the front door interrupted him. John, watching the row, caught the expression as Adam turned away, saying: 'Oh God, not more of them.'

'I'll go.' John's footsteps sounded loud on the tiled hall floor and the front door creaked as he dragged it open. Adam tensed and heard what he feared, the sound of pleading voices and more footsteps. Four bedraggled figures followed John into the kitchen, hobbling, exhausted, feet thick with muck. A young man, clearly injured, was being half carried by a woman.

In their wake a trail of mud and water trickled across the tiles and carpet. Staring at the mess he shrugged. Sally's new carpet -- but this latest assault only blended with the stains built up since the rain began.

His face set in resignation he followed them, his eyes on the injured man. Beckoning John from the room he asked: 'Where've they come from?'

John shook his head. 'Their car stalled in the flood -- they're lucky to be alive.'

Adam noted the unsuitable clothing and light shoes. 'What happened?' he asked.

The three men looked at the floor as if unable to summon the words to describe their ordeal but the woman answered: 'We were trying to get home. The road was flooded but we thought we'd make it -- we wanted some stuff before leaving. It didn't seem that bad.'

She paused. 'I never realised water could be so strong. It was up to the car windows but we kept going. Then it stalled and it wouldn't start again. I was driving, I didn't know what to do. We thought we'd had it.'

Sally turned from sandwich making to eye the woman with dismay.

'What then?' John said.

'A surge of water, like a wave. It smashed into the car and swept us along like a toy. The road was like a river. I was so scared, we all were. I just screamed.'

She began to cry, sobbing: 'I was so scared.'

'But you made it. How come?'

'We were so lucky. A lorry was stuck in the water, jammed across the road -- some cars had already hit it, all jumbled together. The current rammed us into it, side on. That's when Martin hurt his leg. Water rushed in and we thought we'd drown.'

'But you got out?'

She nodded. 'We couldn't open the door, there was so much pressure from the water. But the window broke when we hit and we crawled out and climbed up on the lorry.'

'Christ, you were lucky,' John gasped.

'Martin was in agony, don't know how we got him up on that lorry.' John thrust some tissues at her and she patted her face.

Impatient, Adam demanded: 'But how did you get here?'

'A boat came. There were lots of boats -- it's near the river there -- they were grabbing people. They dumped us at the car park.'

'Car park?' Adam sounded incredulous.

'The multi-storey, near the town centre. You know?'

'No --'

'They said go up through the levels, to the top. And wait.' She shivered. 'It was bitter cold, we were out of the rain but the wind blew something awful. We tried to shelter behind the pillars but that wasn't much help.'

'How long were you there?'

Mumbling, one of the men carried on. Not Martin, he sat huddled, head down on the table. 'We were there nearly twenty-four hours. Lunch time next day they started to move people. More boats and helicopters. Some went down for the boats, some were ordered up to the roof. Then we had to wait another four hours for the chopper -- out in the bloody rain.'

The woman went on. 'They dropped us on this hillside, showed us the road and said some places were taking people in.'

She faced John with pleading eyes: 'We can stay here, can't we? Now we've found you.'

'It's not my home.' He motioned towards Adam and she turned to him.

'Oh please, don't send us back out there. It'd finish Martin.'

'You can stay,' Adam said quietly. 'But we're short of food already. We're doing what we can. But we don't need any more bolshie buggers.'

John grinned.

'Anything you say, we're just grateful to be out of the rain. I'm Maggie, that's Ian and Darren, my husband and brother and Martin's a neighbour.'

'What about his leg?' Adam asked.

'He can't put weight on it, it may be broken.'

Adam grunted.

'Eve'll know,' John said. 'She's worked in the fracture clinic.'

'I'll get her,' Sally said.

Eve frowned as she studied the dejected figure of Martin now stripped of his sodden jeans. His legs looked thin and unhealthy and one bone was at an odd angle. He groaned in pain when she gently manipulated the left leg and she shook her head.

"The tibia's broken in two places, it'll have to be set and plastered. He should be in hospital but that's not possible.'

'We'll get Ron to arrange an air lift. Get him out of here.'

She glanced at him with a cynical smile. 'You'll be lucky with all this going on. I think it'll be down me to try and set it somehow.'

It was Adam's turn to frown and he left them, angered and frustrated by this development, to begin the same tedious routine of constant calling till Ron's line was free.

'You were right about more turning up. Another four, including a guy with a broken leg. He needs to be in hospital, can you arrange an air lift?'

Ron exploded down the phone. 'You're joking, no chance.'

'But it needs setting. He's in pain.'

'Give him some codeine. You'll have to do your best for him.'

'But can't the army send a chopper?'

'Get real, Adam. I've told you how it is. They won't waste time or resources picking up one man. In fact they're more likely to tell you to shoot him.'

Chapter four

What Ron said about Martin's leg really shook me. They won't even consider picking up one man for treatment, it shows how bad things are. I don't think he was entirely joking when he said about shooting him.

Eve's doing her best, she's made him comfortable, as much as he can be here. She thinks it's his tibia and it's a nasty break but without an x-ray we can't be sure. We made a splint and she's strapped it up. We've moved people about to find a bed for him but he's in a lot of pain, poor guy. John and Eve are moving into the summer house. It's small but at least they'll have some privacy.

I find it hard to accept what Ron said but he must be right. He's given me some facts. Most of the hospitals are under water -- they were evacuated early on and anybody needing treatment has to go north or west or even to the continent - if they can get there.

The air ambulances are working on supply drops or collecting people. Someone's made a fundamental decision that individuals don't count any more. It's all about saving the greater number. That means anyone injured or ill hasn't got much chance of survival.

I asked what's happening about missing people. He says they're trying to make lists but it's all so disjointed. I need to know if anyone's looking for a lost child but it's difficult without a name. I don't know what street it was -- names all under water.

There are masses of contact appeals on radio and on line, so that's the best bet, once we can get her to speak. It seems the reality's much worse than they're letting on -- it's all very bleak.

I suppose we should be thankful we're on high ground even if we are hungry. We're hoping for a supply drop tomorrow.

Each time I log in I'm amazed we've still got power -- it can only be a matter of time before it goes. I dread the thought of dealing with this lot without light and heat. They're already moaning about the crockery. If the net goes down I expect real trouble and when the phones are gone we'll have no contact at all.

The thought of his bed beckoned but he knew he wouldn't sleep. With so many sharing the bedroom wasn't the retreat it'd always been. He carried on ploughing through emails, from contacts around Europe and beyond. A rising sense of panic ran through many. After the first few he didn't bother to reply.

Flicking to a news site he saw the same pictures they'd watched on TV -- mile after mile of water with jutting hilltops, church towers and pylons. Then urban shots of flooded streets and high rise blocks like ugly islands. He chewed the end of a pencil as he watched, a long-time habit to help concentration.

He wondered why more boats hadn't featured in the rescue efforts. A lot of people had them parked in drives and gardens, to use on the rivers and at the coast. Had it all happened too quickly, water rising so fast and sweeping them away before they could be utilised?

He started doodling with the pencil, drawing old-fashioned clinker fishing boats recalled from childhood seaside visits to Cornwall and Wales, watching crab and lobster landed fresh from the pots and mackerel gleaming in the light of remembered sunshine.

New images were shown. Violent water like waves on the sea. It was the sea. He turned up the sound and heard the name of a place in Essex where the North Sea had simply merged with the flood water and inundated the low-lying country for more than twenty miles inland. Unprecedented rainfall had combined with an unusually high tide driven by fierce winds. Everyone had fled west ahead of the wall of water rushing in. A grim-faced professor of oceanology, via screen link, said there was no way of knowing when or if the sea would return to its normal limit. He stated, almost with relish, that the map of south east England could be changed for ever, whole towns and villages lost beneath the waves.

Adam was a talented draughtsman and his fingers played over the paper. Balls of waste went in the bin as he amused himself with new ideas. The craft got bigger, with a high prow and a platform at the stern. He drew Tom on one, pointing at the horizon. The sweeping strokes of the soft pencil were strangely satisfying and he recalled bible images he'd loved, Noah sending the birds to seek land and the ark balanced on the stark peak of Mount Ararat. He went on drawing and amending and finally scanned it onto the screen. It was fun and he laughed to himself. The noise woke Sally who came up behind him to look.

'Whatever are you doing? It's two o'clock.'

'Sorry, didn't mean to wake you.'

'Are you working?'

'I was, now I'm having fun -- I couldn't sleep. I'll show the boys before I bin it.'

She studied the screen. 'It's a boat -- the very thing.' She laughed. 'Pretty far-fetched but interesting. It's good.'

'There's several options,' he said. 'Which one do you like?'

She trawled through the evolving designs and chose the basic model. 'That one looks like you imagine an ark but it also looks feasible. Print it off.'

Away from the screen the colourful drawings took on a life of their own. 'It's clever, Adam. The boys'll love it.'

He saved the amended drawing and switched off: 'I think I'll post it, give people a laugh.'

Two hundred miles north in another farmhouse among the Scottish hills, a dark haired woman stared at a laptop, her thoughts far away. Only a small lamp and the screen's glow pierced the darkness. She'd been there from late evening, every half hour trying a number on the mobile beside her but always it went straight to voice mail. She'd tried to sleep but defeated by her fears left the dull comfort of bed for the discipline of work, though she found it difficult to focus her mind. Her thoughts flitted constantly to the frightening scenes of flood chaos on TV. Hearing a sound she turned as the room was brightened by an oblong of light from the opened door. 'What is wrong, Kirstie? Why are you in here at this time?'

'Mr Hassan, I hope I didn't wake you.'

'No, not you, but something disturbed me. I am -- what is the phrase -- just checking, looking around.'

'I didn't hear anything.'

The dark skinned man moved nearer and asked again: 'Why are you here?'

'I couldn't sleep, thought I'd try working.'

'You look very tired, my dear. I ask again, what is wrong?'

'The floods, it's really serious.'

'But you are here and we have no floods. We are safe.'

'Yes, but I'm scared for Hayley and my mother. I've heard nothing -- I can't raise anyone.'

'It is only natural to be concerned for the little one. But she will be safe. You told me her grandmother cares for her when you are away from home.'

'Yes but mum always calls at least once a day, if only to leave a message and Hayley has her own mobile. But there are no messages and I can't raise either of them.'

'You know how poor the signal here is sometimes. You may have missed their calls.'

'But they'd be in my log.'

'Go back to bed, Kirstie. Try to sleep.'

'I can't.'

'Well, if you must work, I have drafted the latest report so you can perform your magic and make sense of my poor English. It must go back this week. Shall I fetch it so you can make a start?'

41

'If you like.'

'Though I think you would be better in your bed.'

He left the room and returned with a sheaf of papers. 'Some of it is written in my hand, I am sorry. I still find it easier to scribble on paper, my thoughts seem to come more clearly.'

She smiled: 'Your written English is greatly improved.'

'Thank you. But I still have much to learn. Without you to correct it and translate when I slip into Arabic, I would not be able to keep these contracts.'

'It's what you pay me for.'

'Yes, that and your charming company.'

She glanced at him, unsure of his flattery, and said: 'You must miss your wife and family, with so much time away.'

'I do. But my wife has expensive tastes and I must make the money to satisfy them. Kirstie,' he insisted, 'leave this now, and go to bed. In the morning, maybe you can contact someone near your home.'

'I don't know who, I've already tried the police and the hospital but there's no response. Everything's down. But you're right. I'll go to bed, I'm doing no good here.' She paused. 'Who were those young men Anton brought back this evening?'

'Oh, he says they are cousins. I never probe too far into Anton's concerns, he is a good driver and I leave it at that.'

'Are they staying here?'

'Who knows but I think so. Now, whatever you want to do I am going back to my bed. Good night.'

'Good night, Mr Hassan.'

She switched off the lights but remained in the darkness, thinking of her small flaxen-haired daughter alone against the floods. The anguish which denied her sleep had grown from the guilt of leaving her. But she had had no choice and her mother was on the way, or should have been. She had to leave when she did, so much depended on being in the right place.

In the darkling dawn Adam emerged from sleep, troubled again by the unfamiliar sounds in the house as he stepped across his sleeping sons. Only a day and the place smelled different. As he opened the door the little girl threw off the quilt to follow him. He went to her, smiling, one finger against his lips to hush her. He knelt to cuddle her for a moment, whispering: 'It's too early for you to be up. Go back to sleep. It's okay, I'm not going far.'

He helped her snuggle down. The rabbit's head peered over the quilt while he stroked her hair until she slept again.

The rain had stopped and he longed to be out. The pensive sky had lightened but the sound of busy water assailed him as he leaned against wet stone and confronted the drowned valley. The flood level seemed the same and as the light grew the whole of the eastern sky turned crimson. The glow from the rising sun transfused the water. He visualised his ship, afloat on that crimson lake.

Somewhere close a bird was singing. He spotted a robin in the hawthorn tree, its throat throbbing with the effort of its chorus, red breast bright in the sunlight as he listened. Out in the fresh air he could make himself believe for a moment that everything was normal. That his beloved home had not become a claustrophobic refuge for unwanted guests.

He'd found it ten years ago. He wanted to be away from crowded towns, in touch with the land and working from home was becoming the norm in his profession. This smallholding on the hill ticked all the boxes, it had seemed idyllic. It was, till now. Nestled on a level stretch of upland, protected from the prevailing wind by the rise of the hill, he'd known at first sight it was the place. And Sally was easily convinced.

Childhood days at his grandfather's farm in the Scottish borders had left him harbouring a dream of farming. But he also wanted to be a soldier, as a way of seeing the world and maybe some adventure. Instead he was persuaded to follow his father, an architect with modern visions and no time for rural idylls. All through the long course he thought of chucking it but stuck it out, consoling himself that his designs would be different. His would complement the land, not scar it.

He managed some of it. He joined a small practice and did well though it caused ripples when he was accepted for the Army Reserve. He enjoyed the comradeship and challenges plus the feeling of real life with the army. But that had ended badly. Coming here with Sally and their two little boys was a new beginning and this view seemed the essence of it.

A wide panorama of hills and valley, from rocky crags to neat cloud-dappled farmland. Cloud patterns often distracted him, now their sombre weight would soon block out the sun. But just then it grew stronger and the colour faded into clear morning.

'Red sky in the morning,' he said aloud, 'shepherd's warning.' He knew how true that was and by seven o'clock a bank of cumulus was building to the west. More rain on its way.

He returned to witness an ill-tempered breakfast, Sally and Eve fielding harsh comments and demands for more. The milk had run out and they could only offer toast with a scrape of butter and a ration of jam or marmalade. Yesterday's good humour had evaporated as people faced another day of uncertainty and discomfort.

Some wandered outside for fresh air but most settled where they could till the next meal. Sally remarked to Eve as they cleared up that everything was starting to hinge on food.

Tom and Ben fussed over Sweet Child. Jane's epithet had stuck and they all used it now. They made her extra toast unseen by the rest. Ben searched among their coats and boots to find outgrown ones of his own. He held out the waterproof for her. 'It's a bit big, but it should do,' he said.

'Come on, Sweet Child,' Tom, whose soft voice was starting to break would soon be handsome. His dark eyes charmed and his smile reassured. Looking up at him she sensed the father in the son and took his out-stretched hand with confidence.

'We're going out to the ponies, mum.'

Inside the barn the farmyard smells of warm dung, horses and hens made it almost cosy and the whinnies of welcome as the children entered surprised the little girl.

She laughed and ran forward, reaching up on tiptoe to touch their soft noses. Ears pricked, one grey head and one brown watched the boys with eager eyes.

'They want their breakfast,' Ben said ladling chaff and course mix into two buckets.

The rustle of bags brought a rush of flying feathers as the hens left off scratching the barn floor. She flinched as the birds fluttered about.

'They won't hurt you,' Tom said.

The small flock usually kept them supplied with fresh brown eggs but the weather had affected them too. Their shed was waterlogged and the boys had moved them inside hoping they might resume laying. One speckled grey hen came right up to them, head cocked expectantly. 'That's Tilly, my best bird,' Ben explained. 'She always lays the biggest eggs.'

The hen squatted down tamely when Hayley reached out to touch it. Her fascinated gaze absorbed everything, the munching ponies and the boys briskly cleaning up droppings and fetching water.

She giggled when Ben stood in a pile of dung. Then a small voice said: 'Would I be able to ride them?'

The boys spun round to stare at her.

Grinning Ben shouted: 'So you can speak! Dad'll be so pleased.'

Tom leant his fork against the wall and dropped on one knee in the straw. He took her hand saying in his sweetest voice: 'Please tell us your name?'

Through large, hazel eyes that would one day be dazzling she looked at Tom and opened her mouth to speak. But nothing came out. Her face puckered on the verge of tears but he said all in a rush. 'Don't cry, it's no big deal. When all this is over we'll teach you to ride. '

Ben said: 'She could have a little go in here now.'

'Why not? It'll do them good to walk about a bit more. You can help us groom them, too, if you like. They're fed up with the rain, like everyone else.'

She whispered: 'They smell a bit but it's a nice sort of smell.'

Ben put a head collar on the quieter pony and lifted her to its back. 'You'll be okay in here without a saddle,' he told her, seeing how easily she sat the animal.

She leaned forward and patted the hairy neck as the boy led them forward. He smiled back at her and she took a deep breath to whisper: 'I've never been on a pony.'

Ron Hutchins' efficient voice on the phone brought good news. 'They've scheduled several drops in your area today. They need to be in and out before it closes in again. The forecast is dreadful with high winds and more heavy rain. You'll need a team ready to shift the stuff. The load's for you and three other places on the hill.'

'Will it be marked who it's for?'

'That's your job, sort it out.'

'That sounds like a recipe for trouble.'

'You'll manage. Get your people in some kind of formation so the pilot can spot them. It's going to be asap -- if the weather's as bad as they reckon they won't be able to fly.'

'Right, we'll get on to it. Is there any word on moving these people?'

'It's fucking chaos Adam, you're stuck with them. And by the way -- you're in charge of the area till further notice.'

'What?'

'They've checked you out, on the Reserves record.'

'I wasn't in that long.'

'Long enough, it seems.

The sun had vanished into grey drizzle and then steady rain as the reluctant crowd waited in the field. They shivered in the rising wind, gusts showering them with harder squalls of rain. They waited. Miserable eyes probed the gloom not knowing which way the flight would come.

In the west another dark, threatening tower of cumulus nimbus was building. They watched it working, a huge tumbling mass reaching thousands of feet upwards, packed with accumulated energy to produce more water to fling at the earth. It rolled in on itself, wisps of white curling over and beneath it, funnels and tassels like a curtain.

John said: 'They'd better hurry or they won't make it.'

Minutes ticked away as the wind roared, tossing the trees while the waiting people grew restless. Grumbling voices muttered and several broke away and set off for the house. Adam was angry that they failed to understand the importance of the drop. He bawled at them: 'Get back here! You must wait.'

'How long for? We're getting soaked,' yelled someone.

'What else you gonna do?' called another.

'I don't know,' shouted Adam 'but if we don't get supplies we'll all be hungry.'

They waited. Then above the billowing wind they heard the heavy throbbing rumble of an engine coming with the clouds and soon the helicopter appeared. He forced down a spasm of panic. He loathed that noise, the sound of menace, the feeling of vulnerability exposed in the open. Without thinking he moved to the hedge, pressing himself against the wet leaves, invisible from the sky.

Breathing deeply he forced himself to stand still and wait. Calmly he watched it come in fast, a blacker form against the dark clouds behind, sweeping in as if riding the wind.

It whirled above them and banked round to check the field, then dropped towards landing. But a mighty gust of wind caught it and it lurched off course. Then he saw how close it was to the power lines that crossed the field. The chopper's door opened and a young soldier with a loud hailer shouted down. Adam strained to get the words.

'We can't land or hover in this wind, sorry. If we're blown on those power lines we'll be toast. Here's something to get on with till we come back.'

Two large packages hurtled down. Thudding into the muddy ground they burst open. One contained tins of grapefruit, the other was cartons of milk, several split by the impact.

In silence the assembled guests watched the white liquid seep into the mud and with disbelief saw the helicopter vanish into the storm.

Chapter five

Another sleepless night, open eyes looking at darkness, thoughts chasing through his brain, including the image of the helicopter tossed close to the power lines.

The lack of food was pressing. For the first time in his life he knew what hunger meant. Not the pleasurable anticipation of a meal but the ache of an empty stomach. If the army didn't return soon they wouldn't eat.

And he'd let his guard down. John had seen him when the chopper came. When they were alone together in the evening he'd said diffidently: 'Do you have a problem with helicopters?'

Adam's reaction surprised him. He'd looked away and muttered something about the noise.

'In Afghanistan they were buzzing around all the time. It made me uneasy.'

John laughed. 'You've never said much about that.'

'It wasn't a good time. I wanted to do my bit so I joined the reserve but it was bad out there. Too many deaths and some of them friends, I don't talk about it.'

'That's fine. I just thought you looked, well, scared, as it flew in.'

'Bad vibes John, that's all.'

He couldn't tell his friend that the sound of them induced only the urge to run. That the grinding drone took him straight back to the desert, to an afternoon when he nearly died, fleeing for his life from that noise, stumbling across sand and rock, desperate for somewhere to hide.

When sleep came it swept him into a nightmare world. Ben had fallen from a boat and struggled screaming in the water.

Adam tried to grab a flailing arm but couldn't reach, struggling while the boy drifted further away. Hearing him crying in the water beyond his grasp was a torment. The crying went on and on, a quiet sobbing which penetrated the dream and brought him awake. He shook his head, entangled in the aftermath of fear. The crying was real and close by.

He listened. The child on the floor whispered between sobs: 'Mummy, mummy where are you?'

He picked her up, pulled the quilt around her and went back to sit with her on the bed. Thumb in mouth she heaved with sobs but snuggled against him. 'Easy, little one,' he said. 'Don't cry, we'll find your mum.'

He held her until the sobbing eased and stroked her hair. 'Hush now, you'll wake Sally,' he murmured. When she quietened he said: 'It's all horrible, I know but we'll take care of you till we find your mum. It'll be all right. I promise. You're not frightened, are you? Not now?'

Feeling her head shake he whispered: 'That's good -- don't want you to be afraid.'

He paused. 'I heard you talking just now and you talked to the boys so if you could tell me your name it'd make it easier to find your mum. D'you see?'

Her head nodded against his chest. Silent in the dark room he waited. The sound of her heaving breaths in the stillness were almost sobs.

'Can't you tell me, it's only your name -- we can't keep calling you Sweet Child.'

'I like it,' she mumbled.

'Do you?'

'Mmm.'

'We can still call you that for fun. But it would help to know what you're really called.'

He longed to close his eyes and try for sleep but rocked her like a baby as long minutes drifted by.

'Are you asleep?' he whispered.

'No.'

The first light of dawn crept into the room and she sat up and looked into his face through the gloom. He roused himself from dozing and heard her say, as if to herself: 'I'm Hayley. Hayley Lomax and I'm seven.'

Everyone in the house knew food was short but the reality of grapefruit segments and half a slice of toast for breakfast was still a shock. Sally watched the various expressions of disgust, waiting anxiously for the complaints to begin. Amy Lock said timidly: 'Is this really it?'

Eve came to back up her friend, saying: 'We've already had all the spare loaves from the freezers. John's gone home to get what's there. But it won't be much.'

'Oh.'

'We've got three loaves left so between thirty-odd that won't last the day,' Sally said.

Marcus Smith appeared: 'You must have more food some-where,' he began. 'You can't expect us to manage on this. You must be hiding stuff.'

Eve, less patient than Sally, stared at him, incredulous. Her face flushed pink in indignation as she listened. He carried on about conditions in the house and the inefficiency of it all till she cut him short.

'What do you think this is? A bloody picnic? You're the most selfish, unpleasant man I've ever met. You know what happened yesterday -- till that chopper comes back, we've got to make do. Get out of here and eat what you've got. When Adam comes in you'll be lucky if he doesn't lock you up.'

'He wouldn't dare.'

'Try him. Now get out.'

'Well done,' Sally laughed as he left then said. 'I've thought of something. There's some mutton left at the bottom of the old freezer in the barn, from two years ago. I've been meaning to clear it out. We'll see if it's still edible. If it hasn't gone off it would make a good stew, I think there's a couple of onions left.'

Jane Bryston was close by, collecting her own and Philip's portion. She said: 'We like mutton. It'd be a treat any time.' Then: 'Don't worry about what he said. We know you're doing your best and we're grateful.'

'That's kind, thanks.' Eve munched her toast and smiled. 'I'd better take Martin's share. Though he might not eat it -- he was sick again this morning.'

Martin looked pathetic -- alone in a room surrounded by untidy heaps of clothes, quilts and blankets, the sleeping quarters of another seven people. At least he had a bed. Eve felt his forehead, certain his temperature had risen. Her medical kit topped John's list of things to fetch from home, including all their crocks and cutlery. Her smile when she brought his meagre breakfast covered her anxiety. He'd been sick twice in front of her and the bucket next to him showed evidence of another bout. The kit should include antibiotics but she feared there might not be enough.

'Can you eat something?' she asked.

'I'll try the toast,' he said. 'I don't like grapefruit.'

She helped him sit up to eat. In seconds he retched and Eve grabbed the bucket just in time.

The entire room smelled foul and her stomach churned as she emptied the bucket down the unflushed toilet.

Inspecting his injured leg, she noted the discoloured skin, reddish and blue with bruising evident above the dressing.

'Does it hurt much?' She asked and he nodded, wincing as she lifted it clear of the bed. But the makeshift splints held it firm.

'You'd be better if we can get you mobile,' she said. 'Adam is making crutches.'

'What's the point? Upstairs or down -- it's just as miserable.'

'You'd feel better with company. I'll send your friends up.'

The animal miasma in the barn was sweeter than the house where human odours combined with damp to produce a fetid stench.

He was contriving crutches for Martin out of wood and sacking. They looked like something Long John Silver might have used but he thought they'd work. His small shadow sat attentive on a straw bale, watching every move. Her eager concentration turned to giggles when he shuffled round the barn on the crutches, one leg off the ground for realism.

She was more cheerful now.

'What d'you think? Will they do?' he asked.

She clapped her hands. 'Like Tiny Tim -- he had a stick like that.'

' I forgot about him. We'd better get some breakfast but there won't be much.'

'Not very hungry,' she said. 'Adam,' she looked anxious.

'What?'

'You said you'd find my mum. Did you mean it?'

'Course I did.'

They heard a car and Hayley ran to greet John who took a moment to make a fuss of her before hurrying into the house.

Eve found what she needed waving a slip of drugs. 'I thought I'd got some left. They may not be the right ones but we'll have to try. If Martin's leg gets infected we'll lose him. '

'What do you mean?' Sally asked, voice subdued with alarm.

'It could turn to gangrene.'

'Does that still happen?'

'Very much so, if we can't prevent infection we'd have to remove the leg.'

'We couldn't, could we?' Sally was appalled at the thought.

'I doubt it.'

'Christ no. Where would we start?'

'We couldn't do it,' John said, looking to Adam who shook his head, 'not without anaesthetic.'

He went out without a word, overwhelmed by it all. Later he found a crowded kitchen with Tom and Ben fussing over five bedraggled girls. Bulky packs cluttered the room. His puzzled frown turned to exasperation. Yet more people to deal with. A dark-haired girl who seemed to be the leader saw his expression and gasped: 'Don't send us away. We're completely lost and wherever we go there's water.'

Two of them sank onto the floor and another said: 'We can't go any further, we're so hungry.'

'There's nowhere to go,' said Tom flatly. 'We're it.'

'What d'you mean?'

'Don't you know what's happening?' Sally asked. 'The country's in chaos, the floods are everywhere. What are you doing? Where've you been?'

One said: 'We're on Duke of Edinburgh. Gold award -- survival test, camping. It's been horrible in the rain. We tried to make our emergency rendezvous -- but it wasn't there -- just water. There was no one to meet us -- nothing. We've been wandering around for two days.'

'Unbelievable,' Adam muttered. Then his crossness softened as he saw the exhaustion in the tearful faces.

'Well you're here now, so you can stay. But you'll have to sleep in the barn.' He went out and left the boys to show them the way.

'We don't mind that,' the girl said to Tom. 'As long as we're out of the rain.'

Tom studied her. 'What's your name?' he asked.

'Abi.'

'Got any food left in your packs?.'

'Not much, just some emergency ration bars.'

'Good,' Adam cut in, 'That'll have to do you for now. We've hardly any food left.'

The girls settled in the hall munching oat bars, eyed by Tom who said to his brother: 'Maybe this flood'll have some compensations.'

'What d'you mean?'

'Well, pretty girls, aren't they.'

'I suppose they are.'

'What d'you reckon to the dark haired one, Abi? She's really fit.'

Ben considered: 'I think the Indian girl's the prettiest. She's got lovely eyes.'

When his father reappeared Tom said: 'Things are looking up, Dad.'

Adam rounded on his son: 'What?'

'The girls, didn't expect a bonus like them.'

'Bonus! You stupid kid, it's just more people to care for. There's nothing good about all this. It's a disaster and people are going to die before it's over. Just hope we're not among them.'

'Oh lighten up, dad.'

'Lighten up?'

'Why're you so angry? I didn't mean anything.'

'Maybe but you don't think. Thousands of people are homeless, starving. Parts of the country might never recover -- just stay under the sea.'

'Oh that couldn't happen,' said   Tom. 'They won't let it happen.'

'They? What have They ever done to prevent it. They've had years of warnings and nothing's been done. We're only safe here because it's high ground.'

Tom started to argue: 'I was only joking about the girls, a bit of fun.'

'Fun!'

Tom stared, bewildered, unable to understand the fury he'd induced. He shouted defiantly at Adam: 'I'm nearly grown up, I have a mind of my own.'

'You think so? No Tom, you're still a silly kid.' Red-faced with humiliation the boy opened his mouth but Adam's anger stopped him and he flung away and bolted out into the rain.

Adam felt the silence, all watching him. Only Sally spoke. 'He didn't deserve that.'

He stared at her and dropped his gaze. 'I'm going to try Ron again.'

John had come in at the end of the row and frowned in concern. He pulled on his boots and raincoat and went after Tom who was crouched in the hay, head in his hands. His wet T-shirt clung to his chest, angry breaths pounding like a runner.

John waited till the boy regained control. 'Steady Tom, it's all right.'

Choking back tears as he raised his head he gasped: 'He shouldn't speak to me that way, Uncle John, should he?'

'I didn't hear it all, don't know what it's about.'

'It was a bit of fun, about the girls. It was silly maybe, but he didn't have to go for me like that.'

'He's worried, Tom.'

'I know but he treats me like a kid. I'm not a kid any more, I'm a man, well -- almost --'

John smiled: 'Almost but not quite.'

'I can't talk to him, not like I can with you -- he can be so sort of, far off --'

'He's a good dad, isn't he?'

'Yeah, he's been great but these days it's hard to get near him. Even before this lot. And now, well, I can't even make a joke.'

'Sons and dads often clash, Tom. I did with mine, still do actually. Though I don't see him much now since they moved. At one stage we didn't get on at all.'

'Really?'

'He expected so much. Men do that, expect a lot from their boys. It's only because he thinks so much of you.'

'Well, he has a very strange way of showing it. He needs to lighten up.'

'I know. But it's an awful responsibility -- for me too, and your mum and Eve. But it's your dad's place so he's lumbered with it.'

'Yes, but -- '

'You've got to make allowances -- try to help him -- try to forget this.'

'Why should I?'

'Tom.'

'All right, if you say so.'

I shouldn't have spoken to Tom like that. The poor kid didn't mean any harm. Don't know why I got so uptight. I can't seem to talk to him like we used to, when he was little -- I think he says more to his mum and John -- he talks a lot to John. And poor Eve didn't expect a badly injured patient. The possibility of gangrene is a nightmare. I just hope we can save his leg. Whatever else I might have to do I don't think I could cut off a man's leg.

Haven't had a peep from Ron, still waiting to hear about supplies and other stuff. I wonder how soon I'll have to start scribbling this diary on paper.

At least we know who the child is. Now I have her name I'll try a radio appeal. They're giving long lists of people trying to get in touch and Ron's got lists as well -- if I could just get hold of him.

But it could make things worse, if there's no response and we don't contact her mother. I'll keep her hopes alive as long as possible but I fear the worst.

Mother and granny may both be dead. So many reports of casualties and trapped bodies, mostly in cars. So far there's no unidentified females fitting the description of Hayley's mum. She seems to have vanished.

Half way down the stairs Hayley was waiting for him.

'Hello, I was just thinking about you.'

'You were cross with Tom,' she said -- an accusation.

'Yes. I shouldn't have been.'

'He's upset.'

'I'll make it right with him. Do you like him?'

'Yes, he's kind to me, like you.' She paused. 'I was thinking about my mum. Have you heard anything?'

Her wide-eyed eagerness pulled at his heart.

'It's difficult Hayley, everything is so disorganised. But I'm going to put it on the radio and on line. Lots of people are doing that. If she gets in touch you'll feel much better even if you can't join her right away. How's that?'

Her pretty face lit up and she eyed him with something like reverence: 'Thank you.'

He laughed: 'We haven't found her yet.'

Sally almost cried watching the little girl's face as she waited close to the kitchen radio.

'Just look at her,' she whispered as Hayley listened intently to the evening update giving lists of names with contact numbers.

She scowled with frustration when interference disrupted the broadcast. Adam and Sally exchanged glances -- there were an awful lot of missing people on that list. The appeal had already run for more than ten minutes and Hayley's disappointment showed as tears crept out and she discreetly wiped her cheek.

'What a brave kid,' Sally said as the radio voice continued.

'Moving on to Shrivenor area, Kirstie Lomax of Dingley and the contact is Adam Woolton ....'

'Yes!' shouted Hayley and ran to Adam. 'Thank you, we'll find her now, I know we will.'

She turned to Sally: 'Thank you.'

Ben was there, grinning, he said: 'Told you it'd be okay.'

But Adam said quietly: 'That's the easy bit. It doesn't mean we'll find her. She may not have heard it. Hayley, it's a real long shot. She could --'

'Adam.' Sally shoved him towards the door: 'Christ Adam, let her have some hope. Time enough when we know the worst. Let her think there's a good chance.'

'It's no good being --- .'

'You can be a real pain, I know the score but let's be positive.'

'If she's alive.'

'Yes, if she's alive.' Sally sounded exasperated. 'Let's assume she is.'

The phone rang at 6am. 'Chopper's on its way, get your people ready. And I have to tell you it's much worse than we thought. You'll have to cope for as long as it takes. They've clamped down on any kind of sensitive information, vital to avoid panic. If people knew the full truth it could be very difficult to control.'

'Is it really that bad?'

'Worse and they've made you group commander with official authority to do anything necessary to maintain order. John is your deputy, though they're still checking him out.'

'Why?'

'Routine procedure, they need to be sure he's sound.'

'You keep saying They. Who are They and how come they give me orders?'

'Special order in council from the government crisis group, the DMD.'

'What?'

'Disaster Management Directorate.'

'Christ, and where might they be, for God's sake?'

'Buxton.'

'Why Buxton?'

'It's a good site. Central in the country and more important, at around a thousand feet, well above the flood level. The Pennine chain has become vital to this country's survival.'

'What about the king and the rest of the royals?'

'He and some of the family were already at Balmoral and they've had a top-class hub system there for years so that was easy. The rest of those that matter are tucked away in Scotland and north Wales.'

'I bet the PM just loves Buxton,' Adam said.

'His opinion is not relevant at the moment,' Ron explained quietly. 'All the important decisions are down to Sir Jock.'

'Not Sir Jock Langdon? Bloody hell!'

The man who nobody wanted to hear, Chief of the Joint Defence Command, who'd warned for years the country was unprepared for any kind of crisis or natural disaster. 'How did that happen?'

'I think the king advised the PM to appoint Sir Jock.'

'Advised?'

'Our new monarch has proved assertive, as you know. Thank God someone is.' He paused. 'It's difficult moving supplies. They're short of air power -- the combined fleet of all three services and the police are overwhelmed. They're juggling food and ferrying people to safety. They've got small planes as well but they're not flexible enough.

'And they're breaking down because there's no time for servicing. Most of my work is organising drop schedules for people like you to minimise time and distance.'

Adam listened with growing alarm but Ron's next words shook him.

'But the main point of my call was to say another consignment is on its way, including weapons.'

'Weapons -- what d'you mean?'

'Assault rifles or pistols I expect.'

'What are you saying?'

'Look, they know your army background. You can shoot so you're in charge. Someone has to be.'

'But Ron --'

'I must go Adam, other people to tell.'

Staring at the silent phone Adam shook his head and sat down in a daze.

Sally was stunned, she'd heard Adam's end of the conversation.

'Did you get most of that?' he asked.

'I heard enough.'

She was trembling. 'Are they saying you might have to shoot people?'

'Sounds that way.'

'But you couldn't. I know we've joked about it but the reality is something else.'

'We'll have to wait and see. Not a word of this to anyone, even John. The guns may not come and if they do we'll keep it quiet .'

His brain churned on this new information. The reasons were obvious, years of cutbacks on military spending, failure to replace old equipment with new and bigger models, reliance on charity to run crucial air ambulances -- the combined inaction of successive governments, now well and truly come home to roost.

Angry men disturbed from sleep were urged outside. The early morning drizzle was enough to soak them but the furious gusts which had battered the hilltop for days had dropped. Grumbling and impatient they waited almost two hours but raised a cheer when the helicopter appeared.

The chopper flew in again from the west, swirling muddy spray across the field. As it settled the door opened and they started to run towards it.

The same young officer from the first attempt called Adam into the chopper. As his crew started to throw boxes and bundles from the open door he said: 'I have to put this into your hands only.'

He handed over a long metal case marked 'A WOOLTON ONLY -- CONFIDENTIAL'. Adam took it and immediately put it down. 'What is it?'

'Two of these and one of these -- and I have five minutes to show you how to use them.'

The captain picked up an automatic rifle from behind the packing cases and Adam gasped. It was the N90, the latest Army weapon used for close quarter combat and crowd control -- when fitted with rubber bullets. 'I can't use that,' he said.

'You may have to -- and the ammunition is live. It's all we've got. Plus you'll have a pistol like mine and I believe you also have a shotgun. You must be prepared.'

'But —'

'There's no time for buts. This is the way it has to be. There's not much time and my orders are to ensure you can use these if needed. No whys or wherefores, just listen.'

Ignoring a sick feeling Adam watched and nodded, knowing he would have to pass on this knowledge to John, as the young captain efficiently showed him how to load, engage and handle the weapon, plus a very quick briefing on maintenance. It took four minutes.

'Now pick up the case. Keep these somewhere secret but handy. And there's this as well.' He handed over a smaller package. 'Satellite phone, instructions with it. Easy to set up.'

Adam stared blankly at the soldier. 'I'm not trained for this. I can't shoot people.'

'You were. But hopefully you won't have to.' The captain's expression softened: 'Look mate, I'm sorry. It's just chance you're in charge here, like it or not it's down to you. You're the man.'

'But--'

'Someone has to make decisions and right now it's you.'

Adam said agin: 'But I can't --'

'No time for buts. Pick up the gear and get off. We must go. We've got five more drops.'

Adam swallowed, picked up the boxes and climbed out beneath the spinning blades. The machine started to lift and was away over the hedge in seconds, leaving him staring in confusion.

He looked at the trail of reluctant bearers shuffling awkwardly across the field with bales and boxes, then up to a veil of cloud creeping across the sky. It was black. Not dark grey and ominous, but black, fingers of darkness darting to the earth where rain was already falling. It moved like a living thing. It was a living thing. The first heavy drop hit his cheek and soon the rain was pouring down again. He yelled at John to go ahead and supervise. 'Stack it all in the barn for now.'

Grabbing what looked like a bale of blankets he slung it across his back and tried to run as hailstones struck the ground around him. Tom came back with Ben and they brought the last box between them, running through a curtain of biting hail, sharp chips of ice which hurt as they hit hands and face.

Chapter six

The barn was crowded, the ponies snorting in alarm at the commotion. People rived at boxes, trying to rip open bales and he was conscious of a cacophony of coughing.

'Stop it, all of you,' he shouted, shoving a way through. A rumble of moans began as he   continued: 'Leave it alone, we need to check what we've got.'

The boys stood back, wondering what to do. He opened a crate of milk and sent Tom indoors with two cartons and the order to make hot drinks.

Marcus Smith was there. 'You're good at giving orders, what gives you the right to tell us what to do?'

'Simple, it's my home.'

John stepped in: 'Why don't you just co-operate and be grateful you're safe. Get yourself back inside for a drink.'

The grumbles eased with the thought of some comfort and they all slipped away, followed by a reluctant Smith.

'What have we got? It doesn't look much,' said John.

Adam sighed. 'No, I'd hoped for more. And it's not all for us.'

He looked at the pile of boxes. 'Let's hope they're planning to return.'

They examined the labels. There were more tins of grapefruit.

Adam stared at the tins. 'They must have masses in store. Is that the best they can manage?'

'Full of Vitamin C,' laughed John.

But there was milk, bread, tins of stewed steak and more baked beans. 'One thing we're not short of,' Adam said.

He listed it all. One sack of potatoes, one of carrots and one of dried soup, sardines packed in twelves and three large bags of porridge oats. He was pleased to see a small net of onions but they were already sprouting and the carrots too showed signs of rot.

He sighed and tipped the carrots into a pile, calling for Ben. 'These have been in store too long, can you sort out any that are usable. The boy nodded and set to work.

The delivery included three shrink-wrapped bales of water in two litre bottles.

'We'll hide those,' he said. 'When the power goes they'll be trouble over water so we'll keep this in reserve. Then we'll have to ration it. In fact we should probably start now, make some rules about it.'

John looked surprised: 'You serious? Water everywhere and you say we're short of it.'

'Short of clean water, yes. Drinking rain water would be a sure way to get rid of people.'

'The borehole's okay isn't it?'

'For now but without power the pump will only work if there's enough UV and there isn't much of that.'

The drop brought a temporary improvement in morale -- people felt reassured. It wasn't just the food but the thought that someone out there -- authority -- was on the case, looking after them.

Eve heard two couples chatting. They assumed supplies would now arrive regularly so there was no need to worry and they'd soon be moved to 'proper facilities'.

She told Adam as everyone settled to watch the latest TV reports. His grimace made her laugh but he said: 'We should stop them watching the news but I suppose that's impossible.'

'It's the one thing they want to see -- to know what's going on.'

'It'd be better if they didn't know,' he said.

On screen repeated aerial shots panned across vast acres under water, hills turned into islands, telegraph and electric poles showing where roads should be and pictures of rooftops surrounded by water. Adam reckoned it was the same footage recycled but it made the watchers gloomy.

Gasps of dismay greeted the apocalyptic tones of the newscaster saying: 'Meanwhile in Europe...' followed by more endless scenes of flooded landscapes. Large parts of mainland Europe were under water -- almost all the Netherlands, northern Belgium and Germany and north east France, as well as parts of Denmark, Poland and the Baltic states.

Adam left the room followed by Sally who caught his arm. 'I'm scared, what's going to happen?'

His face was pale as he looked at her: 'I don't know sweetheart but all that water will take a long time to shift.'

He left them to it and went upstairs where a long list of emails was waiting. His friends had woken to the crisis. A message from Gunter in Denmark told him about conditions there but said their government was handling it well and moving people to higher ground. They'd been working on schemes to shift the population wholesale in an emergency.

'Glad they had the sense to plan further ahead,' he wrote back. 'We've seen this coming for years.'

Not a good day, though at least we've got some food. I have to divide it up and take it to the other groups. Mike Clayton's already been on and he sounded desperate. I'll get over there first thing tomorrow.

Most of them behave well but I can't believe the Smiths. They seem to have no conception at all of what's happening around them. I've never come across anyone so selfish.

Let's hope we never get to the point of cannibalism because I don't think there'd be much doubt about who would be first choice.

I don't suppose the vegetarians would like it. Depends how hungry they are but principles are easily swallowed when it's a case of not swallowing anything at all. The urge to survive is very strong in all of us.

I'm joking -- at least I think I am -- but normality has disappeared.

I long to be rid of them and get some peace. That's why we came here. God knows how long it'll go on. The only good thing is Martin seems slightly better. Eve thinks the antibiotics are working.

I did an ark design to amuse myself when I couldn't sleep. Here's what it looks like so far -- very biblical I think. Might see if I can get some crowd-funding to finance it.

The morning after the broadcast Amy Lock was peeling potatoes in the kitchen with Jock, when a phone rang. The family were busy elsewhere, Adam, John and the boys had taken the chance of a let-up in the onslaught -- just a fine rain coming down almost gently -- to repair a broken gutter. It was letting water pour down the wall and seep into a bedroom window. Sally and Eve were struggling with washing, or the drying of it.

'This is daft, Sal. I think you should give up on it, we'll just have to make do with dirty clothes,' Eve said, struggling to put a sheet on the creel. Sally helped her and together they hauled the damp load to the ceiling,

'Yes, it's hopeless. We'll end up with wet stuff everywhere and it'll take for ever to dry. What a time for the drier to pack up.'

'Listen, that's a phone.'

'Sounds like Adam's,' said Sally 'he should have it with him.'

'He put it down before he went on the roof. He was afraid of dropping it in the muck.'

They hurried through to the kitchen and found Amy staring puzzled at the phone.

'Who was it?' asked Eve.

'Some woman, she just said: 'It's Kirstie' and rang off.'

'Is that all?'

But Sally grabbed the phone and stabbed hard at the digits for recall. 'Number withheld,' she said slowly.

'Who's Kirstie?' Amy asked.

Sally spoke slowly: 'I'm not sure, but I hope it's Hayley's mum.'

Eve gasped: 'Brilliant.'

'It must be, surely?' They were all smiling at the thought. 'It's strange she didn't say more.'

Sally was silent, thinking, then said: 'Don't tell anyone, especially not Hayley, not till we know for sure. She'll try again and if Adam answers, perhaps she'll speak to him.'

Before the gutter job was finished the rain was torrential again and they trooped into the kitchen letting water stream all over the floor. Sally breathed a deep sigh and fetched the mop.

He saw the look on her face. 'Sorry love,' he said. 'We couldn't help it, look at it out there again.' The boys stood with their arms splayed out, dripping into puddles at their feet, reluctant to make the effort to remove their outer clothes.

'It's gone down my neck,' Ben grumbled, hunched against the chill.

'Get it off,' said his mother and helped ease the wet jacket from his arms.

'Ugh, it's so soggy,' he grunted.

'There was a call,' Sally told Adam as she mopped up into an old-fashioned bucket. 'It might have been Hayley's mum.'

'There's something funny about all this,' John said, hanging onto the Aga rail for warmth. 'Why don't you talk to Hayley, find out a bit more about her mum.'

'Where is she?'

'Doing a puzzle.'

Listless, bored people lounged around the sitting room. Some were reading or tapping at mobiles, others were wired into music, watching TV or just chatting. A couple had found the boys' chess set. On the carpet by the window Hayley crouched over a large jigsaw puzzle. She'd completed the frame and half a black and white cow which faced the world from a complex farmyard scene. Big areas of green and brown gave few clues to the pieces.

He squatted beside her. 'How's it going?' he asked.

'A bit slow, I've never done one with so many pieces and they're very small.'

'You're doing very well, it's meant for children of 12 and over,' he read from the box.

'It's interesting.' As he watched her comparing pieces she sensed he had a purpose and looked up quickly to ask: 'Have you heard from mum?'

'Not yet.' He hated the lie but told himself it was only a little lie, a white lie -- to protect her.

'Will you help me with the ponies?'

'It's raining again,' she said doubtfully.

'We can make a dash for the barn and let them out for a bit.'

'Okay.' She got up and dressed in coat and boots.

Sally saw them and protested. 'You're not going out?'

'Going to let the ponies out,' he explained and she caught the meaning in his look.

'Shall we come, dad?' Tom asked.

'No need. Right Hayley, when I say go, run as fast as you can.'

He opened the kitchen door and they both faced the bouncing curtain of water. 'Wait a bit,' he said.

The rain had a pattern, it teemed down with dreadful intensity, then eased up, then came heavy again. Adam watched the sky and the hovering clouds, a paler shade of grey was moving towards the farm. As it approached the downpour lessened to a steady but less violent pitch.

He took the child's hand: 'Now!' And they launched into a race across the yard.

Inside the barn felt warm and the ponies greeted them. Hayley shook off her hood and laughed at him.

'We were too quick to get wet. The poor ponies must be so bored.'

'We'll let them mooch about while we muck out.'

The child looked around her at the piles of droppings littering the floor. 'Will I get dirty?'

'Not if you're careful. You don't mind helping, do you? It's always good to learn something new.'

'Don't think I mind.' There was the doubt again.

'Here's the barrow, look, and a little fork for you.'

He began collecting the droppings and wet straw and Hayley poked about with the fork. 'It smells,' she said wrinkling her nose.

'It's not a bad smell,' Adam grinned at her. 'Don't you have any pets?'

She shook her head, kicked a lump of dung with her boot then forked it into the barrow. 'No, mummy says they're too much of a tie. But granny has a dog, Toby. He's my friend.'

'Do you see granny often?'

She nodded. 'Most days, when mum's away I go to granny's, I have my own room there.'

'So you have two bedrooms, you're lucky, some girls don't have one -- they have to share.'

'I know.'

He finished the first stable and wheeled the manure out to the growing pile behind the barn. It was too far in the rain to take it to the normal muck heap. 'Have we got to do them both?' Hayley asked.

'Of course.'

'Every day?'

'We should do it twice a day but with things as they are it doesn't always get done.'

Head on one side she pronounced: 'It's a lot of work.'

'Certainly is.' He began on the second loose box. 'Tell me about your mum, what's she like?'

'She's fun.'

'Is she?'

'When we're together, she always tries to do something that's fun. We visit all kinds of interesting places and she reads to me and cooks lovely meals for supper.'

'When you're together? Aren't you always together?'

The child shook her head. Adam watched her face and the way she smiled told him this was a happy kid who was loved and cared for and idolised her mum. Probably spoiled but much loved, which made it more strange that she should be alone in such peril.

'What does your mum do?'

'She's very busy, away a lot, that's why I go to granny.'

'I see. What does she do?'

'She's um -- oh, I can't remember the word, it's a tricky one.' She scratched her head, trying to explain. 'She knows a lot of languages, that's what she does.'

'A linguist?'

'No, it's for people who don't speak like us, you know -- they have lots of papers in their language and she puts it all into English so people can understand.'

'She's a translator.'

'That's it. She does a lot of work at home but sometimes she has to go to meetings, conferences and stuff and then she has to say it aloud after they've said it.'

'I get the picture.' He pushed the barrow away and sat on a straw bale, patting it so she sat beside him. It made more sense but still didn't explain why she'd been alone. He tried a different tack. 'The day the flood came, were you frightened?'

Her small face puckered into a frown and she went quiet as she thought about it. She looked sideways at him. 'It wasn't my fault. I couldn't help being on my own.'

'Of course not.'

She kicked her heels against the bale and gazed at her boots, reluctant to say more. She thought about it for a long time and he was trying to think of another way round when she spoke again.

'At the beginning it was exciting,' she said slowly. Then as if a cork was unstopped all her words tumbled out in a rush as she relived the terror of that day.

'Your mum went out?'

71

The child nodded. 'She said she'd be back after lunch and granny was on her way. She was in a hurry, she couldn't wait but it wouldn't be long.'

'But granny didn't come?'

'I rang her but she didn't answer.'

'So you waited?'

'I made beans on toast, that's easy but I started to get frightened. I've never been alone so long and the water at the front was deep. People were all leaving, I didn't know what to do.' She stopped and looked at him: 'I was very scared then.'

'It must have been awful.'

'A big tractor came with a trailer but they didn't see me.' She cuddled closer to Adam as the memory made her shiver. He looked down to see her tears.

'I thought I'd be drowned. I knew I should get out but I didn't know where to go. I opened the door and water rushed in and knocked me over. I got back upstairs and put the sheet out.'

'That was clever of you.'

She brushed away the tears saying: 'Then you came.'

Adam grunted. She'd been so close to drowning.

'Are we going to finish this?' she asked.

'No, we'll get the boys on it. We'll go inside and find something to eat.'

'It's worse than we thought,' he said with Hayley out of earshot. 'I think the granny's missing as well.'

He told them the story. 'The mother was somewhere on business, though what was so important on a morning like that I can't imagine but the grandmother could be anywhere.'

He saw the dismay flash into all their faces but it was Eve who put the fear into words. 'She may've been trapped in the water.'

'Don't say that.'

'One elderly woman on her own. That'll be why she didn't come.'

'It wasn't that bad in the morning, surely she'd have answered when Hayley called.'

Adam tried to rationalise it, that way it seemed less awful.

'She may have been somewhere else and got stopped by the flood. She could be anywhere. I'll ring Ron again, get him to check the lists for Mrs Brogan -- that's the name, not Lomax.'

But Ron was no help. There was nobody called Brogan on his lists -- lists that now covered 500 square miles, as people found shelter where they could or were moved or sent to higher ground. Ron had it all programmed for easy search but his tone was bleak when he told Adam it was far from complete.

'There's so many unaccounted for -- they could be anywhere. We don't know if they're just missing or dead. But anyone trapped won't be found till the water goes down -- if then. It's a grim prospect.'

Adam, thinking as he listened, asked: 'What about the hospitals? Lists of patients?'

'Not yet,' Ron sounded harassed. 'They were all evacuated, moved around the country. The records for the hospitals under water are lost, for now at least. It's impossible to work out who should be where and where they could be now, if you follow that.'

'It's a nightmare. We'll just have to hope the kid's mother calls again.'

He'd always been careless with the phone, disliking the idea he could be reached anywhere, any time. What most people loved, he hated and left it lying around, often switched off. He relented only when this attitude threatened his work. In this crisis it was a vital link.

'You must keep the phone with you,' Sally kept saying. 'For some reason she might only speak to you and we mustn't miss it when she calls again.'

So it stayed in his pocket and every time it rang he grabbed it eagerly. There were eight calls but none from Kirstie Lomax, which puzzled him.

73

'What's the matter with the woman? She can't care much about the kid to be so thoughtless.' It made him angry, he had enough problems without worrying about someone's child.

Sally thought about it, saying calmly: 'Maybe she can't contact you.'

'What d'you mean?'

'Perhaps it's not that simple for her. She may not have the choice.'

'That's a bit far-fetched, isn't it?'

'Who knows? There has to be a reason. Think about it from her point of view, she knows Hayley's safe. And she's told us she's alive.'

'If it was her.'

'Who else could it have been?'

Chapter seven

Driving down the familiar single track lane to Grove Cottage seemed so normal that he almost forgot the hill was an island. The fields looked lush with a cloak of green from the rain-thickened grass. But the runnels of water down both sides reminded him of reality as he peered through the downpour.

The Claytons' cottage stood slightly lower than the road and their pretty front garden had become a muddy swamp. Rose bushes standing in a sad line either side of the path drooped with the weight of brown, rotting blooms. The path oozed brown slime and each footmark filled instantly with water as he approached the front door.

It was a small place, they'd downsized for their retirement. Two bedrooms, a stone outbuilding and a holiday caravan were sheltering fifteen extra souls who spilled from the house when he arrived.

He was suddenly surrounded by voices and people running towards the Land Rover, splashing through the mud.

'Hang on, wait. Let Mike get through.'

'Stop that,' he shouted at a woman tugging at something inside the vehicle. 'Be careful. We can't afford to waste stuff dropping it in the mud.'

Mike Clayton appeared, a man in his sixties. He looked desperate as he pushed his way to Adam.

'Thank God, you're here. They've eaten everything we had.'

'I came as soon as I could. It took a while to sort it fairly.'

Peering into the Land Rover Mike said: 'Is that all there is? It won't last long.'

'They didn't drop much, I'm sorry. I've given you what I could.'

'I don't know how we'll cope, we don't have much room anyway. Some are in the shed and the caravan and all over the house. What are you going to do about it?'

Stepping back Adam said: 'Me? What d'you mean?'

'You're in charge, aren't you. That's what Ron Hutchins told us.'

'I know he said that but it doesn't mean much. I've no idea what I'm going to do. What can I do?'

'We thought you'd know what's happening.'

'I know about as much as you do.' He paused. 'How many are there?'

'Thirteen from the first night and two more turned up this morning. We can't cope, I'm not used to dealing with stuff like this and it's making Nancy ill.'

Frowning Adam led him a little way along the road, away from the watching crowd. 'Look Mike, you've got to cope. You must ration the food -- and I mean that. You'll have to be really tough about it, or it won't last. I know it's hard but you've got to be firm.'

'When will they bring more?'

'Who knows? You've got to eke it out. If you have control problems ring me and I'll do my best to help. We've got to do what we can.'

Torrential rain streamed over the windscreen, delaying his journey back. The wipers could barely clear it as he peered at the road ahead and slowed to a crawl.

He drove into the yard to find chaos. The boys and John waded up to their calves in swirling water, stuffing plastic bags with sand from the bulk bag by the barn. But the sand immediately turned into mud. Tom was probing the water with drain rods and indoors the kitchen floor was already awash. A barricade of clothes and blankets blocked the gap below the door as they dragged the make-shift sandbags into place. The heavy rain bounced off their jackets and ran into their boots. Tom was cursing in frustration and his father smiled at the colourful language.

'Thank God you're back,' gasped Sally. 'The drain's blocked, we're trying to stop it getting into the rest of the house.'

'I'm not strong enough, Dad! I can't get the fucking thing to move. Don't know why it's suddenly blocked but we must stop it or the whole house will be flooded.'

Adam took the rods but found himself pushing against a solid mass. 'It won't give at all, something must be stuck down there.'

He looked around. At the corner a stone wall divided the yard from the garden and the ground was lower there.

'Get the sledge hammer, Tom.'

The boy nodded and ran.

He splashed back through the rising water and Adam began attacking the wall. 'I hate to do this.' He grunted between blows. 'But it's the only way.'

They watched as he rained heavy blows against the stone, gasping with each hit. When he built the wall he'd meant it to last. Gradually the mortar started to crack under the onslaught and the masonry shook.

The first coping stone tumbled into the garden and as the next layer began to crumble John grabbed the heavy hammer while Adam bent double to recover.

'You certainly made it solid,' muttered John as another layer fell to leave a ragged gap.

Water began to trickle through then washed over the top. In turns they carried on till it was at yard level when the pent-up flood rushed through in a satisfying surge and flowed in a brown cascade over the lawn and flower beds.

In the comparative comfort of the back hall he pulled off his soaking clothes and sniffed the air. A tempting aroma of hot food assailed his senses and drew him towards the kitchen. Sally and Eve were in there talking quietly together as they peeled potatoes and things appeared so cosy and normal that for a minute he thought he was dreaming.

They turned to smile at him and he stared in disbelief. 'Tell me I'm not imagining it,' he said 'but it smells like casserole.'

'Yep.' Eve grinned. 'We thawed out the mutton and it smelt fine. So we've cut it up and made a stew. We think it's safe enough and anyone who doesn't fancy it needn't eat it.'

'I can't see anybody turning it down, it smells wonderful, what a treat.'

He was actually smiling as he allowed himself the briefest of showers. An arm down the drain had revealed a stone holding tightly packed leaves and sticks, which puzzled him at this time of year. The incessant onslaught of rain must be pulling them loose before time.

The mutton was a winner. A couple of guests had read about it in glossy cooking supplements but none of them had tasted it. The prospect of a proper hot meal produced an amazing effect on these miserable people who were actually laughing together and chatting, discussing the flavour of the meat in comparison with lamb.

The Smiths and the vegetarians were dubious. Rosanna eyed her plate with distaste and her husband peered into the casserole dish and poked at the meat with the serving spoon.

'Are you sure it's safe?' he asked. 'We could all get food poisoning? We can't get to a doctor, we could die.'

Jock said: 'We'll all die some time, just hurry up.'

Rosanna put her plate down: 'If it's been in the freezer all that time I'm sure we shouldn't be eating it.'

Jock pushed between them and grabbed her plate. 'I'll have yours,' he said. 'Don't force yourselves to eat it.'

'But it could make us ill,' she persisted.

Sally said: 'Totally up to you. It's that or beans on toast.'

The other guests had gone quiet, and stopped eating to watch the Smiths as they dithered. A female voice shouted: 'I wouldn't eat it if I were you' and giggled, 'more for the rest of us.'

Smith took the plate he was offered and lowered his head to sniff the steaming stew. 'It does smell tempting,' he said.

'Could be the last decent meal you get for ages,' called Tom. 'Eat it while you've got the chance.'

'I'll risk it,' said Smith and carried it away, followed by his wife.

The vegetarians had been in a huddle, in a moral dilemma, discussing what they should do. Adam told them. 'It's your decision, I can't make you eat it but in the days to come we may get very short of protein. It might be wise to swallow your principles for a bit. We're talking about survival.'

'I haven't touched meat for nearly twenty years,' said a tall well-built woman, her pale face showing doubt and indecision. 'But it does smell good.'

She smiled at Adam: 'You're probably right. I think I'll try it.'

A cheer went round the room and someone said: 'What a pity. I was hoping for seconds.'

Only the vegans opted for beans on toast.

Jane Bryston had finished hers and was almost ecstatic as she listened to Sally explaining the merits of the meat.

'We haven't had it for years,' Jane said, 'but where I come from in the north mutton's very popular. This is good.'

Sally caught Adam's expression of gratitude because, even if for a brief respite, their guests were happy people.

She'd been telling them how they ran a few lambs on to an older age when they became technically mutton. 'It's all about how you cook it,' she was saying. 'Because it's older, it takes longer and gentler cooking but we love it.'

'It's mouth-watering,' from another voice, in a chorus of appreciation.

'Glad you like it. The last time we did it there was really too much so it's just as well you all came along to eat it.'

Her irony pleased Adam, such a simple comment which eased the strain.

Sally and Eve did a brilliant job with the mutton. It was delicious and something different. I didn't like to mention that much of the national sheep flock is probably drowned and the only mutton around is rotting in the flood. But it was good to see them smiling. The sack of potatoes is going down fast and there may be no more. Most of the crop will be stored in the lowlands and probably lost in the water. We need to eat more of the rice but they're not so keen on that.

I think the water pressure's dropping. I don't know why. It should work as long as there's power and it may be my imagination but if I'm right it's very worrying. It's five days now and the system was never meant to cope with so many people. I'll have to make them use less and they won't like that. It's seems crazy to be short of water when it's all around us.

They're such a mixed bunch, some of them are great but others just don't seem to realise the hole we're in.

Next day's lunch was back to routine and Adam was helping. He muttered something under his breath and Sally struggled to catch it. 'What are you saying?'

She was scraping spread onto toast -- only one slice per person. They were almost ready to serve the meagre offering, baked beans again. She knew there would be grumbles but the bread stock was limited. It was the staple that went with much of what they had -- something on toast. Potatoes were reserved for the day's main meal. Adam had asked for more and hoped for another sack on the next drop but he didn't hold out much hope. He was psyching himself up to announce new rules which they wouldn't like.

'What's the matter?' Sally asked.

'We must use less water,' he said. 'Less loo flushing and no showers or baths without asking. I've got to tell them.'

The guests ate wherever they could find somewhere to sit, spreading themselves across the ground floor rooms and stairs, some more careless than others which made meal times messy.

Amy and Jock had become a reliable part of the team and he admired the cheerful way they got on with collecting plates and cleaning up whatever was smeared on the floor or furniture. They'd started doing this without being asked and Sally was grateful, already very attached to them. It eased the pressure.

He waited till the eating was done and asked Jock to gather everyone together. Straight away he heard Marcus Smith's aggressive voice asking why. Jock shrugged and ignored him.

He stood on the stairs again, hoping it helped his authority and saw the anxiety in many faces as they wondered what was coming.

'I'm sorry,' he began 'but we need to be more careful with the water. I--- '

His voice was drowned by a roar of laughter but it died away when they saw his expression.

'What d'you mean?' It was Phil Bryston with unusual aggression. He was usually unruffled by their plight but perhaps the strain was getting to him as well.

'You all need to think when you turn on a tap or use the loo. Don't flush unless you really need to and no baths or showers without asking. That's it really, I want you to be sensible and careful.'

'Water, water everywhere, nor any drop to drink,' Phil intoned in a solemn voice.

'What?'

'Rime of the Ancient Mariner, remember?'

He smiled. 'Thanks, very appropriate.'

Everyone looked at Phil, many not understanding but some smiling. It eased the tension and he moved from the stairs and waited for quiet.

'It's quite simple,' he said firmly. 'If we run out of drinking water we're in real trouble.'

Chapter eight

John came to at first light with the unpleasant sensation of being forcibly held down, he tried to cry out and started to struggle before opening his eyes to see Adam standing over him. It was his hand over John's mouth that restrained him.

'Sorry, but I need you to be quiet. Come down as soon as you can.'

Outside, grey and chilly in the dawn with a fine, determined rain wetting them Adam led the way in silence to the barn and John followed with a sense of dread. They stood close together just inside the door, well away from the sleepers.

'Sorry about all that but I needed you out here to do what we have to do without rousing any of them.' He gestured towards the house.

'What's going on?'

'That last drop, they brought guns. I was going to tell you sooner but it was difficult.'

'Guns?'

'Yeah, for crowd control.'

'Surely the authorities will be here and sort it all out long before that could happen?'

Adam looked at him but said nothing, the silence was palpable.

'What? What aren't you telling me?'

'Apparently, while this crisis goes on, I am 'the authority' and you're my deputy. That captain, on the chopper — you weren't there when he said it, it was when he gave me the guns.'

'What? Tell me Adam, for Christ's sake!'

'He said 'you're the man, you've been checked'.'

'What did he mean?'

'You tell me. They've checked me out but on what criteria I've no idea. They're checking on you as well.'

'What?' John looked nervous.

'Don't worry, it's just routine. You've nothing to hide, have you?'

'No, of course not but I wasn't expecting all this.'

'Nor me. Ron rang late last night and they want us to take control of the whole area above the flood line and the other camps in our region.'

'Jesus!'

'We're dealing with a series of islands, high ground above the flood line. Our people don't realise how lucky they are, at least the farm is a proper base with some facilities, however limited. Some of these camps are literally just emergency tents.'

'What are we supposed to do?'

'I'm not sure. See how we can help, liaise with the army and show some sort of authority.'

'You mean intimidate people.'

'That's one way of putting it, keep the lid on things so people don't think they can just do as they want.'

'It won't be easy.'

'No, it's bad enough looking after this lot but Ron says there's been nasty incidents in other places and till the police are properly organised to get about, it's down to us.'

'What about transport? You'll need the Land Rover and you won't have enough fuel.'

'Not as it stands but it gets more Boys Own by the minute. They're coming with another drop, in secret. While our happy campers are in the land of Nod they're swooping in with supplies of diesel for the Land Rover and --' he paused for effect as John's eyes opened wider -- 'a boat.'

'What sort of boat?'

'Probably a dinghy, with an outboard motor. So we can go

island hopping through the valley.'

'It sounds like the bloody commandoes to me.'

'Yes, it could be fun.' He saw John's face. 'Joke.'

'When are they coming?'

'Any time now.'

'Shit, this is getting out of hand. How are we supposed to do all this? I'm just an ordinary bloke -- same as you,' John frowned.

'I don't need any of this crap. Don't want these people here, ruining my home, upsetting my wife -- and yours -- I want my life back.'

He paused, rubbing his chin as if it helped him think. 'What we've got here is only a tiny part of it. There are hundreds on this hill alone, from Shrivenor and Beckhill and they've flown in groups from Birmingham. Camps on high ground full of refugees.'

'But it's not down to us,' John protested.

'I'm afraid it is -- for now. But I don't know how long I can stick it -- these people don't understand the countryside, how we live. They've no idea what's going on.'

He looked hard at John. 'Sal and I can't cope on our own, we need your help, you and Eve. We make a good team, the four of us.'

'Do I have a choice? Look's like we're both stuck with it.'

They waited in the barn, with a view over the field, staring through a steady curtain of rain. The path, once laid with lime-stone chips, was a slippery mess of liquid mud, deeper and mud-dier as each wet day passed. Waiting in gloomy depression they heard the familiar sound of a chopper engine.

This time it was carrying something long and bulky, slung beneath the craft. It hovered without landing while the bundle was lowered to settle on the field.

The same young captain called to them. 'There you go. One dinghy with full instructions and some diesel for your vehicle. Good luck.'

The delivery happened so quickly. The chopper was away again, leaving them in a swirl of wind and wetness, whipping off their hoods as they struggled to keep their feet.

In the boat they found a map showing the location of three camps within a thirty mile radius. The nearest and largest was Ruttock Common, an upland ridge covered in heather and bracken from where four counties could be seen.

High and wind-swept they both knew from walking the length of it -- from one valley pub to another -- that there was nothing on it but vegetation and sheep. The idea of anyone living up there apart from a summer camping break was barely credible.

John looked up from the map: 'They can't intend to leave people out there for more than a few days?'

'Who knows? They're out of the flood but that doesn't mean much. Let's find out the reality.'

Driving along the crest of the hill, trying to find a road to keep them on high ground, they used tracks which were bridleways or fit only for mountain bikes. In low box the elderly Land Rover coped as they crossed fields and cut fences to stay on course.

The road ran down into the valley and back up following the contours. Twice they went down too far and it was an eerie sensation to be met by silent water instead of the familiar landmarks they knew. They had to reverse to get back on track, not easy with the boat behind.

But it was stranger yet once they launched the dinghy and set off towards the other ridge. John perched at the back steering and controlling the engine while Adam sat further forward, studying the ordnance map, trying to figure out where they should land. It was weird to be crossing a lake where they should be driving along a valley.

It began like an adventure, new and exciting and brought out the boys in them. Getting used to the craft was an experience for both, neither knew about boats and they nearly fell in at the start as they boarded the rocking craft. The flood had a surprising swell, caused by the wind blowing between the hills and it was uncomfortably cold as they headed onto open water. They talked in loud, sharp snaps but gradually the expanse of water overwhelmed them and the enormity of it began to dawn as the distance to the other side seemed to get no less.

They navigated in silence along what should have been the valley between Rueberry Down and the Maesteg Moors. The hamlet of Lower Downton was somewhere beneath them but they knew it's location from the top of the disused silage tower showing clear of the water. Down there were two farms, with large barns and nine other homes, as well as two caravans.

John gazed at the silent tower stunned and afraid. 'I didn't realise it was this bad,' he said softly.

'It's still rising,' Adam answered.

'It's much deeper than I realised. When you come down this side it's frightening.'

'The hills are steeper here, it's the escarpment. The valley's narrower so it's holding the water.'

They moved steadily on an oblique course along the lake's centre, Adam sweeping the hillside with binoculars. Based at the lower end of the moor, where the land was less craggy on a heather covered open expanse of ground, he assumed it would be easy to spot in the treeless landscape. But the water had changed the perspective of the hills.

What appeared on the OS map and the new reality of the flood were totally different and he was looking too far west. He expected the tented site to stand out easily on the hill but it was John who spotted it.

'There, look, a big tent, more to the east.'

Adam looked more closely and saw a single large marquee, at the centre of a grid pattern of smaller brown tents.

'Army tents. I was looking for coloured ones. Stupid -- there's a lot of them.'

'There's the road, said John. 'if we land there it won't be too far to walk up.'

As they trudged up the steep lane he said: 'Before we get there, what are we actually meant to do? Why are we here?'

'I've no idea. Take it as it comes -- wait and see.'

They were spotted long before they arrived and a crowd gathered round them, jostling and firing questions.

'Who are you? Can you help us? What the hell are we supposed to do here? We need more water. There's nothing here. How long will we be here?' Shouts and demands all round.

'Shit,' said John, his standard response when stuck. 'What do we say?'

'Try to look tough,' muttered Adam, holding up his hand. 'Head for the marquee, it's central.'

They moved on, the press of people almost pushing them along, through the lines of tents, walking on plastic matting oozing watery mud. It was slippery and hard to walk fast. In the marquee, he was relieved to see some organisation, trestles set up and what looked like an army field kitchen. As they entered two soldiers appeared from somewhere, looking worried but pleased. They stayed safely behind the tables as the buzzing throng hung round exuding anger.

'Are you Mr Woolton?'

Adam nodded. 'Glad you're here, sir. It's getting a bit touchy like.'

The soldier had two stripes on his sleeve.

'Is this it corporal? Just you two? -- Just wait, will you -- ' He spun round as someone pushed against him. 'Quiet.' He bawled in his most aggressive tone. 'Just calm down. This racket isn't helping. Hang on a minute while we weigh up what's going on. Back off!'

The crowd edged back and Adam turned to the soldiers.

'Are you armed, sir?' asked the corporal in a low voice.

'No.'

'They told us you'd be armed.'

'We didn't bring the guns, didn't think we'd need them.' He looked over his shoulder at the tense mass, sensing their impatience and frustration -- and understanding it. 'Are you two on your own?'

The corporal nodded. 'We're just cooks, sir, Army Catering Corps. We were dropped here when they set up the camp to provide grub for this lot. But they don't seem to appreciate it, sir. They won't wait for meal times, they keep nicking stuff. I tell you, we'll run out soon.'

'Okay corporal, I get the picture.'

'They don't seem to understand about rations, sir. They think they can just take what they like. You'll have to do something, sir.'

'I understand, we have the same problem at our base.' He glanced at John who shrugged uncertainly.

The corporal went on, muttering: 'You need a gun, sir. They'll understand that.'

'You may be right. Have you got guns?'

'One rifle, sir. But me and Neil, we're not authorised to use weapons except in a combat situation.'

'And you think I am?'

'That's what command said, sir. Take orders from Adam Woolton or John Kerr.'

He sensed the crowd brewing up again and turned to face them, holding up a hand for quiet. 'Should've brought a gun,' he thought, 'the sound of a shot would shake them into quiet.'

He faced them. 'Please be quiet and listen. Is there someone to speak for you.' The whole bunch moved toward him, shouting again.

'Stop it!' He bawled again. 'This is useless. We can't listen to you all shouting at once. If you don't shut up we can't do anything.'

John meanwhile had found a packing case and as he got up on

it the corporal thrust a loud hailer into his hand.

He called through it: 'Let the man speak, will you.'

It took a few minutes but gradually they subsided into silence and waited expectantly.

'Thanks, John.'

'Get up here, Adam. It might help.'

Clambering up beside his friend on the box he said: 'Now then, let's try to make some sense of this and don't all shout at once.'

'Who are you?' called someone. 'What have you come for?'

'My name is Adam Woolton and I live on the other hill. I'm supposed to act as liaison officer to help you till things get back to normal. I need to know what the problems are so I can report back and do something to help.'

'Where shall we start?' Someone shouted and launched a new wave of shouting and abuse.

Adam looked pointedly at the ground, waiting while it carried on until John gave them an ear-splitting burst on the loud hailer which produced enough quiet for Adam to try again.

'Look, I'm trying to help. Just one of you, tell us what's what.'

Furious voices kicked off again but one woman near the front pushed through to stand below Adam and gradually the rest grew still.

'The problem's pretty basic,' she said. 'There's nothing here. We were all brought by helicopter or boat and just dumped. There's the tents and this--' she waved her arms around the marquee where they stood 'and not much else.'

'Have you all got beds?' he asked.

'Sort of. There's some camp beds and those army mattress things, you know, and plenty of blankets but that's about all. These two' -- nodding at the soldiers -- 'they dish up three meals a day but it's awful. There's no proper toilets, just trenches in the ground they call latrines, no washing facilities and no power except in here. Worst of all there's very little water.'

The corporal butted in. 'The engineers set up a generator, sir, to give us power in here. They were supposed to come back and connect the tents as well but --'

'They haven't done it yet, I see.' Adam cut him short.

'I can see it's pretty grim, Mrs?'

'Anne Pocock. Grim, it's hopeless, we can't live like this.'

Adam hesitated to say what was in his mind for fear of starting a riot. He chose his words with care. 'It can't be easy, doing without the basics. Where are you from?'

'All over the midlands, it's impossible. There's nothing but rabbits and sheep.'

He rubbed his chin. 'At least you're out of the flood. They had to put you somewhere and high ground is the only option. We have to make the best of it till the water goes.'

His words prompted a fresh eruption and it took time to regain their attention.

'We'll make a list of what you need -- the most vital and try to get them. The army's very stretched. In the meantime give these lads a break, they're trying their best for you. They can only cook what they've been given.'

The corporal produced a notebook and leaned on the packing case to write down a list of all their complaints and requirements, knowing that few of them could be implemented. Some wandered off, back to their own tents and he questioned the soldiers again. 'Are you in touch with the other camps?'

'Yes sir, we have radio contact and the phones are working okay.'

'We're supposed to visit all three. But I don't fancy a repeat of this.'

'I wouldn't, sir, not unarmed. There's been a lot of trouble at Rowan Hill, they've made the village there into a refugee centre but the locals are cutting up rough. They beat up the cook, a mate of mine. The water's rationed, that's the biggest problem and they don't like it. Same as here, they're supposed to sink a borehole but nothing's happened yet.'

'That all takes time --'

'Yes sir and such heavy equipment is very hard to move by air. We can't see it happening -- not in a hurry.'

'What's the army doing? Can't they keep control?'

'There's a platoon there now, sir, since the trouble. But they'll be moved again. The lads are flat out, sir, rescuing people and trying to keep it all going. There's not enough of us, sir, too thin on the ground. Neil and me shouldn't be here on our own but they can't spare any more.'

They left the camp as the rain increased and the only visible inhabitants were in the marquee. All the smaller tents were zipped up to keep out the deluge.

They surveyed a scene of utter desolation, mud-coloured tents in a landscape of mud, the plastic walkways already swamped and where the heather had been cut to make way for the camp the black peat was oozing through.

'God almighty, you can't blame them for being pissed off.' They looked at each other.

'Do you think we've been any help?' John asked.

'Not really -- the promise of help may have cheered them up a bit. All we can do is pass on their complaints and lobby the army. We'll do the other camps tomorrow but we must take the guns.'

Chapter nine

Depressed by images of misery at Ruttock Common, tired and worried that they'd still heard nothing from Hayley's mum he was in no mood to be patient. He had a foot on the stairs, ready for bed when Smith appeared from the dining room where he was now billeted with his wife.

'My wife isn't well,' he announced. 'She can't get to sleep.'

Resentment welled up in Adam's head but he struggled to control it. He'd watched with disgust at supper as the overweight Rosanna wolfed the pilchard sandwiches which were the evening ration. Then she and her husband snatched the leftovers, without bothering to ask if anyone else wanted them. At every meal they took more than their share and though there had been some angry mutters none of the others had complained. 'What's the matter with her?'

'Stomach pains -- cramps. She's very uncomfortable.'

Sympathy was difficult to summon. 'Sounds like indigestion. She ate a lot of sandwiches.'

'Sardines always upset her stomach,' Smith said.

'It didn't stop her scoffing more than anyone else,' he couldn't help saying.

'That's not true.'

'It is. You two always eat more than anyone, it's not surprising she feels poorly.'

'You're very rude, Woolton. When this is over I shall make a complaint to the authorities.'

'You do that. I'm going to bed.'

'What about Rosanna?'

'Here,' he felt in his pockets where he kept a few basic drugs.

He found some anti-acid tablets. 'Give her one of these and tell her to drink some water. I can't do anything else.'

He climbed into bed and lay on his back staring at the rain streaming down the glass. It seemed for ever since they'd been able to open the windows to let in fresh air, the room was smelly with damp, the unwashed sheets felt clammy and he shuddered.

'Christ, this is miserable,' he muttered and Sally turned over to nuzzle her head against his shoulder.

'What's the matter, love?' she asked.

He laughed at that. 'Where shall I start? The room stinks, we all stink, it's still fucking raining and bloody Rosanna Smith's got stomach cramps. Everything's just great! And don't tell me things will seem better in the morning.'

'Try to get some sleep, it's the only thing to do.'

He grunted and closed his eyes. He was disturbed after what seemed only a moment by the phone buzzing near his head, the blue digits on the clock said 11.47.

He answered wearily: 'Who is it?'

The voice jerked him to attention, a lilting, gentle intonation, soft but firm, a voice that commanded attention. 'Kirstie Lomax, is that Adam?'

'Yes.' He found himself excited, waiting for that velvet tone.

'Sorry to call so late.'

'Mrs Lomax, Hayley's mum?'

'Yes.'

'Where are you?'

'I can't tell you.'

'Why not?'

'Please, listen to me, I haven't got long. You rescued her from the house, right?'

'Yes, through the bedroom window.'

'I'm so grateful, did she have anything with her?'

'Just a rabbit toy, she takes it everywhere.

'That's Benji. Tell her I'm fine, will you and not to worry.'

'She is worrying.'

'Tell her not to. I'll see her soon.'

'You left her alone in that weather.'

'I had no choice.'

'Why?'

'I had to, believe me, no time now for explanations.'

'Why can't you say where you are?'

'I just can't. Tell her I love her and it'll be okay. Say I'll see her soon. Right?'

'I'll tell her.'

'And Adam -- thank you. You and your wife, thanks for taking care of her. She means everything to me.'

'Kirstie, can't you--' She cut him off.

'Gotta go, sorry. We'll speak again.'

And the phone went dead.

They were in the bedroom with the door locked. The four of them and the boys and little Hayley, all eyes on the TV, except Adam who paced the room, face drawn with anxiety. They were waiting for the BBC news.

It began with familiar scenes of flooded landscapes, panning across wide sweeps of town and country.

World events in areas not flooded were featured but the main focus was on human interest stories from all over Britain, much of it about people lost and found.

The filming was minimal, illustrated with stills or recycled clips. So when the familiar face of Lynn Meacham appeared as the third item Adam groaned and next thing there he was scowling into the camera.

The roar of surprise and commotion sounded clearly from downstairs and he went out to listen to the voices, some incredulous, some amused but others angry.

He shut the door and went back to watch. It was a five minute clip of Lynn talking about the potential of his ark scheme to help in the flooding. It showed him explaining that the whole idea was just a joke but the impression she had given of an ongoing project made him very anxious.

She spoke about the group at Down Farm and his commanding role. She also mentioned his wider responsibility 'pending long-term arrangements.' He winced at that and wondered how she'd got the information. But worse, she talked about money and he swore as she told viewers that hundreds of people had already given 'considerable financial support.'

'That's cool, dad,' Ben said. 'All those people reading your blog. When do we start work on it?'

John touched the boy's arm with a finger to his lip, frowning to shut him up. To Adam he said: 'It's not that bad, quite a good piece really. She got most of the facts right.'

He scowled. 'I can only see trouble from this. I wish I'd never thought of it.'

'Calm down. It can't be that bad,' John's voice had an edge of impatience but he caught Sally's eye and the almost imperceptible head shake, meaning: 'Don't wind him up any more.'

Eve, who'd been fascinated by the broadcast, said gently: 'I shouldn't worry, Adam. It'll be forgotten in a day or two when something else crops up and everyone's attention will focus on another issue.'

He was staring at the greyness outside, wondering when some let-up might ease the pressure but he managed to smile. 'I hope you're right. Any minute now the calls will start.'

It had begun earlier in the day as they were getting ready to leave for another of the camps. John took a call on Adam's phone. 'Who is this? I'll find him,' he put his hand over the phone and said in a low voice: 'It's some guy from the Sun, something about an ark.'

'Say you can't find me, get rid of him.'

John lied as instructed.

'What was that about?'

Adam looked sheepish but Sally butted in: 'Something he hasn't told you.'

John looked expectant. 'Come on, tell us.'

'It was a joke. Something I dreamed up to amuse myself, I showed Sally and the boys. Just a joke,' he repeated.

'But what?'

'An ark, a big boat. Something to take my mind off all this.' He waved an arm vaguely.

'So how come the press know about it?'

'I put it on line.'

Eve came into the kitchen and sensed the tension. 'What's this?'

'Tell them the rest,' Sally ordered. 'You won't believe it.'

'Come on.'

'I'll tell you.' She thumped her fist on the table hard enough to make the crockery bounce. 'Do you know what he did? He put his bloody bank details on-line.'

'But surely nobody took it seriously?'

'You wouldn't think so, would you? Tell them.'

Adam looked sheepish. 'I mentioned crowd-funding. A lot of money's come in, I need to send it back.'

'How much?'

Adam sat down at the table.

'Last time I checked it was nearly a quarter of a million.'

'What?'

'I never thought anyone would take it seriously.'

'He's got to refund it,' Sally said.

But Eve said thoughtfully: 'It's a great story for the media. Could you do it, Adam?'

He saw she was serious. 'I doubt it, it's totally impractical. It was just a daft notion that I doodled with.'

'But it shows the desperation,' Eve said quietly. 'You've hit a chord with them. It's like, well, something they can latch onto, a survival option.'

'Don't encourage him.'

'Just looking at the case,' she said. 'Is the cash still coming in?'

'I haven't checked since yesterday.'

'You must take it down, I thought you'd already done it,' said Sally.

'I meant to, but we had to visit the camp and now we need to get to Rowan Hill. We ought to be away.'

But the phone buzzed again and Sally grabbed it.

'No, he won't speak to you.' Adam listened. 'No, you can't. What? Oh, for God's sake, hang on a minute.' She dropped the phone on the table and ushered Adam through the door.

'Who is it?'

'It's the BBC. They're sending two people on a chopper to interview you. I said you won't talk to them but they're already on the way.'

Adam thought hard but John said: 'They're probably your best chance of getting the truth out there.'

'You're right.' He picked up the phone: 'What time will they be here? Right.'

'Within the hour,' he glanced at his wife. 'I'm sorry Sal, I'll sort it, I promise.'

He faced the others. 'We'll have to forget the camp and deal with this.'

'Shall I go alone,' John asked.

'Not a good idea, it could be nasty.' He sighed as he saw them all watching him. 'Sorry about this, I've landed myself right in it. Don't take any more calls, we don't want a swarm of press here.'

The helicopter circled once high over the farm, as John and Adam waved their arms to direct it to the field. They recognised the reporter Lynn Meacham, seen everyday on-line and TV.

She ducked out under the rotors into driving rain to pick her way through the quagmire, well-prepared in waterproof trousers and rubber boots.

The young man trailing after her seemed less organised and John glanced smiling at Adam as he struggled through the muck lugging his equipment. He wore trainers and was soon smeared to the ankles.

'Adam?' Lynn peered out from her streaming hood.

'That's me.'

'Yes, I've seen your picture.'

They followed him to the barn and he said at once: 'How did you get onto me?'

'Not hard, the radio appeal for the little girl's mum. We monitor all that stuff and check names on line to see if there's anything good. You came up as the ark man.'

Adam groaned. 'You read my blog?'

'Of course. Good stuff and the response you're getting is fantastic.'

'It was a bit of fun, not serious, it's not practical. I don't want any more publicity, it'll just make things worse.'

'Look Adam,' the hard-line newshound flashed into action as she said: 'This is a big story. If you don't speak to me you'll get everyone else.'

'Haven't you all got better things to do in this crisis?'

'This is what people want. They're all stuck in camps or in groups like yours -- many much worse off -- wrapped in blankets and drinking a lot of tea if they're lucky. They need some distraction, encouragement. A scheme like yours could be a lifesaver.'

'It's only a boat.'

'To you maybe, haven't you watched the news?'

'I've been too busy here. It's not easy.'

'That's why I'm here with Tommy. The media are pooling resources, it's the only way we get permission to fly at the moment. Small teams fly out on different stories and we share the copy. Apart from the Sun -- they seem to have got round somebody and are doing their own thing.

So,' she faced him, 'do we do a proper interview, filming you and the others or do I make it up from what details I know already?'

'We'd better talk but you must make it clear it's not a serious project.'

'You should be careful how you say that. Look at your site more often -- there's a huge response. This is the kind of thing the Americans go for. Since New Orleans and Katrina they're terrified of floods. With the rise in sea level some of their land is already inundated, they've lost acres of coastline.' She paused: 'A man with an ark makes a big impression.'

'I haven't got an ark. It was only a silly idea.'

'The people sending money obviously don't think so.'

'How do you know about that?'

'They say on the blog, in the chat -- haven't you read it? It's obvious they've sent funds.'

The stunned expression gave him away. 'I haven't time to keep track of it,' he muttered.

'How much has come in?' asked Lynn, latched on to something. Adam's eyes switched to Tommy, the technician was fiddling with his gear.

'Are you recording? He spoke sharply. 'I'm not saying any more.'

She nodded at Tommy: 'Switch off a minute.'

'How much?'

'I was surprised, I've already returned some.'

'Is it a lot?' she repeated.

'Quite a bit.'

'Thousands? Millions? What?'

'Not that much, I can't tell you. It's all got to go back.'

He saw suspicion in her eyes, the cynical expression as she tried to weigh up the foibles of human nature -- his. She was wondering if it was a scam or was he genuine.

He knew what she was thinking because he was thinking it himself.

To people for whom social media was almost life itself the TV and the few laptops were the only thing that kept them in touch with reality. Most of them spent the day looking at screens. When their host appeared it was a sensation.

Adam was right to be worried. The rising sound of argument downstairs shook him. The row was between those who accepted it as a joke that misfired and those who thought their host was running a massive scam.

He was right about the phone. It was Ron, angry.

'I knew you'd call.' Six pairs of eyes watched him as he turned away and went into the bathroom. He closed the door. 'I know what you're going to say. I couldn't help it, I had to talk to them, to get the right story out there.'

'What is this crackpot scheme?'

'It was just a joke. I keep telling people but nobody will believe me. I drew it one evening to amuse myself.'

'Stupid thing to do. Don't you realise what you've done. All this attention will attract more people wanting you to save them.'

'I know.'

Ron went on: 'I called to warn you. The army will be furious, official secrets etc. They won't like the bit about you being in command. Why did you tell her that?'

'I didn't, give me some credit. I don't know how she got it.'

'You'd better have a good story. They'll call you -- and soon.'

'I'm not in the army and I didn't ask them to choose me.'

'Maybe so, but they did and you've got the weapons.'

'What can they do, sack me? That'll suit me.'

'Be careful what you say. These are bad times and they've got powers now to cover pretty much everything.'

'Thanks for the warning. It's a nightmare.'

'That's some understatement but listen, it's the money thing. Be very careful what you say.'

'Wait Ron. There's something else. This child, Hayley, her mother's called twice but there's something odd. Don't know what it is. She can't talk for long and we can't call her back.'

'Where is she?'

'She won't say. I've got a bad feeling about it.'

'The kid's okay?'

'She's fine, less trouble than some of the adults.'

Ron laughed. 'That'll get worse as time goes on.'

'The mother's a translator, or interpreter, I just wonder if there's something in that.'

'What's the name?'

'Kirstie Lomax, have a fish about. See if the name gets a reaction.'

'If it does, they won't tell me much.'

'Try.'

Someone was banging on the bedroom door. 'What's that in the background?' asked Ron.

'It's the guests wanting to give me the third degree about the fucking ark, can't blame them.'

'Stay cool, Adam.'

'I'll try. What with them and the army, don't know which is worse.'

He stood on the stairs again this time faced with anger and resentment. The position at least offered an element of retreat as well as access to the weapons. As he caught the angry vibes he pictured the guns, lying neatly in their box, concealed only by the hanging covers of his bed.

Clearly he heard the words: 'What the hell you playing at?' but the rising clamour continued oblivious of his attempts to speak. He found himself making ineffective flapping motions with his hands and at last gave up and waited, arms folded, assailed by waves of sound.

He watched Jock and Philip doing their best to calm people but they were ignored. He uncrossed his arms and found his fists clenched, nails digging into his palms as he tried to control the sense of frustration and injustice.

He moved back, one step higher and the image of cold metal peeped like a promise into his head. John was close behind him and as if he'd read Adam's mind, he whispered: 'Time to get a gun?'

101

He didn't turn: 'Give it a little longer. You know where they are?' John nodded.

The crowd's fury looked like a taste of the future as events deteriorated. But an ear-splitting din sounded above the rumpus and Eve was there, braced and defiant, drumming a heavy steel serving spoon on the base of a large saucepan. Heads turned seeking the source of the racket.

'Shut up,' she yelled, still crashing the spoon on the pan. 'Shut up and let him tell you about it.'

Like a radio switched off they were silent and Jock muttered: 'Sorry Adam.'

Weak with relief he grabbed the stair rail, smiling at John who said quietly: 'Bloody hell.'

He laughed and said loudly: 'Thanks, Eve. That'd make a good dinner gong.'

The mood changed in an instant and he moved down the stairs. 'I'm sorry about all this. I should have warned you it might be on but I wasn't sure they'd use it as it's all really rather silly.'

'Silly!' It was Smith with a nasty edge in his voice: 'Doesn't sound silly, sounds like you're making a fortune. All that money and you keep us on strict rations and inflict all your blasted rules.'

That created a wave of growling mutters, some agreeing, some annoyed. Philip Bryston turned on Smith: 'Oh do be quiet. Haven't you the sense to see money is totally irrelevant in this? All the cash in the world won't buy food that's not there.'

'Thanks Philip. This is crackers. It was something I drew for fun, to amuse the boys. But I made the mistake of putting it on-line. That's it, it was a joke that's backfired on me. But it really has no bearing on what's happening.' He paused.

Some had that look -- 'yeah, pull the other one, who you kidding' -- but the majority of expressions showed frowns of thoughtfulness, weighing his words.

'Think about it,' he went on. 'I'm stuck here, same as you, trying to hang on till the water disappears. How could I possibly do anything about a project like that while all this is happening?'

'What about the money?'

'It's true that people have offered financial backing--'

'You mean money.'

'Yes, but it's all in the ether. It's only real if I use it and I can't. And I'm trying to send it back.'

I've tried returning the credits but most of them come back unaccepted, the sites must be down. Just think of all those servers round the world made useless by water.

I can't concentrate, keep thinking about what Ron said. I hate the intimidation, waiting for Big Brother to rebuke me. I really resent it. Maybe I should get the guns and chase them all away.

Send them all out into the rain. I can imagine the Smiths shouting obscenities. But Jock, Amy and the Brystons and most of the others are okay. I couldn't do it. They're just frightened, helpless people, out of their comfort zones.

I can see us stuck like this for good, gradually starving, getting weaker, maybe drowning. What if the water never goes down? Maybe I'll end up shooting everyone as a kinder option.

At that moment Sally appeared and caught his distress as he turned away. She saw what he'd written and he looked up and shook his head. 'I don't know if I can do this, it's all too much.'

She held his head against her. 'I know it's hard. But it won't last for ever. You've been so strong, so purposeful. We'll get through it.'

'They think I'm a bastard.'

'Not really, most of them appreciate what you're doing. You and John, you're a good team. You have to have rules in a thing like this, or it's chaos.'

'I don't how long we can keep it up. It'll get worse. There's no sign of a let-up in the rain.'

'It can't rain for ever and the water will start to go down.'

'Will it? What if it never goes down?'

103

The call came in the night, in darkness that these days was total. The constant layer of cloud enveloped the landscape and once the feeble daylight had vanished with the unseen sun the blackness was complete.

The phone buzzed for more than half a minute beside the bed before he registered the intrusion. Shaking his head he felt for the phone.

'Adam Woolton?'

'Yes.'

'Captain Rogers here.'

'Who?'

'Tim Rogers -- I come with the chopper drops.'

'Right.' He was fully awake now: 'What the hell, d'you know what time it is?'

'It's 02.50 hrs.'

'Where the fuck are you?'

'In your field.'

'What?'

'I've come to get you.'

He sat up in bed. 'What are you talking about?'

'We've come to pick you up, you're wanted.'

'Where?'

'Please, I have my orders, just dress and get out here. You've got eight minutes.'

Adam shook his head in disbelief and eyed the silent phone. Beside him Sally had woken: 'What's happening?'

Their window had a good view over the farm. He peered into the darkness towards the field and saw bright lights where there should be only night. 'There's a helicopter in the field.'

'What for?'

'The army, they want me to go with them.'

'They can't make you go, can they?'

'Who knows?'

He looked at her, angry at the anxiety in her face and aware of the cold knot of fear in his gut. 'I think I've got to go, sweetheart. I get the feeling that if I'm not out there pretty smart he'll be in here with that corporal who's always with him and I'll be going out at the point of a gun. We don't want that.'

He was scrambling into his clothes as they spoke, after a splash of chilly water on his face and hands. He hugged and kissed her hurriedly.

'Try not to worry -- I know you will, but it'll be okay. They need me here -- at least, I think they do.' She caught the doubt in his words. 'Love you, darling. I'll call when I can.'

In the chopper's powerful lights the captain eyed his watch impatiently but caught the look on Adam's face and a wincing hesitation as he ducked beneath the rotors.

'Don't you like helicopters?' he asked.

'I can't bear the noise overhead.'

'Why?'

'Unpleasant memories,' he muttered and jumped aboard, one leg still dangling as the machine rose and screamed away.

Chapter ten

On his back in the helicopter, struggling to get his breath, he was conscious of the young soldier watching him.

Captain Rogers waited till Adam sat up before he said: 'Sorry about this, we had to beat the weather.'

'Where are we going?'

'Southern HQ but don't ask me why. I was just ordered to bring you -- some sort of meeting.'

'That doesn't tell me anything. Where is it?'

'A big house they've requisitioned in the Cotswolds.'

He scrambled up and took the seat behind the pilot, staying quiet as he considered his position, wondering if he would come home from this meeting. It crossed his mind that he might be locked up for the duration. He looked out into the darkness: 'It's bloody black out there.'

The pilot heard him and spoke over his shoulder. 'Don't worry, we know where we're going.'

'D'you want to sit in the front?' asked the captain and when he nodded, the corporal, who never seemed to speak, left his seat beside the pilot and motioned Adam to take his place.

'You won't see much in the dark,' said the pilot switching on the down lights. 'How's that?'.

The beams shone bright over an expanse of water, mile after mile. 'We're following the Severn Valley, that's all there is -- water.'

Adam slumped in his seat: 'Turn them off, it's too depressing.'

The chopper landed on the lush green lawn of a stately home, its pale stonework lit harshly by a row of glaring floodlights trained on neat rows of portable buildings and tents. He followed the captain up steps and through a grand hall where two soldiers sat at a desk surrounded by ancient oil paintings, swords, a suit of armour and a stuffed owl. A magnificent carved staircase led up from the entrance hall but they went via a small door down a back stairway and into the large echoing kitchen, now an army canteen.

'Meeting's scheduled for 07.30 so you can get breakfast and a rest,' said the captain.

He was roused from dozing in the room where they left him -- not locked in he was happy to note -- by a boyish private who called him sir and apologised for waking him. The camp bed was hard but he'd made up some of his interrupted sleep. Confidence began creeping back as he followed the soldier upstairs into what he assumed was the main dining room. He gazed in appreciation at the plasterwork and a painting covering walls and ceiling which depicted a battle scene with many handsome horses and soldiers in cavalier dress.

The long, elegant Georgian table had been cleared of its sumptuous silver and dishes, laid out now with laptops, phones, a printer, paper and pens. Overhead hung a chandelier, its romance incongruous. The clock showed 07.24.

The room buzzed with low murmurs from the group of men, mostly in combat uniform, helping themselves from pots of tea and coffee on the dresser. He stood by the door, uncertain what to do until one with a major's crown on his shoulders spotted him.

'Woolton?' Adam nodded.

'Sit down there, tea or coffee?' He was shown a seat and did as he was told, sipping the strong coffee, wondering what came next. At 07.30 precisely a senior officer entered and everyone hurried to the table as he went to its head and sat down without a word.

No introductions, no general information, just: 'Let's get on. Is Woolton here?'

'Yes sir,' said the major and indicated Adam.

'Right.' The colonel glanced at the paperwork on the table and then at the man. 'Adam Woolton, yes? You've been delegated as ground commander for our western C section.'

'I didn't know it was called that.'

The colonel ignored him. 'You were checked and nothing came up, so you're cleared. Now you appear on TV with some scheme about an ark. We need to know about that. Why haven't you informed us? You also told the press about your role with us.'

Adam looked blank, trying to think of a plausible explanation but the colonel was impatient.

'Well?' he demanded.

'The ark thing is a joke, that's the simple truth. And I don't know how Lynn Meacham got hold of the other information, certainly not from me or John Kerr.'

'Information must be kept tight in this crisis. It's a serious breach of security.'

Adam was irritated. 'That's all very well but I didn't ask for this role. It was dumped on me and I can't see what difference it makes.'

The colonel glared at him: 'It might matter a great deal. What about the weapons? Who knows about them?'

'Only my wife and John Kerr.'

'Are you sure of him?'

'Of course I am.'

'How long have you known him?'

'About three years, he's a good friend.'

'We're still checking him. Not easy as things are. We already had your record.'

'I see. I'm sure there's nothing to find.'

'Let's hope not. Things are very bad, Woolton. The greater part of the south and east is either under water or cut off, supplies of everything are low and if it doesn't stop raining soon, we don't know how long we can contain the situation and provide food. Those who can have moved north and west but that causes new problems. The locals in those areas are reluctant to share their dwindling supplies. It'll get very ugly before we're through. Intelligence is on a need to know basis.'

Adam nodded: 'I know it's grim -- our group's lucky, though they don't think so. Those poor buggers on the hill have it really rough. They need help.'

The colonel ignored him, studying his face but Adam met the stern eye and held it until the officer grunted and said: 'Good.'

He paused. 'Now, what about this ark?'

'I told you, it's a joke. I put it out to amuse people, I never thought it'd be taken seriously.'

Another grunt from the colonel as he turned to the man on his left: 'What d'you think, Guy? Could it be feasible?'

Adam gasped when he realised the man, in civilian clothes, had a copy of his drawing.

He laughed. 'You can't be serious.'

The man in civvies looked again at the drawing and said: 'You're an architect, aren't you? You'll know the practicalities. How do we know it's a joke? You may already have a prototype ready for trials.' He leaned forward: 'You may've already done trials and be waiting to offer it to someone. To sell it at the optimum time and make a killing.'

Adam laughed out loud. 'You're mad.'

They ignored him, everyone else was either looking at the colonel or down at the floor. He was reassured to see the carefully hidden trace of smiles on several faces. They at least must see what a farce this was.

The colonel went on. 'The point is, if an ark exists -- built and ready to go -- we must have the plans and get it into production. The army must have control. General Langdon insists."

'General Langdon, does he know about it?'

'Anything of strategic importance goes direct to him. He wants full details.'

Sighing Adam stood up and leant forward for emphasis as if trying to reach the colonel along the length of the table. 'What can I say to convince you,' he shouted. 'It's a joke, there is no bloody ark.'

Everyone stared at him and he realised he was trembling. 'It could never work,' he finished lamely.

'Sit down.'

Adam sat. 'We have no choice but to accept what you say. You seem honest and your record speaks for you. But be sure, if you're keeping a secret from us, the consequences for you -- and others -- would be very serious.'

Adam shook his head in disbelief as the colonel went on. 'Joke or not, we want you to liaise with Guy Cotterill on whether your ideas are practical. When the rain stops and the water subsides, we'll have to begin massive efforts to prepare for the next time.'

He looked around him and said, in a growl worthy of Churchill: 'Because gentlemen, it certainly will happen again.'

The return journey in daylight revealed the full impact of the flooding. Through the helicopter's wide windows he saw for real the scenes he'd watched on TV. The chopper flew in and out of cloud, rain falling around them, cutting down the light but not enough to diminish the effects of the deluge.

The images on screen had given only a limited impression of the floods, from the chopper the vast expanse of the waterscape was awesome. Successive small islands where higher ground stood above the water; no hedges or roads, no clustered houses marking village or town, only the tops of tall trees, church towers or spires and pylons.

Debris everywhere, bodies bloated with decay, animals of all kinds, cattle, sheep, a few horses, smaller carcasses of dogs and cats. And humans, limbs spreadeagled, appearing from above like blown-up dolls, grotesque in their silent reproach to the elements, all detritus from the business of human life.

Stunned, he looked down on the scene of chaos. 'Will it ever go down?' he whispered, really to himself.

'Does make you wonder,' said Captain Rogers. 'It's a frightening prospect to think it might stay like this.'

Sally watched the helicopter land but asked no questions. Her eyes followed him as he made the evening's ritual checks. His drawn, miserable face was enough. He said nothing about the day and she silenced John and Eve with a look when they began to quiz him. John said he'd do the rounds but Adam wanted to check for himself. With so full a house they needed a constant watch on the basics, unnecessary lights or taps left running.

When they were alone in the kitchen he knelt to grope in the cupboard under the sink. It took a lot of finding but his arm emerged with a bottle.

'My Glenfiddich 18 year old,' he waved the bottle at her. 'I need this, do you want one?'

She nodded. 'So that's where you put it.'

'Sharing my home is one thing but I'm not splashing this around for those who won't appreciate it.'

She watched the amber liquid slip gently into two glasses and he fetched a small jug, ran the tap a moment before filling the jug half full.

'I really need this,' he said again, pouring a splash into each glass. He clinked her glass with his.

'Why do we deserve this pleasure?'

'That meeting was an eye-opener -- we think we've got problems but the big picture is appalling. Don't want to talk about it now, I've had enough these last two days. I'll tell you some time.'

'You don't have to tell me anything.'

'It was horrible, looking down on the floods, all that fucking water.'

'It will disappear, sooner or later. It must.'

'It'll take a long time.' He emptied his glass and poured them both another.

'It's lovely.'

'We've earned it.'

They sipped the whisky, content in a few moments of peace as the kitchen darkened into dusk. He'd initiated power saving and banned unnecessary use of light during the day. At just after half past nine the daylight was almost gone, early for a July evening, hurried by the low-hanging clouds that brought the sky to earth too soon.

'I can hardly remember what it was like to sit outside with a drink,' Sally mused. 'It hasn't been that long but it seems like for ever.'

'I thought it was going to be a good summer,' Adam said. 'Everything was looking so healthy. I had big plans for the garden.'

'Yes, before the rain.'

The phrase that said it all, 'before the rain.'

Adam began to massage her shoulders.

'Oh that's good,' she breathed. 'You haven't done that for ages.'

He kissed her neck, stroking her hair. 'We haven't done anything for ages. I'm sorry love, we don't get much time for each other, do we?'

'It's not your fault but it would be good to have a little more of each other.'

'All these people, I know they can't help it -- but it's so tiring.' He carried on rubbing, his hands gently kneading the muscles around her neck. 'You feel tense.' He leaned down and nuzzled her cheek with his. 'Let's have another whisky and take it upstairs. What d'you say?'

'You can't have much left.'

'We can only drink it once.'

'It might relax us.'

He poured two more tots and screwed on the bottle's cap, wrapped it in a tea towel and stowed it away among the cleaning stuff in the cupboard.

'Let's hope nobody else thinks as you do,' she laughed.

They crept through the sleeping children to their bed and lit the candle instead of a bedside light. They sat companionably side by side, enjoying the tawny liquid. He looked at the glass in his hand. 'Do you remember the distillery? First time I'd tried the posh ones.'

'It was only two years ago.'

'Seems like a lifetime,' he said.

'Don't suppose they're flooded.'

'Who?'

'The glen of the stag, you know, or anywhere up there.' Sally loved that description.

'No, they haven't had so much rain in Scotland. '

'Mmm, finish your whisky, I want to snuggle down,' she murmured.

'Sleepy?'

'I didn't say that.'

Smiling he stretched out his arm to deposit the half empty glass. With a sigh he slid down the bed and the same arm found its way to the comfort of her body. He pressed himself against the soft contours of her back to cradle a breast in his hand, caressing the nipple.

Sally sighed and for the first time in weeks he felt the delicious thrill of desire surge through him as his hand moved to the smooth skin of her thigh.

'That feels like old times,' she whispered.'

'Mmm.'

His brain registered a noise somewhere but dismissed it to concentrate on other sensations. But Sally stiffened, her body tense and alert.

'What's that noise?'

'What noise?'

His head came off the pillow to listen, his hardness dying.

'Now what?' Someone or something was banging at the door.

He kissed her on the mouth, a lingering promise to return. 'Sorry sweetheart, it never ends.'

113

He grabbed his clothes and now Tom was awake. 'What is it, dad?'

'Don't know. Since you're awake, go get John.'

The banging was loud and insistent and would soon wake the whole house. Struggling with trousers and sweater he ran downstairs. It was the back door.

'Be quiet whoever you are,' he ordered.

'Come on, open up, we're soaked out here.'

'Who are you? What do you want?'

'Let us in for Christ's sake.' He saw them from the side window, four figures in hoodies, rain streaming on them. He thought a moment and the thought said trouble. But he couldn't leave them out there.

They exploded into the room as the door swung back, water and mud everywhere.

'Get your coats off.' To his surprise they did as he said and dropped the sodden garments in a pile by the door. Three young men and a girl, all with close-cropped hair, wet jeans, tough boots and T-shirts.

'You're not well equipped for bad weather,' he commented.

'We didn't think we'd be out in it like this,' one said.

'Where have you come from, how did you get here?'

'We fuckin' walked, how d'you think?' He had dark hair and several rings in both ears and two nose studs.

'Where from? We thought everyone in the area was accounted for,' Adam tried to be calm and reasonable.

'Walsall,' the girl spoke.

'But surely that area was evacuated days ago?'

'Yeah, but we wasn't, see? We stayed in the flat.'

'Ah,' he tried to picture it. 'That was risky.'

'We thought it'd go quick, the water. Thought they were makin' a fuss.'

'Right.' He waited.

Another youth, dark-skinned, moved closer to the Aga to warm his hands. He said: 'It got bad, mate. Scary, I thought we'd

114

'ad it, sure we were gonna die there.'

Adam nodded.

'Couldn't believe it, the water kept rising, we watched it come, floor by floor up the block. Them towers is fourteen levels. It got to six before we realised we were trapped. The stairs ended in water.'

'It must've been scary,' Adam said. 'So you went up to the roof?'

'Yeah, that's what we did. How d'yer know that?'

'Not much else you could do, is there. What then, your phones still worked?'

They all nodded. 'Two days we sat on that roof, two days in the fuckin' rain. We thought we'd 'ad it. '

'Then a chopper came?' Adam said.

'Yeah!' They seemed surprised he said that. 'Picked us up -- with a hoist -- the bloody army, would you believe.'

'Where did they take you?'

'It was a sort of barn, y'know? Middle o' nowhere, they said it were temporary while they sorted things. There weren't no proper beds, no toilets, nothin', just a big concrete barn.'

'Under cover at least,' from John who appeared through the other door.

'Sort of transit point, I expect,' said Adam.

'Dunno about that. They got us dry an' fed us, lots of sandwiches, nothin' 'ot. They said we'd be sent to some camp, on a moor somewhere. We didn't fancy that -- so we got out an' come 'ere.'

'How did you know about us.'

'We 'eard the army blokes talkin', they said yer name, we'd already 'eard it on the radio. Yer the ark man, ain't yer?'

Adam winced. 'You took a risk leaving them to come here, you may not have found us and you could've died of exposure in these conditions.'

They all grinned and the girl said: 'Could 'ave, but we didn't and now we're 'ere.'

'Now you're here,' John repeated. 'But you can't stay, we've got fifty people here, too many already and we're pushed for supplies. And there's nowhere for you to sleep. Tell them Adam.'

All eyes turned to Adam. The one with the rings said: 'Yer the boss, that's what the army guy was sayin', yer the man.'

That phrase again, it bothered Adam, it had a ring he didn't like. It implied too much. The girl grabbed his arm, he felt her shivering; 'You can't chuck us out, mister, not back into that shit. You said it yourself -- we might die.'

He sighed. 'I suppose you could have the shepherd's hut, it'll be very cramped, only meant for two. Sleep out there and come in for meals. It's not properly finished but it's dry. That's the best we can do. You should've stopped with the army.'

He thought of all the work he'd done on the wheeled hut, building it from scratch as a den for the boys, somewhere they could enjoy sleeping on warm summer nights. That all seemed a distant dream. He should've built a boat.

Sally arrived and without comment made tea for the newcomers. They grabbed it, wrapping cold hands round the mugs but the girl muttered thanks.

John pulled Adam out of the kitchen and whispered. 'You should search them.'

'What?'

'I bet they're carrying.'

They peered round the door, three of them were at the table, the other still by the Aga. Adam moved behind the one with the rings, hands heavy on the shoulders: 'So, do you have names?' He looked down at him: 'Who are you?'

'Gaz.'

'And you?' -- the black lad.

'Brian.'

Adam nodded to the girl.

'I'm Jess.'

'And my name's Les,' said the third boy who hadn't opened his mouth till now.

'Okay,' he still stood close behind Gaz, ready to tackle him if necessary.

'As you seem to know, I'm Adam. This is John, my neighbour and in charge here with me and this is Sally, my wife. This is what we're gonna do. You stay here till I see what can be done. You do as you're told, when you're told and you stay out of this kitchen. Clear?'

Gaz looked up at him. 'We're hungry.'

'You'll have to wait for breakfast. We can't change the rules for you. Now, I want you to empty your pockets.'

'What?' Gaz tried to rise but Adam leaned harder. 'I'm sorry. We can't take chances, if you've got anything offensive on you, you must give it up.'

'You ain't the fuckin' fuzz, you got no right.'

'My house, my right.'

John stepped forward. 'Come on Brian, let's see what you got.'

Brian rummaged in his jeans and moved to the table to drop phone, cigarettes and a lighter, a craft knife and some cash on the table. The boy Les just had a dirty tissue, cash and some mints along with his phone. The girl had a phone, cigarettes and a small flick knife. When Adam touched the button it flashed out, a vicious little weapon with a razor sharp blade. He touched his thumb against it. 'What's this for?' he asked.

'What d'yer think, protection.'

'Okay, now you, Gaz.' He relaxed his hold and the youth stood to bring out a flashy phone, cash, cigarettes, a crumpled pack of condoms and a note with directions to Adam's home.

'Satisfied?' The cocky smirk that lit the grubby face was not lost on John who glanced at the pile of coats by the door. He picked them up, one by one and went through the sodden wet pockets. In the third coat he found a weapon in each pocket, one an eight inch kitchen knife, blade wrapped in a cloth. 'Planning a picnic?'

'Whose coat is that?'

No one spoke as the four looked at each other.

117

'I don't want to be here all night.' Adam's edgy tone made the youth Les nervous. He shifted on his chair and said: 'Everybody carries knives. It don't mean nothin'.'

'No? You haven't got one, have you.'

'Well no, but --'

'Right. This is what happens. Either you tell me who owns that coat or you're back in the rain.'

'You gonna make us?' Gaz turned on him.

Adam moved in close, relieved to find the boy shorter and overweight. John was behind him. 'Yes,' he said quietly. 'We'll make you. Now, whose coat?'

Gaz sniffed, then shrugged. 'It's mine, so what? What's a couple of knives?'

Gaz stood tense in the quiet kitchen, his left hand on the chair back as if poised for attack. The only sound was the incessant drumming of rain on the window.

Adam thought then said simply: 'What indeed.'

John was cool and relaxed as he collected the knives from the table. 'We'll just put them somewhere safe for you,' he said.

Chapter eleven

Bleary with lack of sleep and the frustration of a life spiralling out of control he leaned on the bannister as Sally brought him a mug of tea.

He smiled, the little boy smile which an age ago had first drawn her to him. 'Sorry about last night,' he whispered.

She shrugged: 'Not your fault and we got there in the end.'

'But not like it should have been,' he said. 'When this is over -- if it's ever over -- we'll take some time together and make up for it.'

He sipped the tea: 'I dread going downstairs. Christ knows what we're in for now with those four. I'm afraid it'll unbalance everything. Are they stirring?'

'Not yet, John's down, keeping a quiet eye.' She kissed him on the cheek and stroked his chin. 'Do you know, I hadn't realised you were growing a beard. I only noticed it last night.'

'Sorry, was it like sandpaper?'

'It was rather nice.'

The dark stubble was beginning to show a definite beard shape around his chin. She moved his head to look at the profile. 'I think it'll suit you.'

'I shan't keep it. It's been so hectic I never get time to shave and it saves water.'

'I think you should keep it for now. It gives you an extra something, a touch of gravitas perhaps. Yes, it suits you.'

Rubbing his chin thoughtfully he went to help John and Eve with breakfast but the door flew back with a bang and Sally rushed in, indignant and angry.

'There's someone in our bathroom -- having a bath.'

The bathrooms were open to everyone but showers were limited to twice a week with an instruction to be mean with water and baths were forbidden.

'Let me guess,' Adam groaned and ran to the sitting room where people were starting their day, looking for one person, reading a magazine in the corner, alone.

'Smith!' he shouted, so everyone would hear. 'Where's your wife?'

The man cowered a little at the tone and said: 'I'm not sure, upstairs I think.'

'Get her down here.'

'I can't. I mean, I'm not sure if she's ready.'

'We'll go and see.'

'Wait, you can't --'

'Can't what?'

He headed for the stairs, two at a time, each foot thumping hard making the staircase echo with his anger.

He tried the door, locked -- so he banged his fist furiously against the wood. 'Who is it?' asked the voice he expected.

'What the hell d'you think you're doing!'

'Having a bath.'

'Well get out now.'

'I haven't finished,'

'Get out or I come in.'

'You wouldn't dare!'

Smith had followed him up and tugged at his arm.

'Stop this, how dare you? You can't threaten her like that.'

Adam spun round, grabbed the man's shirt and pushed him so hard he fell against the wall. He pulled him to his feet and slapped his face as John rushed forward in time to grab Adam's arm as he made to hit him again.

'Don't, that's not the way.'

'Get him out of my sight! Lock him up somewhere. We'll deal with him later.'

'I'll have you locked up,' screamed Smith. 'I'll have the law on you, treating people like this.'

Adam put his face very close to Smith's and spat out the words: 'I'm the law while this lasts. You better learn that, fast.'

Behind him the door opened slowly to reveal Rosanna Smith, a pale blue towel draped in folds around her chubby torso. Her crimson face showed fear and fury, a veil of steam wafting round her. Adam pushed her aside and looked in the bath, more than half full of very hot water.

'You selfish bitch!' he shouted.

'How dare you --' she began but he grabbed her arm and pulled her across the landing. 'Get downstairs,' he ordered.

'I can't go down like this. People can't see me like this.'

'They're going to see you exactly like this. It'll be a lesson for them.'

Sally was there now: 'I don't think you should do this --'

'No, these two need to learn. It's got to be fair or it's chaos.'

He pushed the resisting figure before him. The whole house had heard the commotion. They stood in the hall, necks craned to watch, staring in fascinated shock as the pathetic, dripping woman was forced towards them. Her plump wobbling flesh, flushed red from the hot water, quivered with indignation, the towel only just preserved her modesty as tears ran down her cheeks.

Adam resisted the temptation to rip away the towel but said with icy calm: 'Now Mrs Smith, you'll apologise to these people who I expect would all love a hot bath. And by the way, the water's still there so if anyone wants to use it, feel free. You will say sorry and you'll promise not to be so selfish as long as we're all here.'

The guests, embarrassment now dominant on most faces, looked at the woman, stripped of all dignity, staring at the floor, unable to face them.

'Say it,' said Adam. 'Tell them you're sorry.'

She raised her head and opened her mouth but no words came out. Adam squeezed her shoulder. 'Tell them.'

'I -- I didn't think,' she whispered, overwhelmed by the attention. 'I didn't mean anything, I just wanted a bath. I didn't mean to deprive anyone else. I'm sorry.' Her voice tailed off.

Adam released his grip. 'Go and get dressed.'

As she stumbled back upstairs, everyone watched in silence waiting to see what happened next. The new arrivals had watched it all with delight, Gaz eyeing Adam with surprised respect.

He faced them and began: 'I expect you think that was a rotten thing to do but -- '

Gaz interrupted. 'Best floor show I've ever seen,' he laughed.

'It's not funny, Gaz but I'm glad you interrupted. We've made rules to get us through this thing and the rules apply to everyone.'

He pointed at them. 'These four appeared out of the rain last night, Gaz, Brian, Les and Jess. They've had a pretty bad time so we'll try to look after them although we have too many people here already.'

The crowd muttered and eyed the youngsters and Gaz looked sheepish.

'We made the no-baths rule to save water and power, especially water. We've got to be fair and eke everything out till we get more supplies. It's hard on everyone but we can't make exceptions.' He saw most of them nodding or grunting agreement.

'I'm sorry but if you stick to the rules we've agreed we have a chance to get through this. Now let's get some breakfast.'

As the group dispersed, Gaz pushed forward and started up the stairs. 'And where do you think you're going?' Adam demanded.

'For a bath, like you said. I don't mind using the old bird's water, if it's hot. I've 'ad worse.'

Adam laughed at the immediate lightening of the mood. 'Okay, it's all yours. But don't run any more.'

'I wouldn't dare, mate, don't you worry.'

'What about Smith?' asked John.

'Where d'you put him?'

'In the tool shed.'

'We'll talk to him. You'd better come.'

'You shouldn't have hit him.'

'I know, I just lost it. He's such a creep.'

An unchastened Marcus Smith stumbled into the daylight when they removed the padlock and opened the wooden door. He said nothing but the malice written in his expression was chilling. 'What have you done to my wife,' he demanded.

'Just made her apologise. It's only her pride that's hurt.'

'You can't do this sort of thing. It's assault and false imprisonment, it's -- '

'It's simple, we're all stuck here. You and your wife have a choice. You can set off and find another group on the hill or you can stay here and follow the rules.'

'Where could we go?'

'There's a group at my neighbour's, three miles west of here. But they're in the same position.' He hesitated. 'I must tell you that all these groups are subject to my control, mine and John's.'

'What d'you mean?'

'Exactly as I said. I'm regional controller till some other authority can take over.'

'You!'

Adam nodded.

'When?'

'Last week. Ring the army but it won't do you any good.'

The man looked shattered, mouth open in disbelief.

'It's up to you.'

They watched his shoulders sag as he trudged back to the house, rain soaking his cotton shirt.

Ron was no help about the Walsall Four. His answer was brief: 'You'll have to keep them.'

There was no compromise. 'Everything now comes in by air. With Felixstowe inundated the shortages are acute. The country's been running on a just-in-time system for years. But now there's no trucks thundering up the M6, no distribution centres, nothing to fill the shelves in Tesco, most supermarkets under water. You're lucky to be in your own home.'

'I know but where are all the city people?'

'In camps like the ones you've seen, anywhere on high ground, the downs in Surrey and Sussex, all that area west of Oxford, the Chilterns and the Cotswolds, Salisbury Plain. The pretty places are saving lives.'

'It's hard to imagine.'

'You've seen it, it's a mess. Make the best of your extra four and any more that come. Because you will get more, stragglers on their own who don't know where else to go. You've made yourself too well known so the rescue people are bound to point them at your place.'

'I don't know where we'll put them. My biggest worry is old Bryston. He looks very ill now and his medication's nearly gone. I asked for more.'

'What did they say?'

'They said it's low priority. We may lose him.'

'You must face it, Adam, there's been a lot of death and there'll be more. One old man is neither here nor there.'

'It's different when it's someone you know. Surely every life is important?'

'In normal times, yes but not now. It's about making the best of a bad job. Thousands in the cities have died already, drowned before help could get to them.'

'We haven't seen that on TV.'

'And you won't. If people knew how bad it really is we'd soon lose control.'

'The army is censoring everything?'

'Of course.'

'So we've got a dictatorship.'

'What do you expect? Without the army's efforts the country wouldn't stand a chance.'

124

'I knew things were bad but you've made it much worse.'

Ron laughed. 'Sorry but that's the reality. About the Lomax woman, there is something. I got a reaction when I asked. They obviously know of her. I'll keep trying.'

The Walsall Four kept themselves apart, tapping at their phones, or whispering in a huddle, usually finishing in a bellow of laughter. They slept in the shepherd's but spent most of their time in the house.

Their only interests were eating or sleeping. Jess was no good at kitchen duties but Eve did manage to get her cleaning the floor after careful instruction in using a mop and bucket. Sally clung to the idea of maintaining standards but the constant invasion of mud and water and people scattering clothing, magazines and personal items everywhere brought her near despair.

The rain had eased to a drizzle and Adam insisted they get outside for fresh air. They wandered out past the barn and stopped to watch John and Tom cutting firewood. Brian kicked out at a neat pile of kindling, scattering it around Tom who looked up, furious: 'Why did you do that?'

'Dunno, what's it for?' Brian asked.

'What?'

'That wood.'

'What d'you think?'

Brian shook his head.

'It's kindling, fire sticks -- for the wood burner. You'll be glad of this when the weather turns colder.'

'We'll be long gone by then.'

'I wouldn't bank on it.'

'You could help split some logs.'

'No, it looks like hard work.' But he remained to watch as Tom swung the axe with practised precision.

'What d'you people do, apart from choppin' wood?'

Gaz came back. 'There's nothing 'ere. Why d'yer live 'ere?'

John dropped his axe and said: 'Because we like it, different sort of life to yours.'

'But there's nothing here.'

'No? We think there's plenty -- hills and trees, flowers, wildlife. Above all it's peaceful -- or it was till you lot came.'

He looked towards the drowned valley. 'It was beautiful.'

'Couldn't live 'ere,' Gaz said.

'You're here now and glad to be I reckon. Why did you come?' John said.

'To be safe.'

'Exactly, and why is it safe?'

Gaz frowned and looked where the water stretched away as far as he could see. 'Out of the water, 'igh ground.'

'Exactly, we're on a hill. So aren't you the lucky ones.'

The youth pulled a face and moved away.

Angry shouts roused him. He was in the bedroom trying to take a brief rest. It was hard to relax but Sally had sent him upstairs and he dozed pleasantly. The commotion was outside somewhere. He thought it might stop but he couldn't ignore Tom's anguished voice.

He went reluctantly to the window and saw them out beyond the barn, the three lads from Walsall and John, with an arm around Tom, stroking the boy's head. Adam frowned, startled by the small thrill of shock he felt and suddenly anxious to get out there.

When he saw his father Tom rushed towards him sobbing in anger. 'He's killed Tilly.'

'What?'

'Tilly the hen, he's killed her.'

He pointed to where Gaz had dropped the limp grey-speckled body. Adam picked it up. The bird's eyes were closed, the red comb and waffles dulled in death, the neck feathers torn where uncaring hands had twisted the life from it.

'You stupid bugger!' yelled Tom. '

'She was the best bird, our pet.' He lunged at Gaz with his fists and the youth was about to hit him back when John caught Tom and pulled him away.

Gaz looked surprised. 'What's all the fuss about. It's only a chicken. I fancied it for supper and she came right up to us.'

Adam said nothing. It was John who explained wearily. 'She's a laying bird, a hen, they're not meant for eating.'

'What's the difference?'

'The ones you eat are a different type, they fatten quickly. These lay eggs for us to eat. They don't carry much meat.'

Tom had quietened: 'She was the only one still laying, you ignorant prat.'

'Oh.' Gaz looked almost contrite. 'I didn't know, did I. Just thought it'd be a meal.'

'It will, we won't waste her,' Adam said, then, 'I'm surprised you knew how to kill her.'

'Seen it on YouTube.'

'Well -- ' he took the lad's arm, 'you can finish the job. I'll show you how.'

Gaz followed Adam reluctantly to the barn, dogged by Tom, full of the lust for vengeance and the other three, happy to see their cocksure leader lose face. Tom cooled down enough to smile as the chicken killer was forced to the messy task. Gaz struggled for more than an hour to pluck the feathers, shouted at when he tore the skin. When the thin little body was naked Adam said: 'Now remove the head and clean out the innards.'

'How d'yer mean?'

'Cut off the head with a sharp knife, keep the neck to go with the giblets, then pull all the guts out the other end. Then you take it indoors, do some veg and make it into a chicken stew.'

'Can't we just stick it in the oven?'

'No, it'd be as tough as your boots.'

Adam showed him where to cut under the bird's tail.

'Now what?'

'Now you pull out the guts.'

127

'No way, I'm not putting my 'and in all that muck.'

'You won't get supper unless you do. This is your meal, remember.'

'Go on Gaz, get yer 'and in there,' laughed Brian. 'Let's see yer
do it.'

Adam turned away grinning as Gaz pushed a tentative hand
inside the carcass. He drew out a handful of messy entrails and
ducked away gagging. They waited till he recovered and Adam
made one concession, telling Tom: 'Get a bucket of rain water
for his hands.'

When Tilly was finally ready in a dish Gaz was quite pleased
with himself.

'Now you might have some small chance of survival,' said
Adam.

Chapter twelve

A cold breeze washed waves over the tarmac, on the road that led nowhere, where Adam stood with ripples lapping over his boots. He stared at the flood as if by peering under the surface he could discover how soon it might disappear.

He was trying to judge if the level had changed. A metre in front of him the pile of stones the boys had built as a marker was now a tiny island almost under water. The flood had risen by at least half a metre in four days. Rain still fell much of the time but at that moment it was fine. He scanned the sky for a glimpse of sun but saw only dark, looming towers of cloud moving in again.

The last two days had left him badly rattled. He felt control slipping away from him, something he hated. On one side bullying from the army, on the other a struggle to meet the demands of the refugees. For they were refugees, the euphemism 'guests' no longer fitted the bill.

He watched the approaching clouds. 'For fuck's sake go away,' he shouted at the empty air in a futile gesture like Canute on the beach. He heard something behind and blushed with embarrassment seeing Sally there to witness his frustrated anger.

'It's higher,' he muttered. 'It'll take weeks and weeks to go -- once it stops rising.' He gestured at the hills: 'The land is saturated, everything that comes down just adds to the level.'

Sally said: 'You know it's St Swithin's Day?'

'I'd forgotten the date. It may be an old wives' tale but what an omen, another forty days of this.'

'I wouldn't say this in front of anyone else but I'm really frightened,' she said.

'Me too, I try not to think what might happen.'

They stood close together in a hug. 'All these bloody people dependent on us, why did they have to come here?'

'Because we're where we are. One of the reasons you wanted the place. We'll just have to cope.'

'I don't want to cope! I just want them gone along with this filthy water. I want my life back.'

They went in by the kitchen door to avoid meeting anyone but found John there with Philip Bryston, his head slumped on the table.

'What's wrong?' Sally asked.

'He's not well, I brought him in here for some peace,' John explained. 'We need to get him upstairs and into bed. He had almost collapsed.'

'Where's his wife?'

Philip spoke in a strained voice. 'She's gone for her bag -- looking for more tablets.'

John went on. 'They went out for some air when the rain eased. The hill was too much for him.'

Adam gestured John to one side. 'What's he on, do you know?'

'Stuff for blood pressure, statins and some heart drug.'

'I know his heart's pretty bad. I've been asking Ron for medication.'

Philip sat up and leaned back in the chair. 'I'm sorry, you're trying so hard for us.'

Adam smiled: 'You can't help being ill.' He was shaken by the pale face drawn into stress lines, most noticeable about the mouth. The voice was a mutter, broken by small gasps as he struggled for breath.

'Help me, Adam, take his other arm and we'll get him upstairs.'

'Wouldn't he be better down here somewhere?' asked Sally.

'He'll get more rest upstairs.'

Between them they half lifted him up the stairs, resting on each step until they could lay him on the bed.

Jane came into the room frowning. 'I've found some more digoxin. It should be just one but he's had none for three days so we'll give him two.' She brought water and helped him swallow. 'It should help. My bag's been missing' she explained 'but I found it downstairs. It had some cash in it but it seems to have gone.'

'You mean it's been taken, stolen?'

With a bleak expression she nodded. 'Looks that way. But we have the tablets, that's what matters. And I can't spend the money, can I?'

'That's not the point.'

Adam sighed and John said: 'So, now we've got a thief in the house.'

'We'll sort it later, John, nobody's going anywhere. We must get to Rowan Hill.'

'Today?'

'We should've gone before. Ron said it was urgent. Jock will have to manage if the chopper comes. I'll get the guns.'

They knew Rowan Hill. Its pub was popular, offering simple but excellent food, the kind of place for a bite and a few drinks after a cold day's walking or shooting. Many of the villagers were descended from miners, whose community grew up around a lead mine in the nineteenth century, pits long since closed and filled in.

Incomers had a similar outlook, the place attracted a certain type, resilient and self-reliant, undeterred by the near constant wind at over three hundred metres above sea level. Exposed and open to the elements it was chilly for much of the year but they wouldn't be anywhere else

Now its position gave it new importance and the wide expanse of open land around the village was crucial.

After Ruttock Common they knew what to expect. In the first chaos of evacuation the army needed anywhere to get people out of the water.

The hilltop village was ideal and they began dumping people by air and boat with a platoon and a couple of NCOs in charge. Indignant locals had no option but to accept the people billeted on them.

Unwanted guests filled spare bedrooms and dining rooms, caravans and camper vans and the army brought bundles of brown tents.

The NCOs requisitioned the village hall as a command post and central supply point. At the start they did nothing about communal eating, expecting the residents to supply meals. Trouble began when supplies ran short. The small Rowan Hill Stores ran out of food after the first three days and the soldiers were in trouble.

The continual arrival of more people tipped the balance from grudging good humour into resentment and then anger. The army helicopters repeatedly swooped down without warning over the hill, landing briefly to disembark a fresh group before whirling away for more.

And they were still coming.

The friends walked up the steep road from the boat, cradling the automatic rifles. They wanted to seem casual but the weapons belied that image. The village was a haphazard collection of brick terraced cottages from the early days of the mine, with a small estate of modern semis and a few prefabs. On the outskirts they passed several larger stone-built cottages.

In the village centre near the pub the overwhelming impression was of crowds. The rain was heavy enough to keep them in but people were outside, both adults and children, shouting with anger.

'Bloody hell,' John looked at Adam. 'What's the plan?'

Adam grunted: 'Find the hall and the soldiers.'

The village hall was under siege. An angry crowd watched as several men tried to batter down the main door.

Adam asked a woman what was happening. 'Those army bastards won't let us in.'

Hearing the growing fury of threats and obscenities aimed at the soldiers inside he stopped. 'This is no good, we'll never get in from this side. We'll go round and try to get in front of the mob. John --' he paused.

'I know, be ready with the gun.'

'We may need to fire in the air to make them listen.'

They worked their way through the edge of the crowd and people began to notice two men with guns. Heads turned and a buzz vibrated through the pushing throng. They approached close together, ready to swing round with the weapons if threatened. At the rear of the hall they met two middle-aged men.

With eyes on the guns, one said: 'Who the hell are you?'

John recognised him as a farmer from near Brown Hill.

'It's Gordon Finch, isn't it.' The man nodded.

'This is Adam Woolton, from Down Farm.'

'What d'you want here?'

'We've been sent to help but we need to get inside. It's not their fault,' said Adam.

'The power's gone and there's a generator in there,' Finch said.

'Will you help us?' asked Adam.

'What can you do?'

'I don't know but we need to cool it down.'

Finch eyed him. 'You're right, they're likely to lynch those two squaddies before it's done.'

Adam said: 'Come with us. The four of us will have more impact.'

Edging towards the main door they pushed through the crush to appear abruptly side by side, rifles pointing over the heads of the crowd. The noise persisted as if they hadn't been seen. Then all eyes focused on the guns.

An audible sigh went round as people who couldn't see were told by those in front. The nearest group, including three furious women, pushed back to leave space around the four. Backs to the door, they faced the angry faces, hot with sweat and fear despite the rain.

The sudden silence made it worse. The crowd stared, puzzled and uncertain.

Adam started to speak but was instantly drowned in a fresh clamour of questions and threats. He looked at John who raised his rifle and fired over the crowd. The crack was deafening at close range and people ducked instinctively.

But it brought silence and Gordon Finch raised a hand and shouted: 'These two have come to help. Shut up and listen.'

'Why are they armed?'

Adam spoke at his normal pitch: 'We must have some order. Let Mr Finch tell us about the problems?'

'Like I said, the power went off yesterday afternoon, so there's no light and no hot food. They've got a generator but they're doing nothing to help.'

'But you're not from the village,' said John.

'No, two miles away but we've got nine extra at our place and my wife's cooking on a camp stove till the gas runs out. We need a proper meals system . On top of that the water's running low.'

'Are these people local or evacuated?'

'Both but most have been dumped here.'

The other man who'd stood with them butted in angrily: 'Why are you armed, what right have you to interfere?'

'The army sent us,' Adam said.

Gordon said: 'This is Alan Croft from the pub. He's been trying to feed people.'

Adam said quietly: 'Sorry about the guns, Mr Croft. I've been made coordinator until normal authority is back.We were told to come armed. If everyone could calm down, we'll talk to the soldiers and see what's happening. I can't believe they don't want to help.'

Those at the front had listened intently and passed the word that the guy with the gun was taking over. They watched him knock hard on the hall door and call: 'It's Adam Woolton and John Kerr. We have orders to do what we can here. We need to come in.'

A voice through the door said: 'Corporal Evans here, sir. Was that you firing, sir?'

'Yes, only in the air, you must've been told we were coming.'

'Yes sir, I suppose it's safe to let you in.'

'Of course it is.' He called impatiently. 'Get this door open.'

He turned back to the two standing with John. 'I don't want a rush of people pushing in. Can you hold them? Tell them chaos won't help anybody.' He looked at the crowd and realised more had come, all staring at him hopelessly in the driving rain.

'There's a hell of a lot of people here,' he said to Alan Croft.

'That's the problem.The village has about four hundred residents plus others around the district but there must be seven times that now and they're still bringing them.'

Adam shook the door handle impatiently and heard the rattle of bolts being drawn and a key turning in the lock. The door opened a crack and a frightened face peered out.

He pushed through saying: 'Guard the door, John - use the gun if you have to.'

One glance round the hall showed the problem. It was set up with trestles as a make-shift canteen but the floor was strewn with parts.

'Is that the field kitchen?' Adam asked.

'Two of them, sir, we've been trying to set them up. They came with us in the chopper but they need some work and the gas cylinders are only half full. And the generator's packed up too. We've got food here but we can't cook it.'

'Why didn't you tell them that?'

'Wouldn't bloody listen, would they. We tried to tell 'em but there was so much racket they took no notice. I tell you sir, we thought we were done for. Glad you're here.'

'You could've let them in to shelter.'

'No sir, they kept trying to push in, people were falling and being trodden on. We thought there'd be a stampede, people may have been killed in the crush.'

'Is it just you two? I was told a platoon was here.'

135

'They were but they were sent elsewhere.'

'Right." Adam eyed the scattered but orderly sections of the field kitchens in dismay -- it all looked a long way from being able to prepare food. 'How bad is it?'

'Not as bad as it looks. One's the standard job but the other is one of the old Soyers they've dug out from somewhere, uses solid fuel. The gas burner just needs a bit of welding but we've got no gear for that.'

'There must be someone in the village with welding gear.'

Gordon Finch took a look and saw the problem. 'I can sort that, leave it to me.'

'What about the generator?'

'I'll call Eddie to take a look.'

Outside the crowd was smaller and more were drifting away. He beckoned those nearest and explained what was happening.

'Be patient and get under cover. The soldiers are doing their best to organise meals but the cookers are knackered. We think we can fix it. Once they're working we'll get hot food going and I'll call the army for more blankets and bottled water.'

'One of the cookers uses solid fuel so if you can find any -- coal, coke, wood, anything -- fetch it here.'

They listened and began to move away with muttered grumbles. Alan Croft was beside him. 'Water will be a problem soon.'

'Where's it from?'

'Mains pumped into a reservoir up the road and that's topped up by a borehole but with the power gone neither is working.'

'Is there a main stop tap controlling the output?'

He knew how his own system worked though this was water for an entire community. But there had to be a cut-off somewhere.

'Don't know. Could be anywhere, we just ring Severn Trent when there's a problem,' Croft laughed apologetically.

Adam smiled at the irony.

'I think the phone might ring for ever. Think Alan, there must be someone who knows. We've got to turn it off and control the supply, or there'll be none at all. If you think you've had a crisis with no power just wait till they've got no water.'

Hours later they sat exhausted at a wooden trestle eating stew with lumpy mashed potato cooked in large pans from a growing pile of empty cartons. But it was hot and filling and the cooks made tea or coffee to go with it. Like the other damp, tired people crowding the hall they were grateful.

With light and heat the hall had a kinder aspect -- the local mechanic had coaxed the generator into life and Croft and Finch had organised a rota for meals.

The four made a good team and resigned discontent took over from anger and frustration. They'd found the mains stop tap and arranged for stand pipes to be dropped. People soon saw the sense in having a limited but clean supply to drink and rain water for other uses.

The lights in the packed hall were dim and wavering from the variable power of the generator but as darkness fell a gloomy aura of companionable cosiness developed, bringing a sense of safety and reassurance, blurring the edges of reality.

Gordon was worried about the imminent changeover. He feared those in this more comfortable setting would be reluctant to leave and make room for others. An earlier change had gone well but in the evening gloom they feared a new outbreak of resentment.

Phone signal was poor but the soldiers had radio contact with their base and Adam dictated a shopping list for the village. He wondered if the stuff would actually arrive but the information cheered people .

At 21.30 precisely Corporal Evans' banged on his improvised gong to announce it was time to change over. But nobody made a move, the strident command was ignored. John reached for his weapon but Adam stayed his arm: 'Give them time.'

The impatient buzz outside was louder, they'd waited two hours for their turn to eat and get warm.

He told Evans to bang it again and stood up. 'Hurry up please, others need a turn, they'll be hungry.' He raised the metal army cup and drained the last of his tea then slammed it down hard on the table to emphasise his words. 'Time for bed.'

John fingered the gun and saw faces turn to them. Gordon Finch was by the door. 'Come on, Jack,' he called to someone he knew, 'if you get up others will follow.'

The youngish man, Jack, had his wife and little girl beside him. He rose from the bench and took his child by the hand. 'Come on, love,' he said. 'Bed time.'

At the door he grinned at John. 'You've done a good job today, thanks.' He pointed at the gun. 'Hope you don't have to use that.'

The rest began to move after him and filed out as Finch held up his hands to those outside. 'Let them out before you start coming in.'

John smiled as they trooped out but Croft nudged him and over his shoulder he saw five young men still hogging one of the heaters, laughing and talking loudly. One got up and demanded more coffee. 'You've had your ration,' Corporal Evans retorted. 'It's time you went.'

'We're staying here in the warm.'

The hall filled rapidly with hungry, cold and impatient people. The soldiers were poised behind the trestle ready to dish up. The place went very quiet.

Adam had been careless. He'd left the automatic rifle in the kitchen but John was ready with his and stepped towards the five, still laughing their defiance. 'You must leave the hall, others need a turn.'

'You gonna make us?' The one who wanted more coffee was belligerent, cocky, rather like Gaz.

'Yes,' said John sternly.

'We're staying put.'

Almost whispering Adam said: 'I don't want to use force but I will. I have authority to shoot, do you understand?'

138

'Bollocks! You won't shoot us.' All five sat laughing as John raised his gun and Adam stepped back, feeling for the pistol inside his fleece.

He beckoned John close. 'Leave it to me, where can I hit him?'

'Aim for the leg.'

He smiled grimly at the sneer on the lad's face -- he would always remember the rings in both ears. He brought out the pistol and took aim. The boy laughed again and said: 'You're bluffing.'

'I don't want to do this. Get yourself and your mates out of here and we'll say no more about it.'

'It's you who'd better go.' The five of them stood up, arms folded.

The sudden dryness in his mouth made speech difficult. The one facing the gun said: 'Go on, fire it, you haven't got the balls.'

Adam glanced at the soldiers, seeing the doubt. If he let these troublemakers stay he'd lost and anarchy would take over. Corporal Evans caught his eye and nodded as if in approval and Adam stepped back.

'Last warning,' he said clearly. 'Move or I fire.'

The only sound in the stillness was the hiss of gas, all eyes on him as he pleaded: 'Please move, don't make me do this.'

The youth laughed and stepped forward. Adam lowered the barrel and let his finger slide back the trigger. The shot echoed loud in the hall. The body bucked as if tweaked on a wire and hit the floor, blood pouring from a leg. 'He's fuckin' shot me!' he screamed and passed out.

The other four gaped at their friend and backed away. 'Now will you go,' he shouted. 'Don't make me fire again.'

They expected pandemonium but the crowded hall was wrapped in stunned silence, eyes staring in horror at the lad down on the floor.

Mothers covered the eyes of frightened children. They were all transfixed like John and Adam, stranded in shock.

But the two corporals took over, their ingrained training in charge. Evans produced a wound dressing as if by magic and stopped the flowing blood within seconds of cutting off the torn trouser leg.

'What have I done?' groaned Adam but the soldiers grinned.

'Don't worry, sir, it's only a flesh wound. Gone through the outer muscle -- bit like a furrow you might say. Bloody good shot, sir.'

'Lucky shot,' Adam whispered.

'Maybe, sir -- but in the circumstances -- just the job, if you don't mind me saying so.'

John said: 'And after all that the bastard gets to stay in here, so they can keep an eye on the leg.'

'Yes, no question of getting him to hospital. I suppose this is all part of your remit, corporal?'

'Yes sir, basic medical care, first aid, trauma, gunshot wounds and lacerations.'

'Right. Must get out, John, I need air.'

The silent, wary crowd backed off to make way for them. He wanted to say: 'Sorry folks' but he didn't. He'd made the point and it was no good showing remorse.

'You'd better tell someone,' John said. 'Report it, get in first before someone tells it different.'

Outside in the rain he leaned shaking against the wall. 'God I might have killed him -- call Ron for me, will you, my hands are trembling.'

'I'm not surprised.'

It took well over ten minutes to raise Ron. Adam heard him laugh when told what had happened and grabbed the phone.

'It isn't funny, it's terrible. I shot the boy.'

'Sounds like you did just the right thing.'

'It was a lucky shot, I might have killed him.'

'But you didn't.'

'Do I have to fill in a form, some sort of report?'

'No, I'll report it when I'm next on to HQ. Forms are off at the at the moment. Nobody to look at them'.

'I feel terrible.'

'Forget it. It was necessary, that's why you've got the guns.' He laughed again, a chuckle of glee: 'You'll find it much easier next time.'

When the hall was empty but for the injured youth and three couples who'd turned up last thing, he lay on the floor hearing Corporal Evans whisper.

'Don't beat yourself up about it, sir. You had no choice, you couldn't back down.'

'I didn't really think I'd have to shoot anyone.'

'You did well. Not an easy thing to do -- pulling the trigger like that in cold blood.'

'Can't believe I did it.'

'It was the right thing to do. A bad business, all this, lots of people will die before it's over, drowned, ill or shot. Look at it this way, making 'em all realise we need order might just save them in the long run.'

'You may be right.'

'Look at them,' he meant the new couples. 'Quiet, respectful, done exactly what they're told. Someone told 'em before they came in. It'll make things easier, you see.' Then he asked: 'Will you be coming back?'

'We'll try. But the boat is so slow, takes too long to get here. We'll maybe hitch a chopper ride. But you keep dishing up the meals and hopefully they'll stay quiet.'

John was sleeping and they would be away first thing in the morning but he wouldn't easily forget what he'd done.

Staring into the darkness he was pleased to be distracted by the phone vibrating against his thigh. The voice sparked a guilty thrill of excitement, Kirstie Lomax. But this time there was no tension as she began to chat about music.

'I'm marooned up here, it's boring, really missing some decent music, I've heard all the stuff on my phone too often.'

'Can't you download something new?' he asked, irritated by the irrelevance .

'Most sites are down.'

'Shame,' he muttered wondering about such nonsense.

'I really miss my Handel.'

'What?'

The silken voice said: 'You know.'

'Of course I know Handel, I like it, well, some of it, can be a bit heavy -- now, Hayley --'

She ignored him and went on: 'Magnificent music, especially the Coronation anthems, you know them?'

'Yes, I know them.' He was impatient. 'About Hayley, she really needs to know --'

But she cut him off again, still babbling about Handel. He began to be angry.

'That magnificent crescendo in Zadok the Priest, almost orgasmic don't you think, you know Zadok?'

'Ugh? What is this?' he demanded. 'What about your daughter?'

'Yes, that's what I want to hear, some stirring Handel, Zadok the Priest, wonderful music Zadok.'

Understanding dawned. 'Zadok? That means something, right?'

'Yes, wonderful.' He twigged at last that someone was with her, wherever she was, probably listening.

'Zadok is the message?' he spoke quietly into the phone.

'Yes, it'll be great to see her again, it shouldn't be long now.'

'Zadok, who do I tell?'

She was off again. 'Incredible imagination, Handel, I suppose he saw Zadok as leading an army of the righteous, it comes out in the music. Yes, the army of God, that's it.'

'The army, I only know Captain Rogers, or Ron. I'll tell Ron.'

'Yes, tell Ron.'

Chapter thirteen

The sky seemed lighter as they landed to haul the boat clear of the water. The rising wind drove the clouds apart and let a tiny shaft of sunlight pierce the grey canopy. Shielding his eyes from the unaccustomed brightness he stared again at the water. In the brief burst of sunshine a glittering lake stretched away to lap against the hills towards Wales. It snaked through the lower valleys, creeping higher to create a different landscape.

He also marked a change around his home. The sand-coloured stone, already darkened by constant wet had grown a green veneer of algae over every north facing surface, glistening with slime along the walls. Among the tight roundels longer tendrils of sphagnum had taken hold in the lines of mortar.

'Look at this, John,' he called. 'I hadn't noticed before, an unpleasant taste of things to come.'

Inside he started to tell Sally but she immediately said: 'Didn't think you'd be away over night.'

'What's wrong?'

'It's been a bad day. Grumbling and greed and more people turned up yesterday. And poor Philip hasn't moved all day, he's got chest pains.'

'That is bad news. But what people, how many?'

'Eleven, including two kids and one with a dreadful cough.'

'Where have you put them?'

Waiting for the answer he saw her close to tears. He hated to see her so distraught. 'They're everywhere. I'm sorry Adam, I told them to find anywhere they could to sleep. Some are in the barn. There's no more bedding, we need blankets and pads or something. It's a shambles and I don't know how we're going to feed them all.'

'Come here,' he kissed her forehead and cuddled her. 'We'll sort something. Don't worry, I'm sorry we weren't here.'

The hugging made it worse and she began to cry. Not just a gentle weeping but gasping, heaving sobs of frustration. His shirt was wet with it as he held her away from him and peered into her face.

'This isn't like you, where's my brave girl?'

'I'm not brave, I'm terrified. What are we going to do? With no food and no medicine, I think we're all going to die here.'

He held her again, trying to reassure, appalled to see her in this state.

Her muffled voice carried on. 'The drop didn't come and Philip will die if we don't get his drugs.' Again she said: 'What are we going to do?'

'Calm down. We need to stay calm and think how to handle it all.'

She sighed and attempted a smile.

'Now, tell me about these people. Where are they from?'

'I don't know. They were in an awful state -- they were in a boat somewhere.' She swallowed, trying not to cry again.

He caught her mood at once: 'What?'

'The family with the girl and an older son, they lost their little boy, the youngest. He fell out of the boat in the dark, God knows where they were. He was only five. They lost him in the water, he was swept away,' she whispered.

It was startling, frightening even, that another eleven people should make such a difference. He looked at them all and they in turn watched him. The most striking image was the misery in the eyes of another young girl. But where Hayley had been bright and healthy this one looked weak and ill. He heard her racking cough and saw the effort she made to breathe. He knew the sound of that breathing, asthma.

He saw their expectation, as if he would make everything right, produce food, medication and hope — hope above all. But there was nothing to say that would help them.

He retreated to the kitchen as the door banged open and the boys came in making puddles.

'It's so unfair,' Ben complained. 'Polly's shut out in the barn. It's not her fault.'

'I had to put her out,' Sally said. 'She went straight up to the asthmatic girl who started to wheeze. Her mother was screaming.'

'It's not fair, dad,' Ben moaned .

'Your mum's right, if the child's allergic, Polly could make her really ill, we can't risk that. You'll have to spend time out there with her, it's only till this is all over.'

He turned to Eve and Amy who were working on lists. One was food they had left, the other what they hoped they could get on the next drop. Adam saw bog rolls underlined and a drugs section. He added the words 'asthma patient'. The list of remaining food was very short.

'Not much on here, what is there for lunch?'

'Baked bean stew and bread,' Eve said.

'What's that?'

'Dried soup made up with added beans for substance,' she indicated the large saucepans simmering on the Aga. He sniffed at it: 'Smells all right.'

'It's not bad,' Sally said. 'I've eaten worse.'

'What did they have yesterday?'

'The same.'

'And breakfast?'

'Porridge, we've got plenty of that and we've ordered more. Made with water and they're allowed a bit of sugar. It's not very exciting,' -- she saw his face, Adam liked his porridge with cream and syrup -- 'but it's filling and at least the vegans will eat it.'

I haven't told Sally yet about Rowan Hill. I feel so guilty but don't know what else I could've done. Can't forget what Ron said, laughing and saying it'll be easier next time.

Just spoken to him about the old man and the kid. He said he'll do his best to get the drugs but sounded doubtful. If we don't get them soon I'm afraid he'll die. He said I need to be prepared for that.

The extra people have made the house unbearable. It was bad enough but another eleven is far too many. The place stinks. John's out now with the boys trying to rod the drains but the septic tank wasn't built to cope with this volume.

Now I've found three emails from Guy Cotterill. He's coming out here, probably on the next drop to go through the ark plans.

I can't believe they're taking it seriously. It's a nightmare and yet another body about the place.

The money's still coming in though I shut it down, it shouldn't be happening. I just hope the bank site's not working properly and the figures aren't real.

Peering round the door he found Philip Bryston asleep, his wife beside him, her hand resting on his chest. The grey tinge on his face was a shock, especially the lips and his eyes seemed to have sunk. Jane saw him and came out. He noted the extra bedding scattered on the floor.

'How's he doing?'

She shook her head. 'He needs more digoxin.'

'How much have you got?'

'Only another four days at the lower rate then.'

He could only say: 'I'm trying to get more but everything's so disrupted. I'm sorry.'

She touched his hand. 'Don't be sorry, you're doing your best.'

'I wish I could do more and I'm sorry it's got so crowded.'

'It doesn't matter, we're all in this nightmare together.'

'I didn't expect so many,' he said, thinking how lame that sounded.

'I know my dear but I'm afraid there'll be more before it's over. Your idea for an ark, you said it was a joke, but I think you've already launched it.'

He smiled in confusion, uncertain of her meaning and turned to Sally who'd come upstairs. 'John just told me what happened.'

He thought she'd be angry but she wrapped her arms around him in a hug . He rested his head against her, saying: 'I had to do it, it was awful.'

'It was brave, it can't have been easy.'

'Brave? I might have killed him and I couldn't stop shaking. It was pathetic,' he whispered. 'I couldn't help it, it was awful. John helped, he was brilliant.'

'Oh sweetie, it's such a mess.'

'I'm not cut out for this, Sally. I don't want to shoot people.'

A gang of sparrows chattered cheerfully in the bay tree close to the house where they still roosted, sheltered from the rain. He heard them chirping clearly in a stillness he hadn't noticed for days. The window revealed a sky of broken cloud streaked with blue and a weak sun trying to break free.

'It's not raining,' he called. 'It's a nice morning. We must get them out before it starts again.'

Outside he found John ahead of him, looking pleased.

'I know it won't last,' he said. 'I'm not kidding myself but it's good to be out without getting wet.'

Someone inside must've realised it was a fine day and word went round. People crowded out into fresh air, to discover more about their sanctuary.

Sally and Eve went through the house, opening every door and window to let in the breeze and release the smells and stale air of many days. The light wind and faint glimmer of sun was a tonic for humans shut in together for too long. They all had the same idea -- to take their breakfast out to the muddy yard or garden. They ambled about the farm and some headed off for longer walks of exploration.

Philip Bryston stayed indoors but left his bed to sit by the open window. When Adam looked in he apologised for being feeble.

'It's not going downstairs that's the problem,' he said. 'It's the thought of having to get back up here again. I can't do it.'

Adam stayed to chat. He tried to cheer him but knew he was tiring the old man who seemed ten years older than on the night of the evacuation.

'Breathe plenty of that fresh air, Philip. We should get your pills today.'

Another patient waited downstairs. The girl, Kylie, was huddled on the floor alone supported by cushions with an inhaler in her hand.

'Not going out?' He crouched beside her.

'I don't feel well,' she said wheezing.

'You could sit in the garden for a bit, some air might help your chest,' he suggested.

'Got no energy,' she said.

'Shall I carry you out? The helicopter should be here soon, you could watch it.'

'My brother Jason's out there,' she said.

'D'you want to join him?'

'All right, if you think so.'

He carried her out into the warm summer morning, to their little green summer house with its extra layer of damp lichen and a fair view of the hills.

He'd settled her in a chair, wrapped up snugly in a blanket with another round her feet when her mother ran across the grass.

'Kylie, Kylie, What're you doing?' she called as if Adam shouldn't have interfered. But the summer house reassured her and she thanked him grudgingly. 'She must be inside before it rains again.'

A call informed them the helicopter was on its way and John heaved a sigh. 'At least it's not raining. I never thought about the weather that much. But however dry it gets I'll never ask for rain again.'

Adam wondered if this third respite from the rain meant a change on the way. He dared not hope but for now his charges were relaxed, enjoying the sun with quiet pleasure.

But it couldn't last. Tom came seeking him, angry again. The worsening situation was having a bad effect on the boy.

'You've got to do something. They're in the raspberries.'

The vegetable patch had grown in the years after the covid virus. After the difficult time that followed it was soon obvious to Sally, given the space they had, that a productive veg garden would be well worth the effort, even a life saver.

She was right and until now they had needed to buy very little in the way of fresh produce. The lockdowns had sparked a new interest in growing things all over the country and what had been beautiful flower beds now boasted salad crops and rows of carrots and greens. Lawns made way for potatoes.

But the rain had spoiled all that. The patch was waterlogged and any crops not rotting in the ground were ruined by mildew and botrytis. Only the rain-loving raspberries had fruited and ripened defiantly, giving a steady supply of fruit for a month, though some were turning grey with mildew. There weren't enough to share with the guests so the berries were eaten in guilty secrecy.

He shrugged, it was too late to stop them. But he followed Tom through the rose-covered arch to see a dozen or so guests among the double rows, reaching over each other for clusters of fruit which were ripped from the stalks and crammed by the handful into greedy mouths. The canes were being trampled into the soil.

Father and son watched as squabbles began with shouts and swearing as people shoved each other aside, scrambling for the best berries.

The Smiths were in the thick of it. Rosanna, her large mouth framed red with juice, pushed another woman roughly away to reach a lush cluster. She stripped the fruit by the handful, gobbling as much as she could. Adam thought of her, red and steaming in the bath towel and reflected that humiliation hadn't changed her attitude.

He remembered Gaz taking advantage of the hot bath water. Then he saw the youth and his pals who'd followed them through the arch to see what the fuss was about. He expected them to join the raiders but they only watched in amazement at the scene. It occurred to him they might have no idea that raspberries grew on canes and could be eaten as picked.

'Can't you stop them, Dad?'

Adam shook his head surveying the young fresh shoots which would have borne next year's fruit, crushed by careless feet.

'What's the point? They've had most of them and wrecked the rest and flattened the potatoes as well, what's left of them. Forget it Tom, the garden's a write-off.'

'But it's not fair. They shouldn't be here. We don't want them.'

'No, we don't. It wasn't my choice, Tom.'

'It's our home. I wish they'd disappear. I wish you'd shoot them all.'

He looked at his son, full of the anger he felt in himself. 'Don't say that.'

He flicked his hand over Tom's head in mock punishment. 'I know how you feel. I wish they'd all go, anywhere but here.'

'You shot that man at Rowan Hill, wish I'd been there.'

'How d'you know about that?'

'Uncle John told me.'

'Did he! Who else knows?'

'I told Ben of course.'

'Of course.'

Frowning he took Tom's chin and met his eyes 'I don't want you talking about it, not to anyone. I mean it, do you understand? And you must tell Ben that. It's important, got it?'

'If you say so, Dad, but why? It might make them all behave better.'

150

'You might be right. But it could make things worse. You're old enough to realise how bad it is. If they know I shot someone it'll frighten them and I don't want that. It's bad enough already. We have to help them.'

'Even that dreadful woman? Look at her! You could shoot her.'

'Tom!' But he chuckled: 'I won't say I'm not tempted, she does push her luck.' They watched the scavengers trawling through the veg patch, seeking anything fit to eat and saw one man bite into a small green apple.

Tom said: 'Good. He'll get guts ache.'

Adam smiled. 'Never mind, come with me now, we need to round up a gang to meet the drop.'

Dark clouds were back as the helicopter flew in and the dry interlude wouldn't last into the afternoon. Upturned faces showed hope it might stay dry long enough to get the precious stores under cover.

This time it landed, settling onto the muddy ground with the usual spray effect. Seeking the now familiar figure of the captain Adam was disappointed. He found the young officer reassuring and his absence set off a niggle of worry.

'No Captain Rogers?' he said.

'He's on another mission.' This was a different team with a tough-looking corporal in charge. He barked instructions at Adam to get the job done quickly. He stood just inside the door, watching as the handlers scurried around the helicopter with boxes and packages.

Determined not to be intimidated by the soldier's attitude Adam took time to check the stuff. One dark greyish bundle made him pause. 'What's that?' he queried.

The harsh voice made the terse answer more startling: 'Body bags.'

He saw Adam absorbing the implications: 'You'll probably need them before you're done.'

Adam met the challenge in his eyes and shrugged: 'Let's hope not. Did you bring the medication?'

'There's this.' The corporal tossed him a padded package, too small to hold much.

'Is that it?' he asked.

'That's what they sent.'

'Are you certain there's nothing else?'

'That's all that's marked for you. Come on, get out, we need to move.'

Adam was still peering round the interior, hoping for another box when the soldier thrust out his fist and pushed him roughly towards the door. Caught off balance he slipped and landed on his side in the mud. The soldier laughed: 'Sorry mate, you'll need to be a bit sharper to cope in this lot.'

The craft was already rising as he slammed the door and left Adam with the vision of his grinning face. Swearing, he struggled to get up, slipping again on the sticky ground, left knee aching from the heavy fall.

'What a bastard,' John was shocked. 'There was no call for that.'

'Typical army bully, the sort that comes into his own in a crisis.'

'Woolton!' In the rush of the delivery he hadn't noticed the man waiting quietly away from the action, grey-haired, wearing army fatigues but no insignia.

John was puzzled but Adam muttered: 'Oh shit,' and said aloud: 'Didn't see you there. They've gone without you.'

The man nearly smiled: 'I know you're expecting me.'

He nodded. 'John, this is Guy Cotterill. He's come about the ark.'

Unsmiling John raised his eyebrows and said nothing. He turned away saying: 'Another mouth to feed.'

He ignored Cotterill as they lugged packages and said: 'I keep forgetting to ask you, what are we going to do about the missing cash?'

'I'd forgotten about that.'

'We can't let it pass, can we?'

'No, or the culprit will feel they can take other stuff.'

'D'you think it was Gaz and his mates?'

'Could be -- but not necessarily. Because they carry knives, doesn't mean they're thieves.'

The downpour was back as they finished stowing the supplies and the house was noisy and tense with hostility.

Sally and Eve were backed into a corner trying to stay in control. The pleasure of the morning sunshine had turned sour and pent up resentment returned with the rain. They were shouting about the rations, the earlier cheerfulness evaporated, no longer inclined to co-operate.

He saw anger, frustration and fear and knew they'd begun to realise the true state of their situation -- stuck for the long haul in a situation which could only get worse. Fresh supplies made them expect a better menu but Sally was telling them strict rationing would continue. Her sensible explanation was shouted down with wild accusations and threats. When Adam said the same thing the reaction surprised him. Not just the Smiths but several women began shouting and urging their husbands to do something.

'This is bloody nonsense,' called a youngish man Adam recognised as the manager at the garage on the main road. He was one of the vegans and always ready to moan.

'All that stuff's just come, we've lugged it through the mud and now you say it's the same old muck for supper. There's tins of biscuits and chocolate, why can't we eat it?'

'I don't even know what came. If it's stuff like that, it probably means they're running short of staples. We can't just gobble it up. It's got to last.'

'You've got plenty of food, I saw you and him,' he pointed at John 'hiding something in that barn. You must think we're stupid. I expect you'll make a nice profit selling the stuff when all this is over.'

'For fuck's sake, we're trying to help you.'

The noise increased and John moved closer to Adam.

He shouted at them: 'Shut up, all of you! We have to eke it out. This could go on for months, we don't know when they'll come again. Look out there! While it rains we're all stuck here.'

They subsided into sullen hostility and he pictured the guns and the scene at Rowan Hill. He left them in disgust to open the drugs package and examined the contents in disbelief -- a few emergency dressings, three boxes of pain killers, four phials of a morphine derivative with syringes but no instructions and one slip of digoxin -- not even a full packet. There were no inhalers or anything else for an asthma patient.

Chapter fourteen

Cotterill is a bully, he tried to take over as soon as he walked through the door. Wanted me to drop everything and start on the ark plans. Told him where to go but trouble is I'm not sure how much authority he has.

When I mentioned the people stranded on the moor he made some nasty comments. Said I should stop worrying about them, people were bound to die.

He actually said it'd be a good thing if we got rid of some of the jobless underclass. He said the virus year thinned out the world population a bit and this lot will do more. So callous, too pragmatic for me, that may be how he sees the reality but it was hard to take.

It's the bodybags that really bug me, that bundle waiting in the barn. It's all right John saying we're doing all we can but I feel we're letting them down. Ron's so matter of fact about it and that bastard corporal as well, he seemed to take it for granted there'll be deaths.

The only issue is how to handle it when normality is suspended. It comes down to the clinical matter of storing bodies until they can be dealt with. But having corpses stacked in my barn isn't something I can easily accept.

Outside the rain was falling in torrents, darkening the mood but a buzz of fresh resentment puzzled him. But when he saw Guy Cotterill blocking the doorway, broad shoulders thrust out in an aggressive stance, all became clear. He was holding back the hungry crowd, allowing just a few at a time through to get their meal.

Flushed with anger Sally was shouting at him. 'We don't need you here, you've no right. Our system works and you're just making things more difficult.'

His condescending response provoked her to greater fury. 'You need order in this situation. These people need to know who's in charge.'

'We have order, thank you and it works very well. Get out of the way and let us get on with it -- you're just maker it slower.'

They all waited in sullen silence as Amy Lock whispered to Adam: 'He's upsetting everyone, they just about tolerate obeying you but he's treating them like idiots.'

'I'll get him upstairs. I hope he'll be gone tomorrow. Tell Sally to keep me some food, I've had nothing since breakfast.'

Cotterill stared intently at the screen as Adam brought up the ark designs and his calculations. The scientist fired questions at him and made notes on his tablet. 'Good lines,' he muttered.

'It's just a boat,' said Adam. '

'Is that it?'

'Yes, I told them, you heard me. You've seen the plans already, you had them at the meeting.'

'But we thought you had more, that this was just the first theme.'

'No, I told you.'

'But what made you put it out as a viable scheme?'

'I didn't. Like I said, it was a bit of fun, a joke. That's all there was to it.'

'But all that money --.'

'I've already closed the link but it's still coming in.'

'But what made people believe it?'

'You tell me. Your colonel and General Langdon believed it despite what I said. The ark was a bible tale, you don't really believe it could be done, do you?'

'But all that money,' Cotterill muttered again.

'It's like Lynn Meacham said, if people are desperate they'll latch onto anything. But it's still nonsense.'

He eyed Adam with suspicion: 'You know I could confiscate your computer, check it to make sure you're not hiding something.'

'Feel free, take the bloody lot. For God's sake, man, why won't you believe me? When I put out that silly scheme I'd no idea how serious things were. My time is taken up looking after these people. Can't you understand, it was a fucking joke.'

'Don't speak to me like that, I could have you arrested.'

'Go ahead. What matters is saving people. I've already got two set to die. D'you think I'm worried what you think or do. They gave me guns, remember, I might just shoot you. Your damned army has given me authority here and I intend to use it. More people arrived yesterday and more could turn up any time. I know how bad things are but in this place it's down to me. I have to look after them all so go away and leave me to it.'

They glared at each other until at last Cotterill said ruefully: 'I suppose it was a bit far fetched.'

'I was just doodling.'

'That's really all there is to it?'

'Yes, how many times must I say it?'

'Okay, I believe you.'

Following Adam from the room he glanced around at the cluttered floor. 'Pretty crowded in here, must be inconvenient.'

'Just a bit, the boys sleep here and the little girl I found as well.'

'Cosy.' He paused by Hayley's bed and unseen by Adam scooped up the rabbit toy.

'I'll just pop in here before I come down,' he said, shutting the bathroom door as Adam was on the stairs.

The murmur of angry voices was becoming a growl as he surveyed the guests. They'd been asked to wait after breakfast and the idea of another lecture provoked resentment instead of interest. Rain fell again like rods and it was colder with a strong east wind rattling the farm. The daily misery of wetness seeped into

157

clothes and shoes and made the whole house damp. The pleasures of yesterday's brief remission were already forgotten.

He caught mutters of 'What is it now?' and knew his message would aggravate the general ill temper. Cotterill stood at the back of the crowd watching with interest while Jane Bryston beside him looked embarrassed.

'I'm sorry, guys,' he began 'but we have a problem. Jane mislaid her handbag for a while. When she found it there was stuff missing, cash. How much was in there, Jane?'

Her troubled face looked up at him: 'It doesn't matter, I don't need it, I can't spend it --'

'That's not the point -- how much has gone?'

'There was forty pounds and some change.'

'I see.'

More muttering and the groans of exasperation became angry exclamations. Marcus Smith said loudly: 'Now you're calling us thieves.'

Adam glanced around, seeking signs of discomfort which might indicate guilt but saw nothing. He had a plan to make it easy for the thief and waited, arms folded, hoping his body language would control the confrontation. His silence eventually got through.

'Right, money's missing but we needn't make a big thing of it. Whoever took it must still have it, can't spend it here. We just want that person to give it back. We can't have theft, we must have trust among us.'

Smith butted in again: 'You treat us like criminals or children. What if the thief doesn't give it back?'

Adam looked to John for backing and said, very deliberately: 'I don't know what we'll do but we won't leave it unresolved.' He paused: 'I suppose it would have to be some kind of sanctions.'

'What sanctions?' asked Jock. The word worried him.

'Everyone might suffer until we find the culprit. Rations could be cut.'

Hissing anger ripped through the crowd.

Then a soft voice asked: 'Is it true you shot someone?'

The noise stopped as if a button was pressed.

They all eyed him, waiting for the answer and he saw Sally's anxious frown as he said: 'Yes, it's true. I had no choice.'

A sigh rippled through them as they absorbed the implications of that admission.

He waited, then said: 'I don't want to have to do it again.'

'But you would -- if necessary?' It was Smith. 'You'd shoot us?'

He turned to John who said: 'Adam was told by army HQ to take control and do whatever is needed. We were issued with guns.'

'So you'd shoot us?'

John started to answer but Adam touched his arm and said in a voice strained but resigned: 'If necessary.'

Shocked expressions relayed the impact of his words and Jane Bryston caught his arm and whispered: 'There's no need for this, it's only money.'

'No, to get through this we need control and discipline. We can't let it pass. Look,' he had their full attention now. 'Whoever took the cash, we're gonna make it easy. See the hall stand--'

Near the front door an old Victorian hall stand, complete with mirror and brass bowls for sticks and umbrellas, was festooned with hats and outdoor gear.

Its most striking feature was a silk top hat, once belonging to Sally's grandfather which sat, black crown up, in front of the mirror. He pointed at the hat.

'There, whoever has the money, just find a moment when you're alone, turn the hat up and leave the cash inside. Simple, no one will know and that'll be the end of it.'

'You'll leave it at that?' asked Jock.

'Sure, Jane gets her cash and no harm done.'

'It won't be easy without being spotted.'

'It won't be difficult -- they managed to steal it without being seen. He or she will find a way.'

He was saved from further discussion by Sally waving a phone. 'It's Ron.'

He shut the kitchen door against the buzz of speculation and listened. Ron was terse and to the point as ever.

'You're right, Zadok is a code -- you've landed yourself in some serious stuff.'

'What d'you mean?'

'Can't tell you now. But they want you back at HQ.'

'What for?'

'Zadok's something big and they need your help.'

'What can I do?'

'I don't know but that word got a strong reaction.'

'So now what?'

'Be ready, later today. They're coming for that scientist and they'll collect you both.'

'I can't leave here for long, it's not fair on the girls.'

'You should be home before night. And this is the last time I'll call on the mobile. Get your sat phone set up and keep it with you.'

'Why?'

'Just do it.'

Beside Guy Cotterill in the helicopter, he brooded on the reasons for this flight. He'd rebelled and stayed indoors as the chopper landed but when he hadn't appeared a baby-faced private arrived at the door flourishing an assault rifle. Captain Rogers followed.

Fingering the pistol on his belt, he was quiet but firm: 'I'm sorry Mr Woolton, none of us like this. But my orders are to fetch you, by force if necessary.'

Adam sighed: 'Ron said I'd be back tonight.'

'We hope that's possible.'

He rubbed his palms together anxiously, watching the drowned landscape roll out below. In the distance the range of the Malverns stood clear of the water. He gasped when he saw the long upland ridge covered with tents. They drifted untidily

160

downhill, merging with what he could see of Malvern itself and the other communities which hugged the hillside. The sloping land of fields and woodland stopped abruptly at the edge of a giant mere where the famous show ground should be.

Soon they saw the upper walls of a tower with graceful inter-laced arches -- it had to be an abbey -- and he realised it must be Tewkesbury, standing clear of the flood as a pinnacle of hope for normality.

This time both he and Cotterill were taken straight into the Georgian dining room where the colonel was ensconced with two other officers pouring over a set of maps, on paper and a laptop. He found a grain of comfort in the colonel's expression, softer than before with a sense of apology. He half rose and shook his hand, saying: 'Glad to see you again. Sorry we had to drag you back here but it seems you're in the middle of some-thing big.'

He saw the puzzled expression and went on: 'I know you haven't a clue what I'm talking about and that's what makes it right -- that's how we know it's genuine.'

'What?'

'Zadok, it's pure chance you've got into this but the fact is you are. Sit down and I'll tell you what I can. Get him some coffee, Mike.'

'Guy here says you're pretty useful one way and another. The shooting and the money business tells us you're on the right lines.'

Adam realised Cotterill must already have given a full report. Nothing was a secret to these men and he realised his worries about little Hayley and her mother's work were nothing com-pared to the reality.

'Your little motherless girl has become very important, crucial in fact. Her mother works for us, not the army as such -- the se-curity services -- but it's all the same now. It was very inoppor-tune that the flooding began when it did, on the very day Mrs Lomax had her meeting.'

Adam smiled at the understatement. 'But it was lucky for Hayley that you found her.'

Wondering where it was all leading he interrupted. 'I don't know what this is about but I have a family and fifty odd people to care for, I haven't got time to worry about some plot.'

The colonel ignored him and carried on, choosing his words with care. 'Kirstie Lomax is a very talented linguist, in fact she's one of the best in the world and she is also a very attractive woman with a certain lushness about her.' He raised an eyebrow to emphasise his meaning.

He paused and smiled at Adam: 'If and when you meet her you'll understand. She is the sort of woman who can make men -- what shall I say? -- lose concentration perhaps. She has an effect on people, an impact. These combined talents make her ideal for this job.'

'And what job is that?'

'She's acting as interpreter for a leading businessman from,' he hesitated 'let's just say at this stage, a country in the Middle East.'

'You mean an Arab?'

The colonel nodded. 'And she is thought by him and his associates to be part Arab --'

'And have sympathies with that part of the world?' he interrupted again.

'Yes.'

'But she is British? Hayley looks as English as they come. She's fair and pretty -- she'll be a stunner, if --'

The colonel nodded: 'If we ever get back to normal. Yes, Kirstie Lomax is British, English, whatever. But her hair and eyes are very dark, probably way back in her genes there's a touch of something exotic, who knows. Her husband is a soldier, that's how we got onto her, but that all went pear-shaped, though they stay in touch for the child's sake.'

Adam sipped his coffee, disliking the bitter taste of the powdered milk on his tongue. But it gave him the chance to be quiet while he tried to think of a way out.

The colonel pushed back his chair and rose, walking slowly around the table to stand behind him, a hand on his shoulder. If it was meant to reassure it had the opposite effect as he cringed away from the implied complicity.

He tried to shrug off the offending hand but it stayed put and the colonel, having waited for some response, continued in a harder voice.

'The fact is Woolton, we need your help. We need to get the child to her mother and you're the only chap who can do it.'

'What d'you mean?'

'The people Mrs Lomax is with know about the child and that she's stranded with you. So that opens the way to get her in.'

'People? So this businessman is not just that?'

'He's the front man -- or that's how it looks and what Kirstie believes after working with him for months.'

He wandered back around the table and stood again facing Adam who said: 'They'll never believe I just called up a chopper to take a little girl to be with her mum.'

'That's where your ark comes in. There's been so much coverage about it and a lot of people believe it. So we use that, put it out that you're pushing ahead with it. We exaggerate it. I don't think you understand how vulnerable people are. So many of them take what they hear on line as fact. We'll use that and as long as the net is running normally enough people will latch onto it.'

'Do you think people are that stupid?'

'Sadly, yes but not all. Despite everything that's happened these past few years there's still a tendency to accept things. Not from authority so much, the net has changed all that and the WMD business in Iraq did most to make that happen. The notion that the authorities must know something we don't, that's gone. Now it's the stuff on social media we need to use. Then when the systems shut down, anything can happen.'

'Will that happen?'

'Bound to be power cuts before long, only a matter of time,' the colonel said casually. 'It's amazing it hasn't gone already.'

Adam caught the innuendo and gasped. 'You mean it'll go when it suits you. I wondered how long it would be. This really is a dictatorship.'

'Not so! Power will inevitably be lost, it's impossible to maintain it in these conditions. But it must be done in a planned way so we can all benefit and keep control and get it going again. Protect it, don't you see?'

'You'll control everything.'

The colonel leaned across the table towards him, hands resting on the ordnance map, voice hardly above a whisper: 'You know the score, you shot a man to keep control. We're not doing this to please ourselves -- I should be retiring next month -- but someone had to take charge. It's simple, we're trying to save the country. This flood's crippled everything, you know that. And this threat could be the end of everything we understand as Britain, literally. Try to see the picture. We're trying to save it all.'

Adam looked hard at him, forcing eye contact, seeing not a uniformed soldier but a middle-aged man out of his depth and trying to cope.

He sighed. 'Okay, I get it. But what are they and where are they?'

'At this stage I don't want to tell you any more, the less you know the better for us all. But this is deadly serious.'

'I presume you're talking terrorists.'

The colonel allowed himself to meet Adam's anxious eyes again: 'In this state the country is incredibly vulnerable. We must stop whatever they're planning. But that's the bit we don't know, the crucial bit. Our only hope is Mrs Lomax in there with them. And we need to get something to her, something very important -- that's why the child is the key.'

He stood up, brisk and efficient again: 'I want you to go home and let everyone know your ark plan is progressing and that the

Disaster Management Directorate is backing you and mention the cash.'

'But I'm trying to send it back,' he burst out.

'Never mind that! Sound confident, enthusiastic and say the army may fly you north to talk to marine engineers. Keep it vague but keep it running.'

'But it's all nonsense.'

'We know that but they don't. Get it out tonight Woolton, the system could go down any time.'

Chapter fifteen

Thank God nobody realised I was back. Couldn't face a load of questions and anyway I can't tell them anything. I had to sign the bloody act before they'd let me go. The Official Secrets Act, never thought I'd be involved with that. The whole thing sounds crazy but I've got to post the ark rubbish again. Shouldn't say that but this is just a private diary now, I doubt if anyone will ever read it.

What Ron said makes sense now, the sat phone will be vital when the power goes. I dread that, it'll take us nearer the abyss. Without their techie toys it'll be hard to control our growing band of guests. Don't know why I still call them that, sounds less harsh than refugees. But that's what they are, sadly and I have to keep as many of them alive as possible.

I hope we find the money in the hat. We can't let that pass but sanctions could make control nearly impossible without violence. The fact they know about the shooting may help. They know I've done it once so they might think twice about making trouble.

I've done as the colonel said and added new stuff to give the project more authenticity, laid it on thick. But I can't believe anyone will be taken in.

He listened to the sound of his home, thankful to be back and heartened by the captain's parting words: 'Sorry about this, I don't enjoy pointing guns at you. One of these days we'll have a drink together. Things will get better.'

'I'd like that -- if we ever get out of this.'

'We will, trust me.'

The crowded house had a constant hum, a background to everything, voices, real and digital, shuffling bodies, arguments, queries and demands. Only at night was it hushed when sleep took over but even then the mutterings of humanity impinged and made tranquillity impossible.

He opened the ark files reluctantly and turned to see Sally watching.

'You walked right past me,' she said. He rose and hugged her. 'Thank God you're back safe. It's worse every time you go.'

'I didn't see you lying there in the dark?'

She nodded: 'I'm so tired. I needed to get away from them all. John and Eve are on duty.' He kissed her again and noted the dark signs of strain around her eyes that seemed to deepen each day. He held her close, nestled against his shoulder: 'It's very hard on you.'

'It's hard on all of us.'

She glanced at the computer: 'What're you doing?' She looked at what he'd written. 'You're not trying to get more money.'

'It's not what it seems.'

'Why waste time on this nonsense? After all the trouble it's caused.'

'Sally please, it isn't me. I can't explain, not yet, it's what the army wants. They have their reasons, honestly.'

The doubt in her face made him laugh. 'Sally love, trust me. Would I lie to you?'

'Who knows? But this ark thing worries me.'

'I know. But it's why they wanted me again.'

'Just that?'

He paused before he lied: 'Yes. We'll never have a penny of it, don't worry.' Without thinking he added: 'It'll vanish anyway when the system goes down.'

'What?'

'It's only a matter of time before the power goes.'

He saw her fear but knew again why he loved her as he watched her struggle to stay calm: 'Are you sure?'

167

'It's inevitable, we've talked about it.'

'How do you know?' she asked.

'It's been mentioned.'

'You mean they're going to turn it off?'

'Seems so.'

'Why?'

'It's all about control, Sally.'

She slumped into the chair, looking at him as if he could somehow make it all stop but he shook his head.

'Are we going to warn them?' she asked.

'Don't know, let's see what the others think. My gut feeling is it's better they don't know till it happens.'

Waiting for breakfast they'd all seen the clip of Adam repeated on TV with Guy Cotterill speaking about the project's enormous potential and the importance of Adam's work.

He shook his head in embarrassment as Eve laughed: 'Famous again, Adam.'

'It's total crap but don't tell them that,' he gestured beyond the kitchen door. 'Classic fake news.'

'Are you sure?'

'Positive, it's nothing but nonsense and exaggeration.'

'But why?' asked John.

He shook his head again. 'Army orders, I can't say any more.

'It can't do any harm, can it?'

'Probably not, except make me look a bloody fool.'

They had developed a rota system and put a trestle table in the hall to cope with the increasing chaos of meals. When he emerged to take his turn serving the porridge he faced a barrage of questions but Eve called him back, waving the phone.

'It's that girl from the BBC again.'

Lynn Meacham wanted a new interview but he refused at once. All she got was 'the powers that be are interested in my ideas and have asked me to pursue various lines of research in order to facilitate the progress of the project.'

No, he couldn't give a realistic time track for when a proto-type might be launched and he couldn't speculate on how many vessels might be ordered in the initial production.

Her engineering knowledge surprised him when she persisted but he got out of it by referring her to the army.

'But they won't tell me anything,' she exclaimed.

'I'm sorry. I can only tell you that it's out of my hands. I'm sure the army information officer will give you a statement.'

'Huh! About as informative as what you've said, which is bugger-all!'

'That's the way it is.'

Ron was next, via his sat phone, brief and to the point. 'They need you back at Ruttock Common.'

'Why?'

'The soldiers are struggling. They need back-up, moral sup-port.'

'Do you think that'll help?'

'Yes,' he said harshly. 'Go armed and take John. It's all about lessons and like you said, control.'

'I don't want a repeat of Rowan Hill.'

'Could happen -- but don't hesitate. That's why you need to go. They know about it so when you turn up with weapons they might calm down.'

'You hope.'

'The threat of force should keep the lid on things a bit longer.'

'What's their main complaint?' he asked.

'Where d'you start? They're wet, cold and miserable and now they're hungry too.'

'What can I offer them?'

'Not much, unless you're a real-life Noah.'

'I need to tell them something,' he insisted.

'Tell them we hope to get more supplies to them soon.'

'Is that true?'

'Sort of. They are trying but it's getting harder. The in-frastructure's buggered. They're trying to bring in more stuff from unaffected areas but it takes time. The logistics are frightening. Do your best Adam.'

'I don't want to lie to them.'

'Just get the facts for us.'

'We'll do our best.'

'Good. By the way, how's the old man?'

'Philip, not good, his tablets are nearly gone. He's in pain now.'

'Are there any foxgloves about?'

'What?' Adam was puzzled. 'Foxgloves?'

'You know, digitalis, digoxin, that's where it comes from.'

'I know, but what are you saying?'

'Look it up while you still can. See if there's some way you could use the plant.'

He thought Ron was joking but then the man didn't make jokes.

'I'll try but I haven't much time to look for flowers. I'll send the boys.'

He stepped over scattered clothes and blankets to reach the old man's bedside. They'd wanted to keep the room just for him and Jane but space was too tight. She brought his meals on a tray, the stairs now too much for him. Sitting up supported by several pillows, he looked tired but cheerful and brightened when he saw Adam.

'How's it going, Philip?'

'Not so bad, though I hate eating in bed. But staying here saves my breath.'

Adam nodded. 'How many pills have you got?'

Jane passed him the foil strip, only four blisters intact.

He frowned, studying the old man without being obvious. The greyish pallor had worsened since he was confined to bed.

'Two days?'

They both nodded and Jane looked away. He started to say: 'Philip, it's just a thought, probably daft --' then stopped. Why

170

raise false hopes till he knew more. They might not find any foxgloves, the rain had probably made them unusable.

'What?' Jane had picked up a glimmer from him.

'It's nothing. Tell you later.'

The boys weren't great with flowers and his description of the plant seemed meaningless to them. 'You must have seen them, tall things with pinkish bell like flowers.'

'Never noticed,' muttered Tom. 'Anyway it's belting down again, we're not going out in this.'

'It's important, Tom. We'll look on line, find a pic so you know what to look for.'

'Oh Dad!'

He found an image of a foxglove in bloom, the pink flowers bright against a grassy background.

'I've seen them,' Ben said. 'There were some last year in that rough patch near the top wall. Haven't seen any this year.'

'You haven't been up there for ages, there could be some.' He read on: 'They should be in flower now but it's the leaves we need. It says pick them before they flower, we're probably a bit late. But we'll try.'

He swung round in his chair. 'Right. I want you to find some.'

'Dad!' Tom complained again.

'This is serious. Pick them carefully and don't damage the plant.'

'But Dad, the rain, what's this all about?'

'It's for Mr Bryston, it might help him. I'll read up on what we need to do.'

Tom's face was a picture. 'You're having us on, you can't be serious.'

'Please boys, trust me. It's probably crazy but it might just work, you could save his life.'

They stared at him, suddenly solemn as they took in what he was saying. Tom spoke first: 'There's something in the plant like a medicine?'

His father nodded: 'It's worth trying.'

'Is he that bad? Could he die?'

'Yes, his pills are nearly gone, he's in a bad way. His heart needs help.'

They looked at each other and Ben said: 'We'll try.'

'I'm sorry love, we've got to go.'

'But it gets worse every time you're away. Do you have to take John, or couldn't he go instead?'

He shook his head: 'No, it needs us both. We shouldn't be gone too long. We'll try to be back before evening.' He was by the bedroom window, peering through the driving rain for a sight of his sons.

'The rain's heavier than ever, I'm sorry I had to send the boys out in it but we've got to try.'

'Do you really think it will help?'

'I don't know. It's clutching at straws.' He bent to drag the guns from under the bed. He grabbed a bag and fastened a cartridge belt across his chest. Sally winced as she watched him.

'Must you take those?'

He nodded. 'I have to. Try not to worry, I know that's easy to say. It's bad out there. This lot don't realise how lucky they are. I'm dreading what we might find on the moor.'

'Love you, Adam,' she said, kissing him lightly on the cheek. 'I know you won't use a gun unless you have to.'

'I won't. I need to go, John's waiting."

He turned back to the window: 'I was hoping the boys might be back by now.'

He surveyed the rain-swept fields and picked out the figures near the sky line.

He watched them turn for home, on a mission, laughing as they ran down the hill, as he hadn't seen them laugh for weeks. Tom clutched a plastic bag.

They burst into the kitchen, faces alight. 'We found them, Dad,' Tom shouted, thrusting the bag at him.

Adam took a handful of wet leaves. 'Great, were there a lot of

172

plants up there?'

'A few in a patch, all with flowers. And I'll tell you what else is up there -- loads of rabbits. They're everywhere, holes all over.'

'They're digging in under the wall, probably drier for them,' added Ben.

'You'd think they'd all be drowned,' said John.

Adam smiled. 'No, they're survivors, they'll have moved up-hill ahead of the water. They're not stupid.'

Ben grabbed his father's arm: 'There was a fox there, too. It didn't run when it saw us, just sat there, watching the rabbits. And another further along. But the one that stayed put, it was all daggly, y'know scruffy, its tail all clogged with mud.'

Adam and John looked at each other. 'Everything's fleeing the water.'

From their excitement he guessed they had a plan. 'Me and Tom thought we'd try and catch some rabbits -- fresh meat, it'd be great.'

Adam smiled: 'D'you think you could?'

'There's my airgun but I thought I'd try making snares,' Tom said.

John laughed: 'I bet most of this lot've never eaten rabbit. Can you imagine Rosanna.'

Tom was huffy. 'They can please themselves, but we fancy a bit of bunny, don't we Ben.'

His brother nodded then noticed the cartridge belt. 'You two off again?'

'We shouldn't be long.' He turned to Sally putting the bag of wet leaves into her hand.

'Do something with these.'

'Like what?'

'They need to be dried.'

The Lower Downton silage tower looked smaller. They both stared back at it to gauge the degree of difference.

173

'It's definitely smaller so the water's risen since last time,' John was dismayed. 'I thought it might have gone down.'

'Not while it's raining like this,' said Adam grimly. John had to keep a tight grip on the engine as the dinghy cut through the flooded valley. A vicious wind blew down between the hills whipping the water into big waves which buffeted the small craft. They struggled to stay on course. He held firmly to the ropes at the front, kneeling to peer through the grey veil of cloud and driving rain, watching for the way up to the camp.

His head buzzed with possibilities, afraid of what they would find and angry at what he knew must be a futile journey.

They needn't have worried about missing the place -- they'd been spotted and a welcome party had gathered, growing as they approached. As the boat drew in where track met water, Adam jumped ashore, pistol in hand expecting to be surrounded by clamouring people. But the crowd was silent, staring into the boat. Disappointment showed on tired faces.

Someone spoke: 'You've come empty-handed?'

John nodded.

'Why have you come then?'

'Good question,' Adam muttered, as John moved beside him and the watchful group waited. He raised his gun. Someone said: 'Why are you armed?'

'Routine. We've come to see how it's going here.'

Another voice said: 'You two came before and nothing happened, now you're here waving guns about.'

The friends looked at each other, both were wet and untidy from the boat but more or less clean -- these men and women were filthy. They all wore black bin liners with holes for head and arms, tied at the waist with anything that could be found and the longer the better to cover trousers.

Few had boots of any kind, let alone wellingtons which were the obvious necessity in the conditions. Most had their feet wrapped in more plastic bags, secured around the ankles. All looked ill, thin and pinched with cold.

'What's that smell?' whispered John.

'Humanity in the raw.'

'It's awful.'

'Yes. What you'd find in any crowded medieval town,' Adam replied.

'Thanks for the lecture. How can they live like this?'

'Not easily.'

Up the filthy track they passed through bedraggled bramble bushes, their lower stems weighed down by sludge, the higher shoots bearing pathetic clusters of unripe berries grey with mould. They waded through a quagmire of muddy water coming down in a constant stream often up to their knees. The desolation remembered from the first visit was nothing to this.

The plastic walkways had disappeared, sunk into the mire and the rows of brown tents, weighted with a coating of mud into sagging bundles, had merged into the ground outside so the whole site was a morass of oozing slurry. Wide pools of dirty water stretched in every direction.

John lifted an open tent flap to peer in. 'Excuse me,' he said to the woman and her child lying inside but the dull eyes hardly flickered as she said: 'Don't mind us, we don't count.'

They lay on a blow-up mattress only just clear of the mud which went right into the tent. Clothes hung from a string along the apex and he saw no other dry place to keep anything clear of the muck. He backed away and looked around, realising he'd see the same misery in every tent. He hurried to join Adam, heading to the marquee, still in position at the camp's centre.

The only place with even a pretence of normality, plastic duckboards were piled several thick at the entrance and because it was on a slight slope, the floor inside had only a thin coating of mud. The place was crowded, anything that could be used as seating was occupied and people stood around in groups, not talking, just keeping out of the rain. Some clasped tin mugs and the pair were handed the same by the corporal they'd met before.

'Tea, sir, am I glad to see you!'

He sighed. 'Don't be, I've no idea how we can help.' He paused and looked around: 'Is it as bad as it looks?'

The soldier nodded. 'Worse, about as bad as it could be. And now we're short of food. They're here hoping for lunch.'

Adam eyed the miserable gathering, waiting in mute acceptance of their plight. The lack of noise was weird, no conversation and their arrival sparked no interest. They had expected angry demands but the people, mostly men, displayed the dull stupor of resignation.

'It's very quiet,' said John.

'It is now. But a few days ago it was a near riot. Demanding more food, threatening us, shouting and screaming, that's when we asked for back-up. But they seem to have realised it won't help. It's bad for us too, you know. We're in here but it's hard work and not much sleep and we must be alert to stop pilfering. There's a lot of 'em getting ill, sickness and the runs -- you know.' He added this information almost as an afterthought.

'Is the generator still working?'

'Just about, we're low on fuel so we keep it just for cooking and a bit of light in the evenings.' He gave Adam a hard look and said: 'Someone's got to do something, sir. If they're still here when autumn comes they'll all die.'

John was picking up items from the rows of crockery on the trestles, running a finger round the inside of cups and bowls. 'This is disgusting.'

'Hard to keep it clean, sir. Cold rain water's not the best for washing up.'

They stood in the centre of it all with a growing sense of helplessness. 'What the hell can we do?'

A slight stir among the brooding men announced a new arrival through the tent flap. Adam recognised the woman who'd spoken before though the change was striking. The urban assurance and hint of truculence had been wrung out of her as she stared at them in despair.

'It is you two. They said it was.'

'Mrs Pocock?'

She nodded. 'Why are you here?'

'We were sent,' said John.

She laughed. 'You didn't do any good last time, nothing's changed, it's just got worse.'

Adam began to say it was the same for everybody but he knew it wasn't true. Things were much worse here than at Rowan Hill or his home, which was a haven in comparison.

She was saying: 'People will die soon if we can't get away. There's no medical provision at all. We've several children and some old people who are really sick.'

He thought of Philip, dying at Down Farm but at least dying in a dry bed.

He said: 'It's dreadful. We didn't know things were so bad.' How lame that sounded.

She went on: 'Water's the main problem, there's very little to drink, that's what's making people ill. They said they'd sink a borehole but they haven't done it. They drop us bottled water but never enough.'

She detailed the horrors of every day life in the camp. For people long past worrying about entertainment, survival was the thing, simply staying alive.

Cold, hunger, illness, all the tribulations of refugees everywhere but over it all, compounding the misery was the rain; the soaking, drenching punishment of the incessant rain.

'I've watched horror stories from earthquakes and wars and famine and seen all that suffering. I never thought I'd be there myself,' she said.

He saw her eyes fill with tears, tears of desperation and exhaustion drawing lines through the grime of skin unused to doing without the protection of cosmetics.

More women and a few children had wandered in. The child eyes appeared huge in the dirty masks of their small drawn faces, all waiting and listening and wondering if all this raw emotion would make any difference.

John turned aside, wanting to cry with her. Adam's face was shielded by a hand. Neither could believe this was happening in England to ordinary unprepared people.

He reached out a hesitant hand to give Anne Pocock a tissue to wipe her face, afraid she would be insulted.

Softly he said: 'I don't know if we can help and I don't want to raise your hopes but we will try. I promise you, we will try.

Chapter sixteen

Back on the open water a cold fear crept into them. They glanced at each other, wondering if both felt the same, gripped by a sudden dread of the water, the unknown depth beneath them. Reluctant to put it in words each had the awful thought that this mighty mere might never subside.

Hunched in the prow, head bowed against the rain Adam pushed the idea away and tried the sat phone to call Ron. To his surprise he got an immediate answer.

'Didn't think I'd get you,' he said.

'Only a few people have this number, cuts out the crap,' Ron said. 'How did it go?'

'Appalling, the place is nothing but mud and filth, totally insanitary -- vile.'

'That good, eh?'

'I mean it. They'll all die if they stay there. I promised to help.'

'That was rash,' Ron sounded wary.

'I don't care, you've sent me twice, what's the point? The soldiers can't cope, it's hopeless. They must be moved.'

'Easy to say but where? Any ideas? Where are you now?'

'Still out on the water. And it's rising.'

'I know. They're monitoring it closely.'

'What are the weather charts saying?'

'The experts are totally bemused by it. Don't know why it's happening, where it's all coming from. It's one gigantic depression, a continual low and they apparently have no idea how long it might last.'

Adam wouldn't be diverted. 'Even more reason to move them. They could go to Rowan Hill, it's the nearest proper village.'

'Out of the question, the army won't have that. Too big an operation as things are and the village is already overcrowded.'

'I've been there, remember, compared to those poor sods on the hill they're doing okay.'

'They won't stand it, they're already making trouble.'

'They'll have to. At least they have buildings and hard standing, they're not living in liquid mud and sewage. They must take them in.'

'The army won't do it,' Ron said firmly.

'Ask them. And both places are short of food.'

'I told you before, the logistics are frightening. Much of our food still comes over from Europe and elsewhere, a lot of it by sea but the ports are unusable. There should be a consignment from America on the way, US Army rations. They're sending transport planes -- but it's where to land them and then how to get the stuff round the country.'

'There are airfields on higher ground they could use,' Adam said. 'What about Rissington? That was RAF and it's still used by commercial stuff and clubs.'

'That's one place they're looking at but the runway may not be long enough.'

'What about Salisbury Plain or the Berkshire Downs? Surely they can improvise on some open land?'

He heard Ron sigh. 'It's not that simple, those American planes are massive. Then it's got to be unloaded and distributed all over the country. There just aren't enough planes of the right sort.'

'Well, I'm going to tell Gordon Finch to expect more people. And we'll need transport, either choppers, or drop more of these boats and I'll organise it.'

'I wouldn't do that, Adam.'

'Why not?'

'You're exceeding your authority and the army won't take it kindly. Besides, it could all turn very nasty.'

'I could handle that. I've already shot one man, remember. You told me it would be easier next time. And it will be.'

'That's not like you.'

'No but I didn't ask for any of it. They gave me the bloody guns so I'll use them if I have to. I won't stand by and watch people die in that filth when I can do something about it.'

'Okay, okay, leave it with me. I'll get back to you.'

'I'll go direct.'

'No, don't do that.'

Angry and absorbed by bleak visions of the camp, it was bed time before he noticed the small bunches of foxglove leaves dangling above the Aga. He smiled, reminded of hop branches hanging in country pubs in the days when people were allowed to smoke in crowded bars. The precious leaves curled as they dried in the warm air from the hotplates. But this one source of comfort would likely soon be gone.

Cooking for desperate people without it would test their ingenuity. He reached up to touch the leaves, pleased to find them already crisping. Uncertain how to use them he hadn't thought beyond making them into a tea. But he had no idea if this would help Philip's condition -- or even make it worse.

'Thanks for doing that,' he said as Sally wandered in, looking for him.

'Come to bed, you must be exhausted,' she said, slipping an arm round his waist.

Something about her made him pull her close. He kissed her quickly on the mouth and stroked her cheek. 'This could all end badly. You're being so brave.'

'I'm not the only one.'

'No,' he kissed her again, repressing the urge to hug her, cling on and sob his heart out. Startled by his tenderness she kissed him back and said: 'Love you, Adam. It will work out, I know it will.' His silence troubled her. 'What is it?'

'Could you and Eve cook some food to eat cold and dream up a menu with no cooking?'

'The power?'

Nodding, he clasped her hand again, holding it against his face, kissing her palm. Her hands usually so soft and elegant felt rough to his touch. 'I suppose we're lucky that it's stayed on this long.'

'What about the solar?'

'Useless in this cloud. It's hardly pulling anything, we need sunshine, or at least clear light. Sunshine,' he mused, 'if only.'

'Do you know when it's going off?'

'No, but we won't have it much longer.'

'You're joking, it's a nightmare here already, you know that. We can't take any more.'

Alan Croft's voice sounded so desperate it made Adam waver a moment, remembering their visit and the youngster bleeding on the floor. He also recalled the shock to his own body when he fired. He couldn't raise Gordon Finch, a man he felt might show enough humanity to help another group.

'Alan, I know how bad things are but if you saw the state of that hill, you couldn't ignore it.'

'Things are more settled here now, if more arrive it'll be chaos again. Everyone's found a place and it's reasonably orderly. We have to protect ourselves.'

'If we don't move them, they'll die.'

'People are bound to die, it's a disaster. People die in disasters. It's just their bad luck.'

'But you were so keen to help people when this began.'

'Yes but now I'm being realistic. This country's become a very overcrowded island, almost bankrupt and no spare resources. Maybe a lot of them dying will help us all in the long run, like the viruses cleared out a lot of oldies.'

'You don't mean that, Alan.'

'I fucking do. If a boat's sinking, you stop more getting in and you push 'em back in to drown. It's about survival.'

'Christ Alan!'

182

'No, it can't be done.'

Adam changed his tone to grim instruction.

'They are coming and you will find space for them.'

'Or what? You'll shoot some more of us? People here have guns as well, you know, shotguns and a rifle or two.'

'What? Make it a battle? You wouldn't do that.'

'We might.'

'That would bring the army in,' he said, imagining a scenario that could end with a helicopter gunship shooting people indiscriminately.

He had no authority to say that and he would never ask for such help but the threat was powerful.

'But that would kill more people and you're trying to save them.'

'I know. But it won't come to that, will it? Look Alan, talk to Gordon, think it through. Get Gordon to call me on this number. I'm waiting to hear from the army. We'll see what happens.'

There was never enough food. However much they cut the ration, the supplies went down frighteningly fast. Afternoon turned into evening but no call came to prepare for another drop. They had enough bread for one meal but Adam gave instructions to produce a hot meal for supper and save the bread.

'But we've been doing sandwiches for supper -- why change it?' Eve queried.

'We think it best,' John said. 'Don't argue, love. Use the cooker while you can.'

'Oh!' She vanished into the kitchen to challenge Sally. 'You all know something I don't -- he says hot food tonight.'

Sally looked up from the sink. Amy Lock was helping her, tackling piles of dirty crockery from the last meal. While they had hot water they were determined to maintain hygiene and decency. She shook her head and flicked a finger to her mouth to silence Eve but Amy caught the vibes: 'What is it?'

Eve backed her: 'Come on Sal, tell us the worst.'

Sally breathed a deep sigh and handed Amy a towel to dry her hands. 'Sit down a minute.'

They sat, faces anxious and expectant. 'Look Amy, we don't want everyone to know yet, no point until it happens. Things will get worse very soon, we think the power will go any time.'

'No lights,' gasped Amy. 'And we won't be able to cook.'

'They're preparing the camping stoves but we haven't used them for ages and they're not very big. But we should at least manage hot drinks.'

Usually optimistic, Amy seemed stunned at the prospect.

'Everything will go, won't it,' she said slowly as it sank in. 'The net will be down, right -- and all the mobile systems, TV, radio -- we'll be totally cut off.'

'It's not that bad,' Sally tried to sound cheerful. 'Adam's got the sat phone so we'll have contact. It may not be for long -- oh, don't worry, we'll look after you.'

The girl had burst into sobs and Sally hugged her, trying to console and encourage while concealing her own fears, only too aware of the horror lurking at the edge of her mind. Eve watched helplessly, also on the verge of tears.

Sally was saying: 'We will get through this, it will stop raining and the water will go down. You're here with us Amy, and you've got Jock and we're going to manage somehow. We won't let it beat us.'

Eve controlled herself and took Amy's hand.

'Come on, love, cheer up. We're going to need your help with the others when it happens.'

'But when?'

'We don't know. It could be any time.'

'I should have guessed what was going to happen,' Amy said. 'I wondered when I saw you earlier, putting out the new candles in the sitting room.'

'That was just coincidence, they were burnt down anyway,' Sally smiled. 'And I like candlelight.'

'Have you got many?'

'A boxful in the barn, and there's some in here. We'll have to ration them but we'll manage.'

He looked in again on Phil Bryston who was sleeping, his wife beside him, her hand enfolding his. She sat up when he entered and the movement woke the sleeper. Adam held up his hand saying: 'Don't sit up, Phil. How's it going?'

'He's very tired this evening, only one tablet today.'

Adam perched on the bed and Philip, now properly awake, managed a smile.

'This may sound crackers to you but Ron mentioned foxgloves. I don't know anything about them but is it worth trying?'

The old man looked puzzled but Jane latched on at once to the thought of a lifeline. 'Foxgloves, digitalis, the origin of heart drugs -- life savers but also toxic.'

'I looked it up, it's the leaves, dried and powdered. But how would he take it? The only way I can think of is to make a tea. Would you know the safe dosage?'

She shook her head: 'No idea.'

'The boys found some, we're drying the leaves. D'you think it's worth a try?'

Philip looked amused. 'Poor kids, did you send them out in the rain? It sounds worse than ever.'

'They were glad to help. What d'you think?'

'It can only poison me and it might help. My heart won't last long without something.'

The sat-phone buzzed, he saw it was Kirstie Lomax. 'I need to take this, sorry. See you later.'

He hurried away to listen. 'I must be quick as usual. Tell them Zadok is almost ready.'

'What?'

'Just that, is Hayley okay?'

'She's fine. Why didn't you call sooner?'

'You know why. Tell me what's happening your end. They've got the code but I'm in the dark. What d'you know?'

'They want to get Hayley to you -- and something with her -- don't know what. But they want me to do it.'

'Brilliant.'

'Is it? Won't it put her in danger?'

'Maybe, but it could be the answer. The floods make everything so difficult, it was hard before but -- yes, it might work. I need to go, they know I'm calling about Hayley. You bringing her makes sense, they'll believe it because of the ark thing. They don't know if it's genuine.'

'Tell them I sound like a crank. If the power goes how will you contact us?'

'There's a generator here and Hassan has a sat-phone but that would be difficult. If you're coming it must be soon. They'll do it any time.'

'Do what?' he asked.

'That's the issue -- that's what I'm trying to discover.'

'But if the power goes?'

'That would delay them but I'd have to wreck the generator'

He informed Ron that Zadok was imminent. Ron gave him a crisis number, direct to Colonel Harrison.

The colonel said only: 'Right. We'll act on that. Thank, looks like it's time to throw the switch.'

But Adam hung on. 'Has Ron told you about Ruttock Common. They must be moved.'

'Can't be done. Can't spare the men or the time.'

'Colonel, I gave my word. It's not far to move them, a few chopper flights or some boats. They can't stay there.'

'I said it can't be done.'

'And I'm telling you, if you want me to take that child and whatever goes with her, there has to be a return.'

'What d'you mean?'

'If you don't help those people I won't play your games.'

'It's no game.'

'Whatever! It's not that difficult to move them,' he insisted.

'We can't.'

'You must or I won't do it.'

'We'll arrest you.'

'What good would that do?'

The line went dead.

He realised he was trembling and leaned against the wall, wondering what his defiance would bring. A hand gripped his shoulder and John was there.

'You heard that?'

His friend nodded: 'D'you mean it?'

'We can't leave them there, it's inhuman, surely people matter, don't they?'

'They used to, I'm not sure now. The current thinking sounds more like China, it's all about the greater good. Individuals don't count any more.'

'Do you really think that, John?'

'It's not what I believe but it's what's happening. You're really out on a limb on this.'

A text alert made them look at Adam's phone. They read the message together. 'Power shutdown imminent.'

Outside the fading light hid the rain, intensifying the gloom in the house. They stood at the head of the stairs, looking down into the shadowy rooms, darkening despite the lights. Voices and laughter came from one television but most were already settled for another long night.

Mutterings and whispered conversations carried on and somewhere a phone rang unanswered.

'Let's hope it goes off while they're asleep,' said John. 'At least they'll wake to daylight.'

Adam stared into the dusk, hearing the rain, steady and incessant, a persistent patter on the glass.

'I can't believe it can rain like this, day after day,' he said over his shoulder. 'I can't understand where it's coming from.'

'No, but I never did understand the weather. Shall I fetch that box of candles from the barn?'

I've been sitting on the stairs wondering what to do. How can I keep these people going, how can I save them? I feel cold and clammy, sheer nerves. I know too well how my body reacts to pressure. I probably shouldn't have defied the army. I must be mad, I can't be responsible for everybody.

Maybe I should just forget the poor sods at the camp. But I can't. And what about Hayley? Am I really going to fly away with her and take her calmly into danger? It's unreal. And if the fucking rain carries on into winter I can't see any chance of survival. A huge death toll will be inevitable.

This foxglove idea is such a long shot, it probably won't save poor Philip but I must check it out again before the power goes.

The site he'd used before didn't have the answers. Cursing the slowness of his old system, he clicked from site to site looking for dosage details. Halfway through a section on what to do with the dried leaves the screen went blank and the room was suddenly dark.

Someone, somewhere had flicked a switch. As he groped his way out, words exploded in fury. 'Oh fuck it all, God help us now.'

John got it right. Adam came down to find him in the entrance to the main room saying in a voice entirely normal and unstrained: 'Oh damn, looks like we've lost the power for a while, folks. But it's time for bed so let's turn in a bit sooner. The candles are ready.'

With Eve he went quietly round the room putting a match to candles already in place and Sally found Amy and led her to the kitchen. 'Remember, Amy, say nothing. It may be back on by the morning.'

The girl looked hard at her: 'You don't really think that.'

'No but it's best to let them think it. In the morning, in daylight, it won't seem as bad.' Amy was on the point of tears again. 'I'm frightened,' she whispered, turning to Sally for comfort.

'We're all afraid, Amy.'

The peal of church bells woke Adam and he listened to catch the chimes again. But it was a dream, a brain clip from a different time. He couldn't be hearing them because no one could get into the tower, let alone climb up to ring them. The dream stayed in his head, dredging soft memories of warm evenings when the sound would drift up from the valley as the ringers practised. Reluctant to wake to harsh day he dozed, clinging to dreamy warmth, secure from reality.

Sally still slept and he moved close to her, comforted by her warmth, snuggling to the softness. He wanted to stay in bed undisturbed, cover himself and hide from it all. He checked the time and the black face of the digital clock jolted him back to reality -- life without power.

Any time now they would be demanding to know what he would do about it. And the answer was nothing. The challenge was to keep going and survive it.

Then there was the army's wrath in the shape of Colonel Harrison. With a sigh he left his bed and found John waiting.

'You're about early.'

'I thought one of us had better be. And you looked so knackered last night, I thought I'd let you sleep.'

'That was kind.'

'What's the plan?'

He shook his head. 'There isn't one. Cold food, keep the camping gear for hot drinks and those limited to twice a day or emergencies, ration the water. And pray it stops raining.'

'They'll make a fuss.'

'You can warn the Smiths that making trouble will get them locked up. And I mean that. Best if you tell them.'

'Right. Let's go down and face it.'

'John --' He caught his arm. 'While we're alone -- if I have to go away, on this thing for the army -- can you cope?'

'Do my best, will it come to that?'

'Don't know. But I won't go unless they move the Ruttock people.'

Chapter seventeen

He stood dejectedly on the gravel path staring at the garden, Polly sat beside him in the rain. He'd slipped away from the tensions of breakfast, sick of the complaints and arguments which common sense never solved. At least he was alone and breathing fresh air. The pale pebbles under his feet and the lawn were trampled into mud by uncaring feet. The walls behind the flower beds were thick with moss. This desolation depressed him more than the state of the house.

Polly looked up into his face, perplexed by his lack of action. Faced with so many worries he was trying to prioritise the problems. The colonel's demands, the imminent crisis about water and the lack of food and power tormented him. But above all it was the dread that soon he would be dealing with death. He couldn't get away from the image of Philip Bryston struggling to breathe. He had little faith in the foxgloves, at best a very long shot.

The only bright point was Martin appearing for breakfast. He'd seen the young man come painfully down the stairs on his crutch, one step at a time and hobble to where his friends were eating. That was some small gratification. Eve's skill had saved his leg. It would always be crooked but with the infection gone the bone was setting and his appetite had begun to nudge at him.

Polly was suddenly alert and ran to the wall where she began sniffing at something, unwilling to touch it. It was a small brown toad which had emerged from a crack in the wall and sat bewildered in the daylight. Water ran from the crack and the creature must've been washed out. He picked it up to crouch in his hand, its unblinking black eyes inscrutable. Smiling he touched it lightly on its cold, smooth back, as Polly watched in fascination.

'This is one feller who'll be enjoying the weather,' he told her. 'At least someone's happy.'

He stooped to put it down and watching it hop unhurriedly away his eye caught movement in the summer house. He walked over to see John, assuming he was there tidying up. There was just enough room for two whicker chairs and their blow-up beds.

He paused on the steps, surprised to see Tom in there with John. They hadn't seen him approach and leaned close together apparently in deep conversation. About to enter he paused to listen, unable to help himself.

Tom was speaking, saying things he should have said to his father.

'I don't think I'll ever sing in the church again, they won't want me.'

'Why not?'

'You must have noticed my voice, it's so embarrassing.'

'I didn't realise you were that keen on the choir.'

'It was great once I got into it .'

John seemed surprised. 'But you're not into religion, are you?'

'No but when I knew I could sing I enjoyed it.'

'I wouldn't worry, it'll be a long time before anyone sings in there. By then you might have a wonderful man's voice, baritone perhaps.'

But Tom wasn't easily satisfied. 'Sometimes a kid has a good voice but then it breaks and they can't sing at all.'

'That can happen but -- '

'There's other things,' Tom persisted. 'I get these feelings, I've changed, you know, down there.'

'You're growing up, it's normal.'

'I know all about it but they never tell you how it makes you feel in yourself.'

'We all go through that,' John's hand squeezed the boy's thigh. 'It's nothing to worry about.'

Adam frowned. He'd seen them together in a huddle a few times but this didn't feel right. For the first time it bothered him. And it was painful to see his son confiding in another man. Unwilling to hear more he opened the door.

'What was that all about?' he asked, searching their startled expressions.

John grinned at him. 'He's worried about his voice breaking and his balls have dropped.'

Adam ignored him and said to Tom: 'You're the age for it and your voice has been changing for a while. Why didn't you come to me?'

The boy was flustered. 'I dunno.'

He gripped Tom's shoulder. 'Am I so hard to talk to?

'No dad but you're always so busy.'

He left them and hurried away, Polly trailing him in confusion. Sally saw him come in and followed upstairs. He slammed the door almost in her face and she hesitated but took a deep breath and went in.

'What's wrong now?' He swung round from his pensive rain gazing and stared at her as if making up his mind what to say. When he spoke it wasn't in anger, rather a mixture of shock and disappointment.

He said slowly: 'We don't really know much about John, do we?'

'What do you mean? What's upset you?'

'I know he and Tom get on well together and I was pleased. But something doesn't feel right. I've just found them in the summer house, Tom pouring his heart out.'

Her face clouded with concern. 'He's at a difficult age, he started saying something to me the other day, about puberty, you know. But we were interrupted and when I asked him later he just brushed it off.'

'He should have come to me, he's my son.'

'Are you jealous?' she asked.

He dropped on to the bed and looked at her a moment, then in

192

a low voice said: 'Maybe I am. But it's more than that, they were so engrossed, it was the way John touched him, I didn't like that.'

'What are you saying?'

'I didn't like it, that's all. As I said we've taken John totally on trust.'

'He and Eve have always seemed straightforward,' she said slowly. 'I don't understand what you're saying.'

He sighed. 'Perhaps I'm making too much of it but there's been a few times something's niggled me. He never talks about teaching, always changes the subject, you must have noticed.'

'I have but I assumed it's because he packed it in, maybe he regrets it.'

'Perhaps, I hope you're right.'

'You won't say anything to him,' she asked anxiously.

'No, I need his help. If I go on this wild goose chase for the army I need him here.'

Kylie's wheezing cough disturbed the guests. The little girl coughed most of the time but he knew it was getting worse and watched her bend nearly double with each spasm. The child was in pain and he couldn't help her. Now they had two patients in desperate need of medication.

But he was amazed and pleased with the guests, who'd taken the power loss better than expected. They knew there was nothing he could do, coming to terms with the reality of their predicament. They also knew about Ruttock Common and discussed at length the plight of the people stranded there. They began to appreciate what they had at Down Farm.

They'd stuck with the line that it was a temporary blip because, as Eve said, a little hope can go a long way. Better to boost morale than say baldly: 'That's it folks, we're in the dark for the duration.'

The bigger worry was water. The 200 feet deep borehole had never let them down but it needed one vital ingredient to pump it up to the reservoir -- electricity. Drinking water was already rationed but he cut it right back, knowing the reservoir held enough for two days and there was just sufficient power from the solar batteries to pump for one day more.

They were using the rainwater but the difficulty was catching it in clean enough receptacles to be usable for drinking and washing up. Personal washing was more simple -- most of them had given up except for a cursory splashing.

But Jock and Amy found a better way. They'd stripped off one morning in the porch and stood outside in torrential rain with a bar of soap between them. The cold rain bounced off their skin as they scrubbed each other's backs and their laughter brought an audience to the window. They didn't care who watched.

Their pale young bodies frisking in the downpour inspired emulation and soon a dozen more were on show, including the Walsall four, who'd fitted into the system with no further trouble. There was little else to make anyone laugh and the washing antics shortened the long morning.

Tom and Ben joined the bathing party, though Tom kept his pants on. Sally looked on with John and Eve. With misgivings she found herself watching John, wondering if he in turn was watching her son, glad Adam wasn't there.

'You could call it group therapy,' John laughed. 'It must be bloody cold.'

'They're really enjoying it, something positive from the rain for once,' said Sally.

'Are we going to join them?' Eve asked.

'Probably not the right thing for us to do,' Sally said. She was saved from further persuasion by the phone ringing indoors.

Adam was talking to someone and she quickly guessed who.

She heard him say: ' -- as you might imagine it's been a bit busy since the power went, a matter of priorities.'

'Cut the sarcasm, Woolton,' the colonel was angry. 'We have to move on this, we need to get you away with the child. I'm sending a chopper. You'll be briefed en route.'

194

'No.'

'What's that?'

'I said No, negative. I'm not going.'

'We've been through this, you're the only one can do it, the only way that won't arouse suspicion.'

'Colonel, I've told you how it stands. I want those poor people on the hill moved before they die of disease or exposure. I won't help unless it's done.'

'I could have you shot.'

'I know.'

He shut off the call and sank to a chair. 'Oh Adam,' Sally whispered. His hand trembled as he said: 'He really could have me shot.'

'You can't defy them much longer -- can you?'

'Don't know.'

The phone rang again and he listened to Colonel Harrison shouting in a blend of anger and frustration which gave a ray of comfort. 'I'm not joking! I can and will have you shot under the emergency powers.'

'I believe you but I won't do it. Not unless you move them.'

'Why are you so stubborn, it's just a few hundred people. Do they really matter that much when millions are dying all over the world? You have to look at the big picture. Individuals can't be allowed to matter, we have to go for the greater good.'

That phrase again.

'If you believe that what am I doing here, stuck with all these people? These individuals, should I have turned them all away?'

'No but we have to prevent this attack.'

'Colonel, if you'd seen the shit they're living in, you couldn't leave them there.'

'Damn you, man!'

'And you, Colonel.'

Again the line went dead.

They waited but he didn't call again. 'Damn him,' he said. 'I'm going to do something useful.'

Sally had managed to sterilise the old pestle and mortar, an ornament from the kitchen shelf, to grind the foxglove leaves into a rough powder.

'Are we really going to try this?' she asked. The dried-up greenery looked unappetising with a strange aroma. He was worried the leaves were past their best but said: 'It's up to Philip, he must decide if it's worth the risk. Don't know what else we can do.'

'I wish we could come up with something for little Kylie, she needs an inhaler,' she said. 'At least this might help Philip, I'll make it into a tea.'

On the camping stove she boiled a small pan of water and asked: 'How much do I put in?'

From his research he knew it was easy to exceed the safe dose. He'd read 0.3mg daily. 'Not sure,' he said. 'Weigh a tea-spoonful to start with. I'll take it up, then it's only me to blame.'

Philip eyed the steaming mug. 'Well, it's a hot drink if nothing else. I can't get warm, it's so gloomy and the constant sound of rain is depressing. Kill or cure, it'll warm me up.'

Jane smiled and took the mug, holding it steady while he drank. 'Not too bad,' he said and lay back on the pillow. She stroked his forehead, saying: 'He feels very clammy today.'

Philip's legs moved under the quilt as he tried to ease the sores on his skin from lying too long in bed. Adam's optimism faded, knowing this medieval potion had little chance of success.

He looked back at them from the door to meet Jane's eyes and see the same pessimism. 'It's worth a try,' she murmured.

He lingered, reluctant to leave them and heard the phone again.

'Leave it! Let it ring,' he shouted at John, who'd picked it up.

'Hadn't you better speak to him?'

'Not till I'm ready. I need to show you something. Get your coat.'

John followed him through the fields above the house, over the wall onto the moorland beyond.

They'd hardly spoken since the summer house incident, Adam had deliberately kept out of his way and John was uncomfortable. He was puzzled and slightly apprehensive as he followed uphill till Adam stopped and knelt under a grassy bank.

The sound of trickling water was clear above the rain and he began to understand, as Adam cleared moss and long tufts of matted turf to reveal brickwork.

'Is it a well?' asked John.

'Not exactly,' he pulled aside more grass to clear away the muddy earth covering a three-inch pipe and a trough. 'It's the original supply for the farm, what they used before the borehole was sunk.'

'Spring water?'

'Mmm, it comes from further up the hill.'

'Is it pure?'

'It used to be good water, I've drunk it many times.'

'Won't it be polluted by the rain?'

'Maybe, that's a chance you'll have to take.'

'Me?'

'I might not be here. This should be safer than the rain water, it's filtered through the peat.'

'You want me to pipe it down?' He glanced at Adam who nodded.

'There's three rolls of pipe behind the barn and you'll find fittings and some kind of tap. Organise a team and get it set up before the reservoir runs out.'

They came in to the noise of the phone. 'It'll be him again,' said Sally. 'He's tried three times since you left, I told him you'd call back.'

He nodded as she picked it up: 'Yes Colonel, he's here, just coming.'

'What is it now, Colonel Harrison?' Adam spoke irritably, determined not to show any sign of giving in.

197

'Where've you been? I've been trying for ages. You're an awkward bastard but I must give you marks for courage. I've been to the top and back on this issue. You win. I'm authorised to get those people moved.'

Adam breathed a big sigh: 'Thank you, Colonel. So when and how?'

'Immediate, things are moving fast. We're sending helicopters and more rubber boats. Your man Kerr will have to deal with it, we need you on your way. He'll have to supervise the move from the common. The sick can go by air, the rest by boat. Satisfied?'

'Not till I know they're away.'

'What do you mean? You have my word.'

'I'm afraid that's not good enough.'

'What?'

'What's to stop you whisking us away and doing nothing.'

'We wouldn't do that.'

'Well, I won't risk it.'

'I'll get back to you.'

'By the way,' he had a sudden thought. 'Have your security people cleared John Kerr yet?'

'No report yet, it's difficult as things are. Why d'you ask?'

'Just wondered.'

He didn't trust the army to keep the promise and he was uneasy leaving John in charge. His attitude to his friend had changed, the trusting warmth had gone and in its place a gnawing suspicion.

He hadn't told Hayley that he'd spoken to her mother but he needed to prepare her for the journey.

Sally had heard the conversation and when he asked: 'Where's Hayley?' she turned on him angrily.

'You can't be serious about taking her on some army mission.'

'It's not down to me.'

'You haven't said anything to her?'

'I can't. Where is she?'

'Out in the barn with the others.'

198

The others were her sons and the five survival girls who chilled out together and enjoyed themselves despite everything. He heard Ben telling a joke and Hayley's happy giggle at the punchline. Ben had a special voice for jokes, which made them seem funnier than they actually were.

He heard Tom say: 'Don't let Dad hear you telling that one.' Perched on straw bales the kids looked relaxed and cheerful and moved closer to make room for him. Tom, knowing his father's methods said at once: 'What now, dad? You've got that look on your face.'

'Hayley and me might be going on a trip.'

The planned start was aborted and he was left waiting for news which came eventually from an unexpected source.

'Adam, it's Tim Rogers.' He hadn't known the young captain's first name but it had the impact intended. 'You must trust me and leave the camp business to John. I promise you they will be moved.'

'But how do I know that?'

'We'll take him with us and drop him on the hill. The other choppers and boats should be there and you can see it getting underway. Surely that's enough?'

'Maybe, I'll talk to him.'

Upstairs Philip was fading and he wanted to be with the old man. The room was gloomy in the early evening, its dimness eased by candles either side of the bed, casting deep shadows. The candles disturbed him, as if death already hovered over the scene.

At the beginning, Philip had been full of life, eager to back him through the problems but the last few days had worn him down. The lids over his closed eyes looked dry and withered, the bones of his skull too obvious. He was much weaker since the tablets ran out, struggling for breath as fluid accumulated round his heart. He didn't complain but they knew the chest pains were getting worse, the spasms of anguish so evident when he winced and shifted in the bed to ease himself.

He said the foxglove tea made him feel better but Adam doubted it, putting more faith in the tots of alcohol he'd brought each evening. His store of whisky was almost gone and on this night what he brought was the old Glenfiddich.

He touched Philip's bony hand. 'Here, this might help.'

The tired eyes opened and he tried to speak but Adam could barely catch the words. 'Thanks, you're a star. I can't see properly today, everything's a bit yellow but this will help.' He reached for his hand.

'There's nothing you can do, my ticker's had it. It won't be long now, I feel so weak.'

'Try to rest, we might get more supplies.'

Philip smiled: 'All I do is rest. It's too late for me now.'

He supported the old man as he struggled to sit and sip from the tumbler, watching the trembling hand try to grasp it.

'I'll join you,' forcing a smile he poured a tiny measure for himself, clinking the glass against the other. 'Cheers, to better times.'

'Ah,' Philip savoured the spirit in his mouth before he swallowed and leaned back. 'That's a good medicine. I'm grateful for all you've done and I've grown fond of you. I could've chosen many worse places to die,' he whispered. 'I feel among friends here.'

'I'm so sorry we couldn't get your tablets.'

Philip smiled again: 'Put it in perspective, I'm one old man who's had his time. The biggest toll was among the old last time, remember? But this is much worse, so many dead already and millions struggling to survive. It's about priorities.'

'You're very calm about it.'

'What else to do?' he whispered. 'I'm far too weak to rage against the dying of the light.'

The allusion was too much for Adam who fought against the tears he felt welling inside him, raising an arm to hide his face from the old man's eyes.

'Oh Philip, I wish I'd known you before all this. Why did we meet when it's too late to be friends?'

'We are friends and I'm glad of it. And I know you'll help Jane when I'm gone.'

'Of course we will. It's hard on her -- she doesn't find the prospect as easy as you seem to.'

He woke with a jolt as Sally shook him and groped half-asleep for the light switch before remembering and found his torch under the pillow.

Jane was in the room, Sally's arms wrapped round her as she wept quietly.

'Philip?'

Sally nodded and whispered: 'She thinks he's going.'

They stepped silently across the landing, over bodies huddled in their way under blankets, quilts and old coats. Philip was alone in the bedroom now, because nobody wanted to share with a dying man. Fresh candles lit the room but Philip's eyes were closed, his breath uneven in gurgling gasps. Adam feared it was the death rattle.

'Philip?' his whisper was unanswered. 'I think he's unconscious.'

He stood by the bed to take one thin hand in his. Jane was huddled close to her husband, holding the other hand against her cheek. He laid his head on Philip's chest, listening to faint beats which became more intermittent, the rattling breaths more difficult, longer between each one. When it stopped he said nothing. The struggling heart was still. He raised his eyes to Jane and shook his head. 'I'm so sorry.'

At a loss what to do Sally said: 'Will you come into our room? I'll make you a drink?'

Jane held fast to the dead hand: 'No, I'm fine. I'll stay here with him for now.'

They waited unhappy, unsure what to do till Sally said: 'We'll leave you then.'

When the door closed and she was alone with him Jane stood and looked long at her husband. She leaned down to kiss his eyelids, then his lips. 'Goodbye my darling,' she whispered. Then she sat again, still holding his hand. She stayed beside him until dawn lessened the gloom, when she blew out the candles and pulled up the quilt to cover his face.

In their room Sally lay beside Adam, holding his trembling body as he sobbed into the pillow, desperate not to disturb the children but unable to control himself. Sad and tearful herself the effect on him appalled her, realising the old man's death had unleashed all the fears and pain he'd been bottling up.

'Why?' He sobbed. 'What have we done to deserve all this?'

She couldn't answer him.

'I've seen death in battle but not this. All it needed was a few pills. He didn't need to die.'

In the morning the body had to be moved. Jane was persuaded away from the room but the death couldn't be concealed. John and Jock struggled to get the dead weight into the thick plastic bag and down the stairs.

A subdued and silent crowd waited and watched as they brought him down. Everyone stepped back with heads bowed to clear the way as he was carried out. Jane walked behind with clasped hands. Several people followed the grim cortege like mourners, across the muddy yard to the barn where they'd cleared a discreet place to lay him.

Adam glanced at Jane, shame-faced: 'I'm sorry, he'll have to stay here for now until --'

'I know,' she interrupted. 'It's all right, Adam. There's nothing else you can do.' She stared at the long grey bundle. 'This is why they sent the bags.'

Chapter eighteen

He lifted Hayley into the arms of Tim Rogers who met her with a broad grin: 'Hi Hayley, I'm Tim and this is my whirly-bird,' he joked as he carried her to a seat behind the pilot. On the ground John waited quietly for his turn to board, watching Adam jump in, uncomfortably aware of a new unease between them.

Earlier Adam told her: 'We're going to find your mum. Would you like that?'

'Is she a long way away?'

'Quite a way,' he answered.

'Are we going in the sky?'

'In a helicopter, is that okay?'

She'd looked at him with solemn eyes and said: 'I expect it'll be dangerous.'

He couldn't lie to her. 'Maybe, these are dangerous times, but' he added 'look what you've survived already.'

She nodded. 'Is mummy in danger?'

'Well,' he hesitated -- 'kind of. But we plan to fetch her home.'

She'd looked hard at him and asked: 'Why can't I wait for her here, if she's coming back?'

'Good question,' he thought, struggling to reply. 'You see, we think, that is, the soldiers think, you can help us.'

'How?'

'It's to do with her work -- you know -- the translation stuff. She's been helping the army.'

'Will it be an army helicopter?'

'Yes, they'll take us. It'll be fun,' he tried to emphasise the up-side of the plan. 'We'll look down at the floods and see where people are staying to escape the water.'

But she wasn't impressed by that.

'Poor people, they're not as lucky as us.' After a moment she said: 'I don't mind going -- but I'd rather stay here.'

'All set?' Captain Rogers leaned over, gripping her shoulder in a little hug. 'Can you see okay? Can the bunny see all right?'

'Don't be silly,' she was sharp. 'I'm not a baby.' But she took a firmer hold of the rabbit on her lap.

'Course you're not,' he looked contrite. 'But are you comfy and ready to go?'

Adam saw the strain on her face and watched her hands clench hard on the armrests as the craft whirled into the air. She looked back and waved to Tom and Ben standing at the field edge in the rain.

They'd told her they wished they were going. As the chopper headed into the weather and swept over the hillside she realised for the first time the vast scope of the flood.

'It's like the sea, or those big lakes in America.' But they were soon back over land, to a muddy scene where dirty, torn tents flapped in the wind and a line of people waited to clamber into rubber boats bobbing in the water.

They circled the hill, seeking somewhere to land and came down near a Chinook, also waiting for a group straggling towards it. They touched down and John approached the door.

'Good luck,' Adam said.

John turned with a sad smile. 'I think you'll need it more than me. I'll do my best here.' Their eyes met and John said: 'You know that Adam, you can trust me for that.'

'I hope so.'

Adam watched him hurry away with mixed emotions.

'Satisfied?' The captain asked but the chopper was already rising.

'I suppose so.'

'They're getting into the boats, what more do you want?'

I suppose it's enough.'

'Is this the bad place?' Hayley asked.

'Yes, he said, craning his head to look back at the crowd of people moving on the ground.

The captain said quietly: 'They really are moving, they won't take the boats away without them. You were right to push it. I don't think the boss had any idea how bad things were, it's appalling.'

'He either didn't believe me or thought it didn't matter. I couldn't leave them, they'd have died there.'

'You did well.'

'He's good at saving people.' She sounded so sure he had to look away. But he turned it into a joke. 'Thanks for the vote of confidence, hope I can earn it.'

'You will,' she said. 'That's why they're sending you -- isn't it captain?'

'Of course.'

'Where we going?' Adam asked. 'Can you tell us now?'

'North,' he said. That was all.

They watched the changing landscape unfold below, fascinated by the new map carved from the waters. Up through the Cheshire Plain the expanded Mersey had turned into a lake, the Lune and the Ribble estuaries had obliterated most of western Lancashire, Morecambe Bay stretched all the way to Kendal, and the new coastline followed the edge of the Pennines, where they met the Cumbrian mountains.

Far to the west, the unmistakeable tower at Blackpool stood in the sea, lapped by waves covering its lower levels and most of the town.

Minutes later he saw the ancient abbey at Cartmel, now on an island surrounded by the extended waters of Windermere.

The rain eased and Hayley shouted in excitement: 'Look, over there, the mountains.'

The range of peaks to the west crouched like giants as they had done for millennia. But they seemed to be somehow smaller, because the lakes were deeper, swollen by the incessant rain brimming the countless streams that fed them.

'Thought Hayley would like to see them, it's quite a sight,' said the pilot. 'Might as well make the most of it.' Then he said: 'Look at Carlisle.'

The historic city was under water, swallowed by the Solway Firth, inundating the lowlands across the border into Scotland. The tops of taller buildings and the outline of the castle were visible but the city as such had disappeared.

'Where've the people gone?' Adam asked. 'I didn't realise it was so bad up here.'

'Inland, to higher ground or further north. The city spent millions on flood defences but nothing could hold out against this lot. Yet further north, they've had less rain than normal. It's strange.'

With Carlisle behind they turned inland and he showed Hayley the line of Hadrian's Wall clinging to the rugged ridges north of Hexham.

'Imagine what it was like when they built it,' she said. 'Mum's told me about it. She said we'd go when I'm old enough to walk some of it.'

'Do you go out much with your mum?'

'Sometimes but it's often granny who takes me.' She hesitated. 'I wish I knew where granny was, I expect she drowned.'

He held her hand. 'She may be safe somewhere, we'll find her when all this is over.'

But she wouldn't be comforted. 'No, you'd have heard something. I expect she's dead.'

In silence they watched the immense landscape of Northumberland pass beneath. The rain stopped and the clouds opened to allow a brief spell of sunshine. Hayley squealed with pleasure when she spotted the shadow of the helicopter racing over the ground.

She couldn't watch for long before the clouds rolled back and a fine rain returned.

They were heading north east, the land rising along the chain of the upper Pennines and ahead the range of the Cheviots, choppy on the horizon. He told Hayley they'd soon be in Scotland

The captain had been sitting quietly but suddenly he passed a phone over to Adam saying: 'It's time to contact Mrs Lomax and let her know we're close.'

A male voice answered his call.

He kept his voice casual and friendly. 'Sorry, I thought this was Kirstie's number.'

'We share it. Who are you?'

"Is Kirstie there?'

'Who is it?' The voice sounded English but with an odd accent.

'It's Adam Woolton, I'm bringing her daughter.'

Silence. Then another voice came on. 'Are you the ark man?'

'I suppose I am,' he said it casually. 'Can I speak to Kirstie.'

The voice said slowly: 'That will be all right. I'll find her.'

Down the line he heard footsteps echoing, on stone flags perhaps, then a door opening and the same voice.

'There's a man calling about your daughter.' After a pause more words he couldn't catch.

Then Kirstie's voice, tinged with excitement: 'Is that you Adam? 'Where are you?'

'We're just flying over the Cheviots.'

'What are you doing there?' Her feigned surprise was effective, meant for other ears. 'Where're you going?'

'A naval base on the west coast. I'm meeting their top engineer about the ark scheme. Thought we'd find you and bring Hayley. She'll be safer up here.'

The irony of the lie was frightening.

'Brilliant, I didn't expect that.'

She was the anxious mother thrilled to see her child. 'Anton, guess what?' He must be close by. 'They've brought my little girl. We can find room can't we?'

He heard reluctant agreement and something else.

'He says you must be important.'

'Tell him I could be. How's it going? Are they nearly finished with you?'

'Pretty good. Mr Hassan has almost finished his submission and I'm translating as it goes along. I think we're getting there.'

He heard more footsteps, this time going away.

She spoke quickly in a whisper: 'He's gone. Tell them Zadok is imminent. They must do something.'

'That's why Hayley's here but I don't know any more. Is it safe to speak?'

'Yes.'

"She shouldn't be involved in this.'

'It's the only way. They know about the ark, it'll seem natural. We'll say you'll collect us on the way back.'

'Where exactly are you?'

'In the hills above Ettrick, a farm they've leased, middle of nowhere.'

She gave him the co-ordinates then a door opened and he heard the footsteps returning. The voice said: 'Say we'll meet them in the village.'

A burly pick-up was already there as the helicopter circled to land on the grass of a school playing field. He jumped out and lifted Hayley down. She saw the woman running towards them and called in excitement: 'Mummy, it's me.'

He turned to meet her.

Face to face at last with Kirstie Lomax he saw at once what the colonel had meant. Windswept and out of breath she was still stunning. Raven hair, luscious eyes and an indefinable exotic quality that made him reluctant to take his eyes off her. Captain Rogers stared with the same expression.

He understood how her looks would convince these people, whoever they were. A man sat in the truck, dark-haired and swarthy, watching the greeting.

Kirstie low to the ground, hugging Hayley close, eyes bright as she turned to Adam: 'Thank you, for looking after her so well and bringing her. I've missed her terribly. I never thought that morning it would be so long before I saw her again. This dreadful rain has made life so complicated.'

'And how! You've no idea, it's dry up here.'

'I'm so grateful,' she said.

'It's good to meet you but we have to go. I don't understand any of this but I know it's bad news. I pray you can get out when the thing kicks off, whatever it is?'

'I hope so. But they think I'm part of it, remember, one of them. But even Mr Hassan isn't involved in the real plan. He's part of their cover, they're supposed to be helping with his deal.'

The swarthy man left the car and came over, pushing back his sleeve to check the time.

'I must go,' she said, seizing Hayley's hand.

Captain Rogers hurried forward to hand the child's bag to Kirstie and put the floppy rabbit into Hayley's arms. 'Don't forget this feller, look after him.'

Hayley smiled at him, nodding. She cuddled the toy under her chin and moved close to her mother.

The helicopter veered north west and he closed his eyes trying to sleep. But he couldn't shake off the image of the little girl walking away, nor the impact of her mother. He couldn't forget her eyes, the way they looked at him. Tantalising eyes that could pierce a man's soul. Their brief meeting left him wanting to see her again.

'You okay, Adam?' Tim Rogers interrupted the reverie and got a grunt in reply.

'What's the matter?' He patted Adam on the shoulder, meaning reassurance but his hand was swiped away with a growl. 'Leave me alone.'

'What's up?' persisted the captain.

'This is all wrong, they shouldn't be in such danger.'

'She knows what she's doing.'

'But the kid doesn't, she trusts me. I've betrayed her.'

'There was no other way, Adam. It was the perfect answer.'

'I don't believe that.'

The captain took a seat beside him. 'Look, the stakes in this are enormous and -- you'll hate me saying this -- two lives at risk to save thousands is a no brainer.'

'That doesn't make it right,' Adam whispered.

'It's because you know them, it wouldn't matter if you didn't.'

'But I do know them!' The landscape of jagged peaks and lakes beneath couldn't salve his fears.

The pilot's voice cut in saying: 'Here we go.' They looked ahead as the helicopter swooped down over mountains towards a long sea loch with installations around the bay and two grey naval vessels moored some way out.

It seemed familiar and he recalled a visit to this coast years before, trying to spot sea eagles which had been reintroduced despite the opposition of disgruntled farmers who said the birds took too many lambs. From the helipad on top of a low concrete building Adam was hurried inside, reminding him of previous visits to armed authority, only this time the combat wear was dark blue. He followed Captain Rogers and a woman officer a long way down a metal stairway and through a heavy reinforced door. Everything was metal and concrete inside a massive bunker.

'Have I got to stay down here?' he asked.

They nodded.

He said: 'I hate places like this, I need fresh air.' He baulked at the thought of a prolonged stay underground.

The woman said: 'Stay calm, you'll be okay.'

'But can't I be put up somewhere above ground?'

'No, this is where it's all happening. We need you here.'

'I don't think I can stand it, I get claustrophobia.'

'It's not so bad away from the corridors. Come in here,' they took him through another door into a big room with comfortable furniture and a large television on one wall.

'This is the mess, make yourself at home. You're an honorary officer for the duration.'

Air-conditioning made the room less oppressive and clever lighting created the effect of daylight. He relaxed a little. The captain said: 'It shouldn't be for long. Rachel -- Lieutenant Watson -- will show you round. Stay cool, Adam, it'll work out.'

'Are you going?'

'Got to -- but I'll be with you when it matters. Stay cool.'

'I'm used to fresh air,' Adam turned to the girl. 'I spend most of my time outside.'

'Sorry, just try to relax but if you start feeling bad the doctor will give you something to help.'

'I don't want to be a zombie.'

'No, we need you alert. Come on, I'll show you what's what.'

'Isn't all this classified? Secret?'

'Of course. But you're part of it and you've got clearance. As the man said, stay cool.'

He wished they'd stop saying that but he looked at his hands and laughed at himself. His clenched knuckles were white and he made a conscious effort to loosen them, stretching each finger in turn, taking deep breaths in and out.

'What're you doing?' she asked.

'Trying to relax!'

'Come on.'

'I'm hungry.' His stomach reminded him he hadn't eaten since they left home hours before.

'That's a good sign. Don't worry, the rations are good here. You'll enjoy supper.'

She took him into another corridor, opening the door to a small bedroom. 'You're in here,' she said, 'number eleven.' He shuddered, a small tweak of panic back in his gut at the thought of being shut in here.

'They're not so bad,' she said. 'Well designed, you'll be surprised how comfortable they are, en suite of course.'

Through another door: 'This is where we eat.' It looked civilised despite the steel table and he noted the crockery was china, not plastic. The sight of bottles and real glasses was reassuring.

'This is the important bit,' she said, opening half a double door and standing back to let him pass onto a low balcony surrounding an operations room.

It looked almost familiar, as if he'd seen it all before, oddly reminiscent of World War Two scenes where young women moved markers representing ships or aircraft around a huge table.

But there was no table here and the only chart a huge map of Britain -- just a dozen or more men and women with screens and a tiny earpiece, listening. They were all listening, tuned in to information from everywhere but especially from a small village in the borders.

'This is where the rabbit talks or we hope he will,' Rachel whispered.

'What?'

'The child's toy, Benji, haven't they told you?'

'Nobody's told me anything except to bring her.'

'Benji has a secret, a piece of very sophisticated technology -- top secret and this is it's first outing.'

'What is it?'

'It's smaller than a blackbird's egg, inside the rabbit's head. Don't ask me how it works -- I'm not a techie, I just take orders. It listens, it gathers all sound in a two hundred metre radius.'

Adam interrupted him: 'But how does that help, you'd just get a garbled mass of noise.'

'That's the clever bit. It has the capacity to filter sound, so that everyday noises are separated into different sections. It picks out the human voices and divides and amplifies them so they can be heard and analysed.'

Puzzled Adam asked: 'But how did it get there? When? She had that toy when I found her, it can't have been in it then.'

Rachel grinned. 'I think your friend Guy planted it.'

'Guy Cotterill, he's no friend of mine. Of course! In the bedroom, he went for a pee, or so I thought. The sneaky bastard, so it was all a ploy.'

'I assumed you knew.'

He shook his head. 'Does Kirstie know?'

'Probably, depends how much chance they've had to speak.'

'Have they heard anything worthwhile?'

'Not yet or there'd be an alert.'

'So, what now?'

'We wait and we eat. They'll change shift in half an hour and you can meet some of them. The screens are never left unmonitored.'

He thought about it all. 'They might suspect, surely, if she's always got it with her?'

'Once in the house she can leave it anywhere, carry it or tuck it up in bed. It'll do its work. Two hundred metre radius, remember, that's a big area.'

'It's hard to believe.'

She laughed. 'Yes, it's pretty impressive tech, leaves me way behind.'

But Adam scowled: 'Bombs and gadgets, but they didn't see this lot coming. Nobody warned us about the bloody rain.'

For a man used to starvation rations dinner was sumptuous. A thick steak of beef fillet topped with herbed mushroom sauce and a choice of fresh vegetables, something he hadn't tasted for weeks. He wondered as he ate that the navy was so well supplied. But to his surprise it seemed that here in Wester Ross there was little sign of the national crisis. There would be plenty of local farms and gardens still selling the usual summer veg.

He managed a very small portion of the cheesecake that came next, along with apple pie and ice cream. But his tightened stomach couldn't take it and he turned down the cheese regretfully, despite seeing his favourites on the crowded board.

His companions were a group of friendly young officers, male and female and most drank freely from a range of malt whiskies that made his taste busts hum. But before and after the meal he was alone, shut in the small bedroom. It had everything he needed, with great attention to detail, but was totally utilitarian, without the smallest touch of character. The base was unaffected by the general power outage, with massive generators running the state-of-the-art surveillance kit they operated, so he had a choice of digital entertainment.

He watched the inevitable coverage of the floods but turned it off, depressed. Alone and unoccupied he had too much time to worry especially as he'd had no contact with home. He'd left the sat phone with Sally, praying its powerful battery would last but had to give back the captain's. Twice he'd asked Rachel to get a replacement.

Three times during the evening he left his room to visit the operations centre. But it was always the same, quiet figures listening intently, making notes on a keyboard. He walked up and down the balcony waiting for action but nothing changed, only the same intense concentration on each face.

Rachel collected him around seven for breakfast. He hadn't slept well and his head felt heavy, the dry atmosphere brought lethargy to a body used to fresh air and rain. Rachel was brusque and efficient. 'Don't be long, they want you in the briefing room.'

Another steel room next to the ops room, linked by a sound-proofed window. He noticed first the impressive layer of gold braid which decorated a cap on the desk. Commander Harry Wallace, tall and well groomed, nodded at a chair. 'Coffee?'

Adam left the drink on the table, his attention on the listeners beyond the window as Wallace spoke.

'It's time we told you what's happening.'

He paid no attention and Wallace said sharply: 'Mr Woolton.'

Still staring through the window, he said angrily: 'That would be courteous, if nothing else.'

Slowly he turned to face the officer.

'You and Harrison dragged me into this. It's not my concern but I'm stuck here waiting for what could be doomsday and I haven't even got a fucking phone!'

The Commander smiled: 'We can soon remedy that at least.' He pressed a button on the desk and Rachel Watson was there instantly.

'Get him a phone,' he said, then, as she turned to go. 'Hang on.' To Adam: 'Are you armed?'

He shook his head. 'I left it for John, in case.'

'A phone and a pistol, Rachel, then come back and take him up.'

'We didn't want to involve you but we had to.' He paused: 'How much do you know?'

'Not much but I assume Kirstie Lomax is at the heart of it.'

'Yes, she's worked for us a long time in very deep cover. She's monitoring a group we think is a terrorist cell, translating for Abu Ben Hassan, an Egyptian businessman.'

'Or pretends he is?' Adam cut in.

'No, he's genuine -- and the deal he's working on. Hassan is cover for the group, she does all his secretarial work. We don't know if he's an innocent tool or the leader.'

'What are they planning?'

'That's the problem, Kirstie had all the info. They intended a toxic attack on the water supply for London, Birmingham and Glasgow. It was well advanced and we were ready to grab the lot of them. Unfortunately--'

Adam butted in again: 'It started to rain.'

'Yes, rain like we've never known and then the floods.'

'So they moved on?'

'They were based in the midlands. Kirstie was with them part of the time with a meeting the day the floods began. They bolted north and took her with them. We know they abandoned the original scheme but she couldn't keep us informed. We lost them, that's why when she contacted you it was so important.'

215

'I see,' Adam mused. 'That's explains Hayley being alone.'

'You finding the child gave us the perfect contact. What could be more innocent and understandable than a mother's concern for her child?'

'What indeed?'

'But when she gave you the Zadok code we had to act fast.'

'So my idiot scheme was the ideal cover.'

'You told the world about it so we had to check it out. Whizzing you up here and dropping the child on the way is just sufficiently plausible.'

'You hope.'

'Well, from what Benji's told us they're not suspicious.'

'You're getting stuff through?'

'Yes but nothing yet to tell us the actual plan.'

'So it really works?'

The commander nodded. 'Every word in that house comes through to our ops room.'

'You think they're waiting for something?'

'Mm, maybe some instruction but everything's on hold. Kirstie asked when they're moving.'

Adam frowned: 'Do they really think she's one of them -- a terrorist?'

'It's confusing. We reckon the group thinks so but she's not sure about Hassan, or if he realises what's going on.'

'Maybe he's innocent?'

'Could be. But we have to count him as an enemy, guilty till proved otherwise.'

Adam studied Wallace, picturing Hayley with her floppy rabbit, the innocent pawn. He wondered if he'd ever see her again.

He chose his next words with care: 'It sounds highly improbable, messy and very dangerous. The child's in there and you don't even know what's happening.'

'We have no choice.'

'I keep hearing that.' In the brief silence a nasty doubt crept into Adam's head. He looked at Wallace, weighing up probabilities. In a quiet voice he said: 'You're certain Kirstie's on our side, you're sure of her?'

'Of course! Why do you ask?'

'I can't believe a mother would put her own child in such terrible danger.'

Wallace turned his back on him and stood watching the adjoining room. 'The people in there are listening to that house. Kirstie Lomax is a very brave woman, we've no reason to doubt her but if she was turned, well -- she knows about the rabbit and she'd have warned them.'

'Maybe she has.'

The commander spun round. 'How could she? It's been operating since the child arrived. Its range is huge, any sound is picked up.'

Adam gazed into the piercing eyes that studied him, probing the thoughts conjured in his head and said softly: 'Maybe she wrote it down -- you must've thought of that.'

Clearly not. Adam couldn't believe it but the doubt and near panic he saw in the man's stare told him someone had overlooked that simple possibility. Controlling himself the commander said: 'I won't believe Kirstie is anything but loyal, her record proves it. Why would she suddenly betray her own people?'

Adam shrugged: 'Just my cynical mind, I suppose.'

Chapter nineteen

As Sally replaced candles in the sitting room she listened to Kylie's tortured cough. The child coughed all day and much of the night, an audible whistle with every breath and every few breaths the cough, a constant irritation to everyone.

Something about the attitude of mother and child struck Sally and she went back to them. 'How is she today?'

Hazel glanced up, her auburn hair straggled in grey-rooted wisps round her tired face.

'She didn't eat breakfast, the porridge makes her feel sick.'

'There was bread and jam.'

Hazel shook her head. 'She wasn't hungry, she's worse today.'

Sally touched the child's forehead. It felt clammy and her eyes seemed too large though half closed as another coughing fit racked her body. 'Are you warm enough?' she asked and Kylie shook her head.

'I'll find something.'

She came back with one of her own fleeces and helped the child snuggle into it.

'Thank you,' said Hazel, 'sorry to be so miserable. It's not your fault, but it doesn't look very bright for us.'

'We'll be okay. If we can just hang on till the water goes. I'm sure we'll make it, it's a matter of time.'

'But it's still raining. Look at it.'

Kylie doubled up in another spasm, with short, rapid breaths as if she couldn't absorb the air quick enough. Hazel gathered her daughter closer and shook her head. 'She can't last like this.'

Shocked by the implication Sally didn't answer, then whispered: 'Is she really that bad?'

218

'She should've seen the doctor last week, she needs stronger stuff, they change it around when she's bad and stress makes it worse. She keeps talking about Darren, when he fell in the water. She was holding his hand -- he just slipped away, like and she can't get it out of her mind.'

'I'm so sorry,' Sally was helpless. 'It's all horrible. I wonder, I've got some chocolate in my room -- would you like that Kylie? Would it make you feel better?'

The girl's eyes lit up and she nodded.

They heard a shout from Tom: 'Ben! Grab Polly, quick!' The bitch bounded eagerly through the open door into the room, tail wagging in delight. She launched herself at the nearest humans, spraying doggy wetness and went to Kylie, the only child there, pushing against her for attention. Horrified the girl shrank away, cringing with fright as the dog tried to lick her face.

Hazel let out a screaming sob as Eve rushed in to grab the animal but the damage was done and Kylie was immediately convulsed by a coughing bout and gasping for air.

'You should shoot that bloody animal. This could kill her.'

'Get her out, Tom!' Eve shouted, dragging Polly away and Tom grabbed her collar to haul her outside.

Ben watched the turmoil and Kylie struggling to breathe. He ran sobbing to his mother. 'I didn't mean to let her in, the door didn't shut properly. It's not her fault, she just wants to be back where she belongs. It's not her fault.'

John pushed through the crowd round the gasping child. 'For God's sake give her some space,' he shouted, shoving them aside.

He took Kylie gently in his arms and carried her away from the staring faces, her dangling thin arms seeming to him more bone than flesh.

Hazel followed, her hand in his back as if to push him up the stairs but when he went into the only room with any space she screamed and tried to pull him away: 'No not in there, that's where the old man died.'

Ignoring her he set Kylie down on the bed, where she lay semi-conscious as he opened the windows for fresh air. Hazel held an inhaler to her daughter's mouth moaning: 'It's almost empty, this is the last. Please help her.' She looked at John as if expecting a miracle, repeating her frantic pleas for help.

When Eve appeared she said: 'You must have something that can help.' But Eve could only watch helplessly.

The frail girl became more conscious and tried to speak. Between breaths she whispered: 'My chest hurts, it feels so tight.'

Eve said: 'Isn't there anything we can do?'

'Unless you can magic up a chopper and a hospital bed to take her, I can't think of anything,' John said.

'She should be in hospital.'

'I know.'

'Sorry, stupid thing to say,' Eve said quietly.

They listened to the sounds from the bedroom, the house was quiet as if everyone held their breath to catch each anguished cough and the child's struggling breath seemed louder in the stillness. Phil Bryston's death had shaken everyone and now another life hung in the balance.

John asked: 'Do you think she's got a chance?'

Eve sighed as she answered: 'Short of a miracle, no. She needs medication and we don't have it -- same as poor Philip.'

They took turns to stay with Hazel as she watched her child slip in and out of consciousness, gasping for each breath as she struggled for life.

Just after ten, Eve moved through the dark rooms with a candle, checking everyone before night. Most were already asleep, some talked in dull whispers, one girl was reading a paperback by torchlight. Eve hovered close and the girl saw her and said: 'I know what you're thinking but I want to finish this bit. It gets me out of here, if you know what I mean.'

Eve smiled. 'Yes, I know what you mean.' Behind her she sensed rather than saw movement in the hall and turned in time to glimpse a figure scurrying upstairs. In the darkness she couldn't tell if it was man or woman. On the hall stand the black silk topper was turned crown down. Eve felt inside, touching paper. The candlelight revealed Jane Bryston's missing cash but the thief had vanished in the shadows. She ran upstairs but no movement anywhere gave a clue to who it might have been.

A little after midnight Hazel's scream announced the worst had happened. She was out of control with grief, saying wildly: 'That dog did it, that dog killed my baby.'

John turned from the dead child, his voice low with suppressed frustration: 'You can't blame the dog, Hazel. This is her home, she didn't know. It's the weather, the bloody rain and the floods. And whatever power made it rain like this -- man-made, or God-made or just bloody bad luck.'

They left her with Kylie and fetched her partner Joe. Through the events of the past few days he'd seemed disconnected to his family as if the shock of losing home and small son had numbed him into insensitivity. He sat by the bed in silence and they realised nobody had heard him utter a word since he arrived.

At dawn John and Jock came with another body bag and Hazel began screaming again. 'You can't take my baby, you mustn't take her.'

'We have to move her,' said John and Sally took her away, sobbing and disoriented. The small body slipped easily into the tough plastic, the bag loose around her. It needed only one of them to lift her and John gathered the pathetic bundle in his arms, holding it tenderly as if she still lived.

He and Jock stared at the two bags side by side in the barn and Ben crept in to stand beside them.

'I can't believe all this,' John muttered.

'What can we do with them?' Jock asked.

'Nothing till the water goes. It's horrible. And please God there won't be any more.'

'It wasn't Polly's fault,' Ben whispered. 'She didn't know.'

'Course not, Ben. Kylie was very ill.'

221

Ben sighed. 'At least she can come in now. She's so miserable alone out there.'

The steel stairway seemed steeper and longer than he recalled and the echoes of his footsteps made him uneasy. Out on the helipad a hectic scene unfolded, a huge helicopter centre stage, hunkered down on the giant white cross.

He shivered as he took in the sinister shape and armoury of the helicopter gunship, streamlined cannon turrets bulging like frog's eyes, menace in the squat outline. Designed as an advanced battlefield helicopter the Merlin MK5 was much larger and designed for longer distances, capable of carrying a heavy load of men and equipment. This wasn't a flight to pick up passengers, this was a military mission to destroy a threat to the nation's safety.

Men were assembled around the machine, loading equipment and starting to climb in, quietly one behind another. From behind Rachel shoved her hand in the small of his back and pushed him forward.

'What is this?' he swung round.

'Training flight, they want you on it.'

'You can't make me take part, I'm not in the navy.'

She held his arm and led him forward: 'My orders are to get you on that chopper. Move.'

Beneath his feet the massive engine vibrated, growling like an animal, unnerving. 'I hate that noise,' he said.

'It's just the engine,' she sounded annoyed.

He started to approach the door but halted, dismayed at the sight of the soldiers silently climbing aboard. Men dressed as he was but with blackened faces and dark hoods. Several glanced at him with unfaltering expressions, not one gave the slightest recognition of his presence, no smile or greeting.

In his head the memory of other men and another take-off made him tremble and gasp for breath. He shuddered and turned hastily to face Rachel. 'I'm not going in that.' She took hold of him again but he pushed her roughly aside to fall heavily on the concrete as he dashed for the bunker.

He heard the thunderous roar as the machine lifted and whirled away and saw Rachel, back on her feet, holding onto her cap as the chopper rose and the windsock whipped horizontal in the downdraught.

He wasn't stopped as he rushed down the stairs back to his room. He waited, expecting any moment a guard to appear or to hear the sound of the lock being turned. When neither happened he relaxed and remembered that at least he had a phone. He could relieve one anxiety by contacting home. But he couldn't raise either the farm or Ron.

He didn't think about Sally and home but about Kirstie and why he'd questioned her loyalty. Did he really mistrust her? Why had that idea suddenly appeared? He knew nothing about her, only what Hayley had said.

Was it her beauty that made him suspicious, the lushness as Harrison described it? He so wanted to be wrong and forget the impulse which questioned her.

He drowsed and paced the small room, not daring to brave the corridors outside. When the phone rang he hesitated to answer but was relieved to hear Ron's familiar voice.

'Got your new number at last,' he said.

'I couldn't raise home, d'you know how things are?'

'Not good, Sally and your boys are fine, coping. But more have turned up and there's another death. I'm sorry.'

'Was it the child, Kylie?'

'Didn't get her name but John said it was a kid with asthma.'

Adam sighed.'I thought she would die, she was sick when they came. Like poor Philip, we had no meds for her.'

'Nothing you could do about it. But that's not why I called.'

'Oh?'

'You won't like this but I've now got the lowdown on your friend John.'

'They found something?'

223

'Yes, I'm sorry to say.'

'Bad?'

'Bad enough,' Ron sounded reluctant to tell him. 'It turns out he was sacked from his teaching job, the stuff about being tired of the red tape was all cobblers. He was caught with a pupil, a boy, not exactly in flagrante but enough to get rid of him.'

'You're saying he's a paedophile.'

'That maybe a bit harsh, the boy was well in his teens, not really a child and apparently a willing partner.'

Adam was silent, anger rising as he remembered the sight of John with an arm round Tom's shoulder. What he'd hated to think now revealed as truth.

'Adam, you still there?'

'Yes, I'm here. I've had doubts about him for a while but Sally laughed it off. Now I'm thinking about that bastard back there with my sons. Was he prosecuted?'

'The police tried to bring a case but the boy wouldn't cooperate, said it was no more than cuddles.' Ron was almost laughing now.

'It's not funny,' he shouted into the phone.

'He seems a decent guy, maybe he's got over all that. But they can't find any record of him working at a proper job since, only some private tutoring since he moved here.'

'Huh, living on his wife's income I suppose. Christ, he really took me in!'

'D'you think she knows?' Ron said, then, trying to soften the news. 'They've been a big help to you and your wife in all this. Could you have done it without them?'

'Not really. You're right about that but if I'd known I wouldn't have let them talk me into this.'

To change the subject, Ron asked: 'How's it going?'

'Badly for me, I'll be in the shit now, I wouldn't do their training trip.'

'Well, there's a bit of good news, your place and the others on the hill are getting priority for supplies because you're helping.'

He brooded on Ron's call, and kept trying to raise someone at home. He told himself Sally wouldn't let anything bad happen to the boys. He was left alone, shunned, Rachel didn't appear to take him to lunch nor was any brought to him. He wanted to see her, to apologise. Then in the afternoon as he tried to sleep someone knocked at the door. He didn't answer, waiting, until it opened to reveal Tim Rogers with a bottle in his hand.

They looked at each other, hesitating to be the first to speak, the captain looked uncomfortable. 'How are you now, Adam?' he began.

He shrugged and after a long pause said: 'I must apologise to Rachel. I didn't mean to knock her down, I just couldn't get on that machine.'

'She's wasn't pleased but she's fine. She was following orders.'

'They shouldn't have asked me to go, I'm not here to fight, in fact I don't know why I am here.'

'Shall we have a drink and you can tell me about it.' Tim picked up two glasses from the small side table and opened the bottle.

'It's Old Pulteney, from Caithness, I think you'll appreciate it.' He took the room's only chair and drew it closer.

'So what's it all about? What's your problem with choppers? You seemed fine on the flight up here.'

Adam went to the bathroom for a dash of water in his drink. He sniffed it and took a swallow, smiling. 'That's lovely, so smooth. Helicopters -- I don't mind the small ones, like you use for the drops. I quite enjoyed our flight. It's the noise they make, those massive double rotors and that thing out there this morning, like a much bigger Apache. If you'd been chased by one you'd understand.'

'Chased? You were in Afghanistan, is that right, serving with the reserve?'

Adam didn't answer.

'PTSD?'

'I've never called it that, just bad memories. And after all that happened since you have to wonder why any of us bothered, what the hell were we all doing there."

'Yes, it did end badly, it all seemed such a waste.' He paused. 'But didn't they offer you treatment or counselling?'

'I didn't talk about it, I treated myself. We bought the farm -- that was my treatment and I've been all right. Peaceful place like that, it cures the soul.'

Tim leaned forward: 'D'you want to tell me about it?'

'Not really. I've tried to forget it but I still have to hang onto myself when I hear a chopper. The noise makes me want to hide.'

'It could help if you tell me.'

Adam sighed. 'Okay, if I must.' He took a big slurp of the whisky. 'Our spies had whispers of a pending attack at Kandahar. They wanted volunteers to check out a suspected Taliban base between Bastion and Lashkar Gah, four men plus an Afghan guide. We were all Reserve men, young, looking for adventure. Big mistake. We were dressed as locals, Pashtuns -- I fancied myself in those caps -- we looked the part. I was in charge, a lieutenant, with a sergeant and two men. We were dropped to proceed on foot, no problem. We found the place and the info was correct, it was a Taliban hotspot. It seemed easy, we radioed the coordinates back to base. It'd all gone well, we were pleased with ourselves.'

He stopped and smiled at the captain. 'We thought we were real soldiers then.'

'You were, the Reserve does a fine job, too many soldiers were lost out there.'

'Regular troops might have taken more care,' Adam said it slowly. 'Hubris, that's the word, we were too cocky.'

'You're very hard on yourself,' Tim said kindly.

'I don't think so. It was about five miles back to the rendezvous where a chopper would pick us up. We followed the road, just a group of local Afghans going home.' He was silent, musing, seeing himself back on that dusty track.

'We were actually laughing, Josh the sergeant had told a joke, we were laughing,' he frowned at the memory.

'We were armed and now, on the return we carried the rifles openly, loose in our hands. We heard the Apaches before we saw them, the unmistakeable grinding noise in the distance. We watched them approach, two of them, just kept walking. They came in low for attack. We looked about for their target, then realised it was us.'

He trembled, whispering. 'They came straight at us, firing, lines of bullets exploding across the ground behind us as we ran. The only cover was an outcrop of rock maybe fifty yards away. Josh went down and the guide, the three of us were almost at the rocks when Brian was caught and I felt this appalling pain in my leg. With Peter, the other private, I dived behind the rocks and lay doggo.

'My leg was pumping blood but we daren't move. The choppers came round for another pass and we just prayed. One of them fired another burst but that was it.'

'What then?'

'Peter was hit in the hand but he managed to get a dressing on my leg and his hand.

'We crawled out to get the radio from Brian. He was dead, a ghastly mess. Peter was so brave, he sprinted across to help the others but they'd both had it. That was it, we radioed and they picked us up.'

'Bad business,' Tim said. 'Here,' he refilled Adam's glass.

'I was the officer, we should've been more alert, it was my fault. I knew it was dangerous, dressed like that, showing the rifles too. But I thought the Yanks would've been told about the op. Mown down by our own side, that shouldn't have happened.'

'Friendly fire, it happens a lot, easy to make mistakes in combat conditions,' Tim said sadly. 'A lot gets covered up. But you made it, was it bad?'

'Not that bad, I was lucky, a nasty wound, took a lump out of my leg and chipped the bone. But it healed. '

'Was that it for you with the army?'

'I wasn't fit for active service after that. Now I look like a coward.'

Tim said: 'I'd say you'd done your bit.' He saw Adam's anxiety. 'Don't worry, you've got reason, we'll explain it to the boss later, he wants to see you. It's not so bad, he can't court martial you. Cheer up.'

'It's not just that, I had a call from Ron.'

In the early evening the captain returned to collect him. His stomach by now was recalling last night's supper and he hoped the coming interview wouldn't mean he'd miss another meal. In the ops room Commander Wallace was hunched over a screen, leaning on the operator, listening directly through an earpiece. He beckoned to Adam.

'I think you're wrong about Kirstie.'

'I hope so. About this morning, I --'

'We'll talk about that later. Kirstie was on the phone, talking to her mother about music.'

'Her mother?'

Wallace grinned. 'She called HQ direct with the Zadok code. Then a man's voice told her to clear the line.'

'Is that all?'

'No, talk of helicopters, seems they can fly them.'

'That's ominous,' muttered Adam.

Another operator was waving for attention and Wallace hurried to look at the screen transcribing an incoming message.

Adam read it over Wallace's shoulder.

The message was simple: 'Mr Hassan's equipment will be at Aberdeen airport in the morning. Flight arrives 04.30.'

'Where's the call from,' demanded Wallace. 'Can you tell?'

'Somewhere in north Africa, can't be more precise yet.'

'Sir, look at this.' A female operator called and simultaneously on three screens appeared transcriptions of what was being said away in the hills.

228

'Put it on broadcast,' ordered Wallace and all clearly heard the exclamations and garbled conversation, some in French, and in the background voices from TV or a laptop.

They heard Kirstie ask: 'Does this mean you've given up on the poison?'

Someone said: 'Can't be done now, impossible.'

'So what next?' she asked again.

'That's my girl!' shouted Wallace. 'She knows we're listening, she's no traitor.'

'The equipment has come,' said a heavily accented voice.

'Equipment?' Kirstie sounded incredulous, naive.

'Explosives, lovely one! For bombs! We shall blow them to hell.'

'But how?'

'We shall be as birds, my dear.' Adam recognised Anton.

'You mean we'll be flying?'

'You're very slow tonight, Mrs Kirstie,' said the heavy accent.

'I'm tired, I walked too far today. I'll make some coffee.'

The sound of a door closing followed by two voices speaking in whispers, Anton and the man with the heavy accent.

Anton said: 'The floods have helped us, made it easier, not so many targets.'

'No, Allah has blessed us with this water. It is a fitting punishment for them,' he laughed. 'They're more vulnerable isolated on high ground.'

'Will we attack the castle as well?'

'Most certainly, it is what they call a sitting duck, an easy target.'

Then he called in a louder tone: 'Hamza, Ahmed, turn that off and listen.'

Wallace pulled absently at the small beard covering his chin as they heard Anton issue orders to leave at once to be at the airport in Aberdeen when the cargo plane landed. Tim Rogers was studying the huge map of Britain which took up half one wall. It displayed the country as it now presented itself, showing the full extent of the flooding and those areas left above the water line. Prominent on it large red dots marked the site of the government emergency headquarters at Buxton and the military command bases on the downs in north Wiltshire and Oxfordshire. Other dots indicated places of safety for the royals -- among the hills of Wales and Scotland and Balmoral itself.

Minor centres of communication and control on high ground were also marked and the underground base beside the loch was a large red star.

'It's simple, sir,' Rogers tapped the map. 'It's obvious. Knock these out and they've crippled the country at a stroke.'

As Wallace studied the map, Adam wondered if all this was credible. 'Would they know about these centres?'

'Of course,' snapped Wallace. 'You can't keep something like the Buxton move a secret for long.'

'They'd have to be efficient with their bombs,' Adam said.

'Not difficult with the latest smart devices, a place like Buxton could be easily wiped out. If they incorporate a poison or radioactive element it would finish off any survivors from the initial attack. With things as they are it would be very difficult to help them.'

'That's what's at Aberdeen,' the captain said, 'the fucking explosives waiting for collection. The crates won't be big, packed as machinery or electrical goods. Christ sir, they can really do this!'

'Yes, and with the government and military eliminated once the water goes, they, or whoever is backing them, can establish a new state.'

'Do you think that's what it's about?'

'I can't see what else is behind it, assuming they are Islamists, that was always the aim. We thought we'd defeated ISIS, got rid of them but the ideology lived on, this looks horribly like a revival.'

Wallace rubbed his chin again. 'We must stop them before they leave the farm or find the explosives before they get them.'

Rogers said slowly: 'But then they'll know we're onto it, any sign of a search will spook them.'

'You're right, so we stay with the original plan.'

Adam chipped in impatiently: 'Surely you can at least move the royals?'

'Of course.' Wallace was irritable now.

'That's routine but with Buxton and the army HQ it's more difficult. We can't shift the whole town, they'd die, along with all the refugees in the area. They're sitting targets. No, we must stop it before it starts.'

Adam stayed silent, thinking of the soldiers in black-out on the huge helicopter. Now he began to understand.

Chapter twenty

Recalled to the briefing room after supper, he faced fierce scrutiny from the commander while Tim Rogers hovered near the door.

'So, you didn't fancy the training flight. You struck one of my officers, knocked her down. We wanted you on that mission, it was important.'

He tried to look contrite. 'I didn't mean to knock her down, I couldn't bring myself to get on that chopper.'

'You panicked?'

'I suppose so, sorry to be a disappointment but I'm just an ordinary guy, nothing special.'

Wallace smiled. 'Not so ordinary. I'm told you've done well so far in this mess, taking care of survivors. But we still need your help.'

'I don't see how I can help,' he said with relief, 'it sounds like fighting from now on but I'm not a soldier any more.'

'Not officially but they say you were a good one.'

'No, I messed up.'

'That's not what your record says -- Tim's explained the problem. Understandable in the circumstances, it seems to me you should've had more help.'

'It's history, I got over it, more or less. I brought the child, why do you need me now?'

Wallace was watching the ops room through the window and turned back. 'We want you in that house with them. The idea was to drop you today, have you arrive at the farm by taxi.' He frowned. 'But that didn't happen, you're still here.'

'They won't want me there, they'll be suspicious.'

'You're be there to collect the child.'

Wallace looked back at the telltale screens, stroking his beard, a finger moving from side to side thoughtfully. Then he faced Adam saying: 'It's bombs, you heard most of it.'

Adam nodded: 'An air attack, helicopter or maybe a small plane.'

'It's got to be helicopters. The sky's never been so full of them -- a few more won't be noticed. Air traffic control is hopeless, it's impossible to keep track of everything.'

Tim Rogers said: 'They must be planning to steal one or more helicopters, from the airport maybe.

'Nothing at the farm when you were there?' Wallace asked.

'We didn't get that far, they had us land in the village and the kid was collected by truck,' explained the captain.

Adam said: 'From what they've been saying my guess is they haven't got the wings yet. Kirstie would've made some reference surely.'

'Okay Adam,' Wallace had come to a decision. 'We'll send you by road in the morning.'

They told him to be ready for 08:00 hours, the Navy truck would take him to Selkirk where they'd booked a local taxi to turn up at the farm. He had nothing to prepare but one urgent call to make. He sat impatiently on the bed calling constantly until at last Sally picked up.

'Adam, at last, darling how are you?'

He almost snapped at her. 'I'm fine, it's all a muddle but I must speak to John. It's what I thought, he's a bloody paedo. I haven't got long, get him on the line. And Sally, I can't do a thing about it, I'm five hundred miles away so it's down to you to watch him, watch him with our boys.'

'What?'

'No time now, get him, quickly.'

John was eager to talk, beginning an account of Kylie's death and the water problem.

'The boys have been brilliant,' he began.

A blast of anger cut him short. 'Don't talk about my boys. I know what you are!'

'What're you talking about, what's wrong?'

'You know. The army checks came back. I know what you are, not the man I thought at all. A fucking paedophile and you're there with my sons — and I'm fucking miles away.'

'Christ Adam what do you think I am? What d'you think I'm going to do?'

'I don't know what you might do. I trusted you, thought you were my friend in all this. I've seen you with Tom, god knows what you might do while I'm not there.'

'Adam please! I am your friend.'

'Are you! I tell you this John, you lay a finger on those boys and I'll kill you.'

'I made a mistake but it wasn't as bad as you think.'

'Are you queer or not?'

'It's not a crime.'

'It is with a young boy, my boy.'

'The truth is I'm bisexual, Eve knows what I am, she accepts it. We've dealt with it and it works for us. I love her.'

Adam said again: 'I've seen you with Tom, the way you look at him.'

'I made mistakes,' John repeated, 'ruined my career -- I was a bloody good teacher. But I wouldn't touch your boys, I'm fond of them, especially Tom but I wouldn't sully them. Tom has no idea about me, not like that, believe me.'

'I've no choice, have I. But I meant what I said, try anything and you're dead.'

Anton was outside as the taxi approached, he'd seen it for half a mile making its slow way on the rough, narrow track to the farm. He hurried forward as Adam got out, intending to send him away but the driver had his orders and followed them to the letter, turning double quick to get back to Selkirk.

'Why are you here?' Anton asked, his tone unfriendly. 'We are busy and don't need more visitors.'

'Sorry, shan't stay long. I've come to pick up Hayley. The Navy kicked me out,' he said.

'They got what they wanted from my plans and told me to leave. Bastards,' he grinned, 'I don't think they trust me, they've got a lot of secrets there.'

Anton look dubious, saying again: 'We are very busy, we have to leave here soon and Mr Hassan is anxious to complete his project. You must keep out of the way.'

He stood blocking the entrance while Adam hovered, wanting to get in and find Kirstie.

The man scowled at him: 'It is very inconvenient.' But he moved aside to let Adam pass and he couldn't resist saying: 'Thanks for the welcome.'

Anton led him to the kitchen and told him to wait. Very soon he heard a child's shout and a rush of footsteps and Hayley dashed into his arms. Kirstie followed, a quizzical expression showing her surprise.

'How come you're here?'

He'd rehearsed his act, looking at her hungrily. 'Couldn't keep away, I wanted to see you both again, especially you,' he said softly as he took her hand, imagining what the listeners would make of it.

Kirstie had the grace to blush which suddenly made him think he meant it.

Outside the sun was shining and in any other situation he would've thought it a charming place to visit. Usually a holiday rental the old farmhouse sat on flat land by Ettrick Water. The rushing river tumbling over boulders made a constant murmur in the distance. The garden was equipped with a swing and other play equipment for children. Seeing this he said to Hayley. 'Let's go outside and enjoy the sunshine.'

The noon sun was hot on their faces. He couldn't believe the contrast. Scotland, usually afflicted by abundant rain, had escaped the worst ravages of the storms. He could tell by the rich green of the grass and the volume of river water that it had rained enough but not with the persistent onslaught in the south. Hayley laughed, delighted to see him again, as he pushed her backwards and forwards on the swing.

In the ops room they heard Kirstie clearly, speaking anxiously to Anton. 'We need to know why he really came and what he knows. It's very strange he should come like this.'

"We need to get rid of him, he says the Navy people don't trust him -- and I certainly don't. He's bad news, I don't like it. But we can deal with him.'

'It may just be because of me, he fancies me. I'll take him out, show him the hills and the view, find out what's going on, you can rely on me.'

Anton's voice was doubtful. 'If you think you can.'

'He's out there with Hayley, enjoying the sun. Leading him on will be easy.'

Hayley took Adam across the grass to the river. In the fast flowing water she spotted small fry in the shallows. He was startled to see an angler standing up to his knees in the current, casting for salmon. The tranquillity of the idyllic scene brought a lump to his throat when the man turned and raised his hat in greeting. Kirstie strolled casually down to join them and they stayed watching as the rod dipped in an arc and he began to reel it in.

Hayley bounced with excitement but the line went slack and they saw the silver body of the fish dart away downstream. The angler turned with a rueful grin and smiled at Hayley who watched him choose a different fly from his box and fix it on the line. They waited while he cast again.

'Shall we go up the hill?' Kirstie asked, holding out her hand to Hayley. 'The heather's almost in full bloom, it's quite a sight.'

They kept well apart until a belt of conifers hid them from the house, both wary of watching eyes. Unused to walking uphill in such heat he felt hot and sweaty in his heavy fleece. Beyond the trees the rolling landscape opened into a stretch of heather moorland, a purple haze against the blue sky. It was beautiful and romantic. He was very conscious of being alone with such a woman in such a place. A pile of rocks ahead looked inviting and he made for them and sat. She stood looking down at him, as if assessing the man.

'So what are you doing here?' she began, the silken voice firm and decisive.

He blew a deep breath and half laughed. 'You want the truth? I have no idea.'

'That makes no sense. You shouldn't have come. You're in danger, Anton will kill you if they can't find a use for you.'

'All I know is they want me here so I'll pretend it's because of you. That's easy for anyone to believe. But for now it's great to feel the sun's heat again. I'm baking.'

He stood up and wriggled free of the fleece, revealing the automatic pistol strapped against his chest.

Her eyebrows rose, studying the weapon. 'I wondered why you were wearing that, at least you're well armed -- but we must hide it.' She was emphatic.

'Why don't we relax a while, enjoy this wonderful day and consider what to do,' he said. The sun made her raven hair glossy with light and the wide dark eyes studying him intently were disconcerting. He tried to think of her as the security agent that she was but her proximity as a woman unsettled him. After a moment she sat, yards away, looking into the distance towards the river, alert for any approach from the farmhouse. Hayley was busy gathering small bunches of heather.

'Being here it's hard to believe much of the country's under water,' he said, glancing at her. 'Are you afraid to come near me? Sitting so far apart reminds me of the virus year, they called it social distancing, no hugging allowed.'

'Yes, my husband and I were together then, in Estonia of all places. He was stationed there and I'd just been recruited to the service. When we came back here everyone was wearing masks.'

Adam nodded. 'We hadn't long bought the farm, nobody took much notice of some new disease in China. We didn't think it would affect us. Then it all blew up and the country was totally shut down.'

Kirstie moved to lean against a closer rock as he mused, more to himself than her.

'It was April, a warm, sunny spring, beautiful. I remember a sense of guilt because it didn't really affect us much, we just carried on more or less as normal. It was incredibly still, no wind, the turbine in the valley unmoving, no traffic, only the sound of a tractor in the distance. In the evening the lightest breeze rustled the trees and the birdsong was so distinct -- it was a different world.'

'A lot of people died,' she said.

'Yes, we were lucky, that was the guilt."

'You shouldn't feel guilty, we missed the worst of it too.'

'They created such a terrible climate of fear and the media made it worse. Everybody was wearing masks, people were so scared, some never regained the confidence to live normally. We just stayed on the hill and got on with it.'

Kirstie turned from her vigilance to look at him, admiring his strong profile but hearing the note of reticence and self blame. 'But now you're helping, looking after those people. Because you live up there you can help them.'

'It's been hard going but I guess it's payback time, a chance to do my bit.'

'This ark of yours, I know it's all nonsense but don't you see it's real? Your home is the ark, saving all those people from the water.' She saw his expression change and he looked sideways at her with moist eyes.

'That's what she said, I didn't understand what she meant.'

'Who?'

'Jane, the old woman whose husband died, you don't know about that. Now there's two bodies in the barn, the kid with asthma died was well.'

She'd listened patiently at first to his worries and his fears about John but soon cut him short, dragging him back to the present.

'Okay Adam, I get all that but you're here now and the lives in danger are yours and mine, real and present danger. We may not survive but we're going to try and you have to trust me and more importantly obey me. When we go back down there you follow my lead, don't show surprise or any sort of dissent. Two of them went to Aberdeen last night. They were back first thing this morning with explosives and they're in the cellar right now, making bombs.'

Anton looked anything but friendly on their return. She took Adam directly upstairs to a bedroom, with Hayley's pink patterned pyjamas folded neatly on the single bed.

He was embarrassed when she said: 'You'll have to be in here with us, there's nowhere else. Did you bring any stuff?'

'Only this rucksack.'

'But you've got a phone?'

He nodded.

'That's a bonus, there's only one between us since the power went and Anton's got that.'

'I thought there was a generator.'

'There was. I spiked it, given orders, though it's actually made things more difficult for me.'

'At least we can contact the base,' he said

'Give me your gun.'

'Why?'

'To hide it, they may search you.'

'Do you have a weapon?'

'Yeah,' she smiled ' a neat little job in my wash bag.'

He handed her the gun and watched as she pulled up the carpet by the wall. She took a knife from her pocket, inserting it in the line of the floorboards to prise up a small section. His automatic pistol sat neatly in the space.

'That's clever,' he said.

'Not really, basic stuff, take a closer look.' He squatted and saw a cluster of hand grenades in the hole.

'Stay here with Hayley while I report to Anton.'

They came together in the early evening for an uncomfortable meal, five dark men, all but Anton obviously of Arab origin, plus Mr Hassan, who ate next to nothing. He met them warily but the atmosphere had improved and he wondered what tale she'd spun to explain his presence and keep him alive. The role played by Hassan was a puzzle, the man must surely realise what was happening around him or was he totally duped by them.

There was no alcohol in the place but he took his coffee mug outside to be away from them, wandering back to the river to stare into the clear water and think about home, wishing he was away from this place, whose beauty belied the true menace. He tried calling but it dialled unanswered which launched him into frustrated anxiety.

He called the base, to speak to Commander Wallace, waiting on the line as the sun began to set.

The commander was unavailable but Tim Rogers came on, sounding cheerful.

'You're in place Adam, that's good. The Commander's tied up so you've got me.'

'Fine, but what am I doing here?'

'Waiting, my friend.'

'What for?'

'I hate to tell you this but we've set a trap for these buggers and you're the bait.'

He stayed by the river hoping she would come. The sun was well down behind the hill among streaked wisps of cloud which had blown in as the temperature dropped. Shivering he watched the dying rays deck the clouds with tints of pink and gold as she strolled down to join him.

'I thought you weren't coming. I expected one of them down here to get rid of me -- and my gun stuck up there in the house. I'm amazed they left me out here on my own.'

'They won't kill you, not yet, they have a use for you.'

'That ties with what Tim Rogers just said, it sounds like bad news.'

'It's quite simple. They need a helicopter and I pointed out the army will be collecting you and Hayley on the way south. They mean to have it.'

'You mean hijack it?'

She smiled, nodding.

'That sounds too easy, surely they suspect a trap?'

'Not necessarily, remember, they've no idea their cell is discovered.'

'They trust you that much?'

'Yes, we laid a complicated background story for me before I took the job with Hassan. They think I'm an Islamist zealot like them.'

'But doesn't Hayley make it difficult?'

'They know I was married to an infidel.'

He stared at her in the gathering dusk. 'You're really something else, a scary lady.'

'It's what I do,' she said.

He turned back towards the river. She followed as he said: 'You don't seem to give a shit about the risk.'

'Oh I do, I don't want any of us to die but we have to stop them.'

'But surely they know there'll be armed men on that chopper? It won't be that easy.'

'They're ready for that and remember they have a hostage, you.' She tugged at his arm: 'Best go back, it's nearly dark.'

Hayley was tucked up in the single bed, in deep, untroubled sleep. He contemplated the child, his mind on the terrors ahead, noting that Benji was nowhere in sight.

241

'Won't they think it odd she doesn't take the rabbit to bed?' he asked.

'She carries it most of the time, I doubt if they notice.'

'Can it really pick up over such a wide area.'

'The base may not have heard all we said by the river, the water was noisy. But they'll have got all I said to them after you went out.'

'So this was the plan all along.'

She moved close to him. 'I'm sorry you got dragged into this.'

Perched on the bed and awkward at being alone with her he found refuge in talking. He went back to the year of the virus, contrasting the weather then with this new catastrophe.

'It was beautiful. All through March and April and into May it was dry, really hot much of the time. The weather was on our side, they said the heat helped kill the bug. The stillness was amazing, the quiet.'

She watched him as he babbled on, knowing why but listening patiently when his voice grew softer sinking into memory.

'Most nights were cloudless, a mass of stars and there was Venus, sparkling low in the evening sky, looking down at us. Sally and I stood outside, gazing up at her, like she was telling us there was more to this world than us.'

Downstairs a sudden outburst of noise from the kitchen made them alert. Raised voices sounded like an argument. 'What do you think that's about?'

'Probably something on Al Jazeera, they monitor it all the time or it could be anything on the net or TV.'

They heard a door bang and more voices below. 'The others have come in, they may have finished. Not easy making bombs in bad light.'

'Any idea when they'll do it?'

'It won't be tomorrow.'

'Why not?' He sounded puzzled.

'It's Friday -- they're believers.'

'Of course.'

'Adam, it's down to us when they do it -- or rather when the army decides to collect you.'

He thought about that but said nothing and reverted to his rambles. 'People hoped that somehow it would make a difference, things might change, it could be a more caring world. It brought everyone together, made them kinder for a while. But it didn't last and all the promises were forgotten. Back to normal was what everyone wanted. The billions they spent had to be recouped and the promised cash for flood defences was soon forgotten. Now here we are with half the world under water. Normal won't be so easy this time.'

Kirstie let out a very audible sigh. 'Talking about all that doesn't help us now.'

'There are parallels. You've been up here, missed the worst of it. This is different and much worse. When everyone was told to stay home, it was fine for us but dreadful for people in towns, shut in for weeks. That's what started the move away from the cities.'

'It was hard,' she said 'but at least they were in their own homes, not stuck on some bleak hilltop like you told me.'

'Worst thing was, when people started being let out they headed for the beauty spots, the mountains and the coast and polluted them. Acres of rubbish dumped, that was dreadful. The beauty of the place obviously had no impact on them, it was like they were a different species.'

'I don't remember all that, we were busy keeping an eye on Putin, the neighbours weren't being too friendly.'

'Yet now I feel I must save the same sort of people. I couldn't believe the state of that hill camp and the army meant to leave them there.'

'But you got them moved. Good for you, now forget about the past and concentrate on this. You feel things too much, you need to harden up.'

'I'm not soft, I was in the army, the reserve anyway .'

'I know your record, you were injured.'

243

'Not badly but friends died that day and I don't want a repeat.'

She left the armchair to sit beside him, close enough so he moved away for space between them. 'It's awkward being here with you,' he said. 'Isn't there anywhere else I can doss down tonight?'

'Not really,' she said, 'you're safer here with me. Hayley will share my bed and you can sleep over there.' She laughed and added: 'It's okay, I won't climb in with you if you don't want me to.'

The scent of her and the sensuous voice made him flush and stirred feelings he didn't want. He stood up to get away from her and she watched him, an amused smile playing about her lips.

She tried to catch his eyes but he looked down, afraid to meet them.

'What's the matter, are you afraid of me?'

'Not afraid but you know very well you're gorgeous, desirable, that's why these men are fooled by you.'

'Yes, you know they think you're my lover.' She came close to him. 'Can't I tempt you?'

He stepped back but she reached for his neck to pull him close.

'Please don't,' he said .

'You know you want me. We could make it real.'

She said it softly but he was thinking of that room away on the coast. How much they would enjoy hearing this.

'Does that damn rabbit hear everything?' he said.

'Pretty much, they seem delighted with it. Are you frightened they'll hear me making love to you?'

He shrugged: 'I expect they've heard worse.'

She stood on tiptoe suddenly and kissed him. He was startled and appalled by the impact of it. The wild thrill of heat through his body was frightening as he realised how much he wanted her and he let her pull him towards the bed.

He kissed her briefly on the mouth and nuzzled her neck but then stepped back sharply from her.

'No, we can't do this.'

She frowned. 'I know you want to.'

'No,' he stood up and backed away. 'I'm sorry, I can't.'

'Why not?'

'We have a job to do, we can't be distracted. And I love my wife. It may sound corny but I do. I can't betray her.'

'Betray!' She laughed. 'She'll never know -- I won't tell her.'

He sighed. 'But I will know. Every time I touch her the guilt would be there. I would always know and if there is life after this I want it to be as it was before.'

'Christ Adam! We could both die soon.'

'I know that.'

He trailed a finger across her skin and kissed her lightly on the lips.

He whispered: 'I'm so sorry but I can't.'

The rueful smile came again. 'You're a lovely man Adam, probably too good for me.'

She went to the door. 'I'll go see what they're up to now,' she said.

Left alone he lay in turmoil conscious of an unsatisfied ache in his loins. He pulled himself together and tried calling Sally. It was late but to his relief she answered and he felt shame at the sound of her voice.

'Is everything okay? How are things?'

'Not good, I'm trying to sort out extra bed spaces,' she said.

'More people?'

'It's the barn, they won't sleep in there now.'

'Oh?'

'The smell from the body bags.'

'The plastic should stop that.'

'Well it doesn't.'

'I'm sorry, I should be there to help.'

'Has something happened?' she asked, catching a nuance in his voice that troubled her.

'Nothing yet, it's what might happen that worries me.'

Chapter twenty-one

The new day brought only anxious suspense. He would wander up through the heather, constantly looking over his shoulder for any sign of activity at the farm, then return to check with Kirstie; then off again, mooching without purpose, in a different direction or along the river bank, taking Hayley with him on shorter walks.

He couldn't bear to be in the house, despite Kirstie's plan and his role as hostage he was constantly aware that any moment could bring him face to face with an Arab intent on murder.

The hidden gun, out of reach if he needed it, didn't help his peace of mind. But they couldn't risk it being found.

He wondered why they didn't keep him guarded but she told him in the early morning when he woke alone in the single bed that she would tell them about their night of passion.

Wide-eyed he watched her dress, half wishing he'd made a different choice. When she went down he stayed upstairs with Hayley, listening at the door to the voices below.

'So, pretty one, did you take the infidel into your bed?' It was Ahmed. 'Allah will forgive your sin for you were made to trap men like him and his lust for you will keep him close to us.'

He heard her say: 'Yes, I did as you asked, he was satisfied. He is an Englishman.' Their laughter unnerved him and for a moment his trust in her wavered before he smiled at the lies she was telling.

Anton was more practical. 'We are ready to leave. The devices are prepared, all we need now is the aircraft. We will try your plan Mrs Kirstie but we need to know what time they will come, so we can be ready. What does he think we do here?'

246

'I'm not sure,' she said. 'You all work with Mr Hassan on his project, that's what I've told him. He may believe it or he may suspect something, because of what you are.'

'Huh,' Ahmed laughed again. 'It doesn't matter what he thinks, he will die before we leave. Tell him Mr Hassan has finished and you are ready to leave with the child. Tell him to call and fix a time to fetch you. Then we shall take their wings, inshallah, and become demons in the air.'

Heavy rain had fallen in the night, he'd heard it as he lay awake, thinking about the woman in the bed across the room. In an obscure way the rain pleased him as some small justice. The river ran wild in torrents flushed by water flowing down from the hills and he was careful to keep a tight hold of Hayley's hand as they walked along the bank. The angler was there again, taking advantage of the fresh flow which attracted more fish in the warmer water. The man nodded a greeting to Adam and the little girl.

'Any luck?' he asked.

'It depends,' said the fisherman, 'the way they're running I could get several but I'll only take one home — I have to keep my wife happy and justify the time I spend here.' He winked at Adam and nodded towards Hayley. 'Your daughter?'

'She's just a friend. I envy you, I've always fancied trying.'

'What's stopping you?'

'Not a good time, right now. I'm up from the south, escaping the floods for a while. I can't believe what it's like here.'

'I've seen the pictures. Are you moving up here?'

'No, I'm,' he hesitated 'sort of on business.'

'I see. Are you involved with those people at the farm, they look a bit shady, foreigners, Arabs I should say, they never speak.'

'Not exactly involved but I'm staying with them a couple of days.

The man frowned and wound in his line ready to cast again as

Adam watched him, wondering. Then he asked: 'Do you fish at night?'

'Sometimes, why do you ask?'

He pondered what to say but the man seemed genuine. He looked back at the farmhouse, gauging distance to the river and imagining possibilities.

'Might be a good idea to avoid this spot for a few nights,' he said.

The other cast again, concentrating as the fly landed on the water and without turning said: 'Oh yes, why?'

'They're leaving soon, they'll be a lot of comings and goings, you won't get much peace.'

He glanced over his shoulder at Adam. 'I haven't been at all comfortable with those people around, it seems odd, strange. Are you warning me?'

'Just better to be out of the way, maybe.'

They walked on downstream where the river ran more gently over smaller stones. Releasing Hayley's hand he rested on a rock, troubled by cramps in his gut which he recognised from old as pure nerves. The child trotted onto a tiny beach where she spotted another shoal of small fry darting after larvae in shallow water at the edge

He gazed up the river where the fisherman had waded further out into the current, struggling to wind in the straining line as a salmon bolted for freedom.

This guy has a privileged position in life he thought but his pastime in peaceful concentration harms no one. If the terrorists succeed and build the world they wish for the fisherman and his kind would get short shrift, himself included.

Adam had no doubt about what was intended for him once the helicopter landed.

He thought about his home and the floods and how the country had already changed. The rain must eventually stop and the water would go down. Some parts of the lowlands might remain underwater but essentially Britain would recover and return to some semblance of normality.

But if these fanatics accomplished their murderous mission nothing would be the same. The dreadful atrocities shown on screen over the last decades would become reality in a new and alien lifestyle. God only knew what would happen to a child like Hayley. He was saved from going down that road by the phone grunting in his pocket. It was Tim Rogers, his voice sounding full of laughter.

'You gave us an entertaining evening,' he began.

'I suppose you heard it all,' Adam grumbled. 'It was extremely embarrassing.'

'What Benji gave us this morning was even better. Full marks to Kirstie, she plays her part well, they really believe she's one of them.'

'I find it quite frightening, sometimes I'm not sure what to believe.'

'Bloody hell Adam, you must have been tempted.'

'Of course I was but I just couldn't -- and knowing you were all listening didn't help.'

'No, okay, looks like we're getting near boiling point.' Now he was serious.

'They want the chopper, we want them, preferably eliminated, no buggering about with trials, no publicity. They want you to call us, so pretend you have. I'm going to brief you now.'

'We'll come late tomorrow, after dark. It's nearly full moon so we must hope for cloud cover, the darkness will help us. I'll be in charge of the op and I want to impress on you that whatever command I give you, obey it without question. It's life or death and I want us alive.'

'Okay, she's already told me I must obey her so now I'm getting orders from two of you. What if it clashes?'

'It won't.'

'Is that all you can tell me?'

'It's better you don't know any more. We'll make contact when we're close so you're ready for a routine pickup, you, Kirstie and the kid. But you won't be getting on that chopper. Got it?

Another day of waiting, the sunny morning changed to an overcast sky in the early afternoon with intermittent showers of rain. Again he welcomed the rain, musing on the irony after the weeks he'd endured from its incessant onslaught. But rain meant clouds and clouds meant cover.

The Arabs were in high spirits, almost chummy after he'd told them what time the helicopter was due. If they'd been drinkers he'd have said they were intoxicated. Kirstie said they might have taken some drug but most likely they were high on religious fervour and the prospect of achieving their goal. The young one Fahad was pleased with himself, he'd mended the generator in the cellar so the house had power again -- and light.

She and Hayley walked with him again along the river bank and Adam noted the absence of the fisherman. One thing had puzzled him and he asked her. 'I've hardly seen Mr Hassan, he doesn't eat with them any more. Is that significant?'

'He is genuinely tying up loose ends on his deal but he isn't well. He has an ulcer which he's neglected and his appetite is never very good. And he doesn't like Hamza and Fahad.

'Is he part of it?'

Kirstie sighed. 'I honestly don't know, I wish I did because he may pay the price either way.'

'The commander said guilty till proved otherwise.'

'It's a pity,' she said. 'I like him, he's been good to work for.'

They strolled on in silence as Hayley danced ahead of them. 'She loves it here,' Kirstie said.

'She doesn't seem to mind about them, you'd think she'd be frightened.'

'After what she's been through she probably thinks she's on holiday.'

'Some holiday!'

She stopped and called to Hayley. 'When we go back, Adam, keep out of their way,' she warned. 'And get your gun.'

He obeyed, staying put in the bedroom trying to concentrate on a holiday novel from the bookcase but as the day progressed he grew increasingly agitated. His heart raced and he clasped his wrist to feel the quickened pulse. He could almost taste the adrenaline pumping through his body.

He was afraid.

Towards evening he heard movement and bumping noises downstairs. Peering from the landing he watched them bringing up equipment from the cellar, to the room nearest the door, packages and assault rifles. He watched Anton lock the door.

His tension became almost unbearable as dusk turned into true darkness. No stars were visible but the moon was a pale spectre behind the veil of cloud. Each time he crept outside, the clouds seemed to be thinning, skeins of cirrus opening patches of sky. A little before eleven the phone vibrated in his pocket with the expected message.

He went to Kirstie, sitting with the Arabs in the kitchen. 'They'll be here soon, better wake Hayley, they won't want to hang about.'

To Anton he said: 'We'll be out of your way soon now.'

The dark face broke into a sinister smile. 'Our thanks Mr Adam, we will see you safely aboard.'

'I'll listen for the engine,' he said.

He felt safer outside, more in control but a worrying wind had risen making the moon sail in and out between fleeing clouds. Its brightness revealed the landscape for a moment then dimmed again.

He headed towards the river, across the flat space where the helicopter would land, noting that it offered no cover between house and river.

Looking north towards the hills his ears strained to catch the first sound of an approach. Soon he heard the unmistakable drone of a powerful engine and saw the chopper's lights flashing below the clouds.

Suddenly they were swept away and in a moment of full moonlight he saw what looked like giant moths silhouetted against the sky. A cluster dropping rapidly towards the heather covered slopes beyond the farm. Then they were lost in darkness as the moon disappeared again.

He began to run towards the house but stopped to draw the gun from inside his fleece.

He checked the magazine was full, smiling with satisfaction and carried on at walking pace to tell them the transport had arrived. He hung about near the door, not waiting for Kirstie and hurried back into the open air.

The helicopter circled above the farm, down lights illuminating the landing area. He heard the engine change tone as it slowed for descent. It came down swiftly and settled, engine throbbing, the double rotor blades still whirling. He saw Captain Rogers in the open door, smiling at him.

'Here we are, as arranged, are you afraid Adam?'

'Shit scared actually.'

'No shame in fear, it helps the adrenaline kick in. Makes you sharper. Things may move very fast now, we don't know how they'll tackle us so we must think on our feet. Quick reactions needed.'

Adam nodded with a deep intake of breath.

'Try to keep it normal, we're simply collecting two passengers. Get going. Be as quick as you can. And do exactly what I say.'

Everything now was bright from the helicopter's big lights and the farm floodlights. In the yellow oblong of the door he saw the waiting figures, the woman and child and two men.

He walked back to them, calm and casual and Hayley ran to him. Anton and Ahmed watched him approach. Anton flashed him a beaming smile, incongruous in that face. Hanging back he spoke to Kirstie: 'Are you ready?'

'My bag's just here,' she followed Ahmed inside.

'We must hurry, they're on a tight schedule.'

'It's a big machine,' said Hayley, staring at the helicopter.

'Much bigger than the other one,' she peered up at him. 'It looks kind of fierce.'

'It's just ordinary,' he said hurriedly, feeling the sweat damp in his armpits.

Kirstie came out carrying her bag. Ahmed brought two large holdalls, handing one over to Anton. The three of them trooped across the grass behind Adam with Hayley bouncing in excitement, oblivious of the tension. Adam managed to laugh at her, desperate to appear relaxed.

Kirstie said lightly: 'Can they find room for Anton?'

'You must ask the captain. Where's he going?'

'South,' said Anton. 'Transport is difficult with the floods.'

An implausible request but Adam maintained his assumed naivety.

He took Hayley's hand, saying over his shoulder: 'We must hurry.'

In a backward glance he saw the other three Arabs come out from the house, standing back to watch.

The pilot had climbed down and was standing by the tail fin, examining the fuselage. The only man on board was the captain, waiting by the open door.

He frowned as the Arabs approached but greeted them politely, listening to their request. They stood smiling up at him but he told them firmly he couldn't take unauthorised passengers on a military aircraft. They wouldn't take no for an answer and the smiles faded into agitated argument, some of it in Arabic to each other.

'I'm sorry,' he said dismissively, beckoning Kirstie to get aboard 'but I can't take anyone extra without clearance.'

It was high off the ground so he leaned down and took her arm to pull her up. Anton and Ahmed exchanged a sharp look but made no attempt to stop her and Ahmed lifted Hayley to join her mother. Adam put out a hand to climb in but Rogers hissed: 'No!'

Obediently he stepped aside to wait.

The captain was emphatic he couldn't take them but still they persisted. Adam couldn't see the pilot. A single shot sounded from the buildings and suddenly the floodlights were gone. He saw dark shapes moving fast in the shadows and asked: 'Where's Mr Hassan?'

'In the house, his journey is already taken care of.'

To him something jarred in that statement.

'Has he finished his work? Is that why you're leaving?'

'Yes,' Ahmed said with a strange smile. 'His work is finished.'

For a moment the only sound was the chopper's engine then everything changed as the three young Arabs emerged into the light, aiming automatic rifles. Anton whipped out a gun, pointing it at the captain and a heavy pistol appeared in Ahmed's grasp.

Anton spoke, his tone harsh and threatening. 'Okay Mr Captain, we asked nicely and talked long enough, now we will come aboard.'

Adam saw Ahmed take aim at him and ducked, two bullets flashed close as he threw himself to the far side of the chopper. A barrage of shots sounded but he had no notion of what was happening as he rushed back. Ahmed and Anton jumped into the craft as Tim Rogers backed off. They shouted for the other three who came at a run, bundled the holdalls through the door and leapt in. He heard Anton ask: 'Where is the pilot?'

'Checking the fin.'

'We don't need him.'

He nodded to Ahmed who hurried to the controls. Adam heard the engine noise change and raced back as the helicopter began to rise. It all happened so quickly that later he couldn't remember the precise sequence but in that instant the captain flung himself forward, grabbed Kirstie and pushed her out. He saw Hayley crouched close to the captain. The little girl was terrified, screaming, as a spray of bullets passed over her head. Rogers bellowed for Adam and threw the child out into the air. He dashed forward to catch her in his arms, more shots spattering round them. He hit the ground, rolling over and away, hugging

254

her to his chest. An instant later he found himself held firmly by a burly sergeant

Gazing skyward he watched horrified as figures struggled in the open door while the machine rose to tree height and gathered speed. Then a body leapt clear and almost in slow motion fell towards them, legs paddling the air, to land with a sickening thud in the grass. It was Tim Rogers.

Adam tried to get up and go to the silent figure on the ground but he was held in a harsh grip.

'Don't touch him,' shouted the sergeant, speaking rapidly into his phone as more soldiers emerged from the darkness, some running with a stretcher, while others headed for the house.

The noise of the engine was loud in the still night air, heading fast north over barren moorland. The sky was lit by flashes from beyond the farm, sounding like surface to air missiles. His eyes followed the helicopter's lights, diminishing into the distance, the craft unscathed. But then the air seemed split and the ground shook from the force of a massive explosion, an ear-rending blast that made Hayley scream. The hills were illuminated by a huge ball of fire in the sky which continued some way on its course before plunging into the heather.

'Gotcha!' said the sergeant with a grin and in the distance they heard a chorus of cheers.

Stunned, Adam stayed put but Hayley's sobbing brought him back to the moment.

'Where's mummy?' The child's voice wrenched at him: 'Is she dead?'

The sergeant's flashlight ranged across the ground until they spotted Kirstie's body near the trees.

'Stay here, kid,' he ordered but they couldn't stop her running to the unconscious figure. Adam knelt beside her, feeling for heart beat or pulse, then the paramedic was there, pushing him out of the way.

'This arm's broken, maybe an ankle, not sure,' he said. 'She's luckier than the captain.'

Kirstie groaned and her eyelids fluttered.

Hayley was beyond tears, dumb in shock, her face pale with fear. But the soldier ruffled her hair and said: 'Cheer up, sweetheart, she'll be okay. She'll mend.'

Two soldiers carried Kirstie on a stretcher. Adam followed to find others working methodically through the house as they checked for booby traps. He waited by the silent form of Tim Rogers.

'Is he alive?'

'Just about, he's in a bad way -- don't let the kid go in there, sir!' Hayley was headed to the open door of Hassan's office but Adam caught her arm. A soldier took her hand while Adam went through. Hassan was at his desk, face up, head thrown back over the chair, the wall chart behind him splattered with blood and part of his brain.

Adam closed the door hastily: 'So he wasn't part of it.'

'Seems not. We couldn't get inside quick enough to save him. They shot him as they left.'

'Poor guy.'

'He must've had some idea.'

'Perhaps he just trusted them.'

'Maybe. Keep the kid with you, sir. We're out of here soon as.'

Chapter twenty-two

He leaned back dejected in his seat after glancing at the mountains below. Overhead a mass of clouds swept in from the Atlantic. He wanted to be heading home but instead was stuck with the soldiers facing a debrief from Commander Wallace. Hayley was beside him in the helicopter which had landed by the river soon after the other exploded in that ball of fire. Somewhere behind them lay the silent forms of Tim Rogers and Kirstie, sedated for the journey.

The sergeant took the other seat next to Hayley, chatting to them both. Adam didn't want to talk but asked the sergeant: 'How many millions were wasted in that explosion? Surely there was a better way.'

Shrugging, the soldier said: 'HQ must have thought it worth the price. The plan worked well. That chopper was due to be decommissioned anyway, it did the job in one strike, no messing about with trials and evidence. I must say I got a real buzz pressing that button.'

'You detonated it?' Adam thought the missiles had brought it down, his mind on the lives snuffed out. 'What a dreadful responsibility.'

'I don't see it like that,' replied the sergeant. 'It was orders. I wouldn't waste your sympathy on them. They planned to kill millions.'

He didn't reply, thinking it over before saying: 'You're right, they were totally ruthless. There was no need to kill Hassan and they would've killed me. What about the captain, what are his chances?'

'I don't know, I'm not a medic but he's in a bad way. But we've got some of the very best doctors, if anyone can save him, they will. We'll be there in a few minutes.'

They circled over the base and he watched the white cross on the pad grow larger to meet them.

They were there three days while he fretted, shut in underground, wistful for the sunlit days in the heather at Ettrick. He answered a lot of questions but got no answers, either about Kirstie or Tim Rogers. Hayley occupied most of his time. After her initial excitement she was bored and anxious to know about her mother. He couldn't understand why she wasn't allowed to see her. On the last evening at supper Rachel, efficient as ever, said casually: 'They've done with you now, sending you home tomorrow. Be ready for 08:00 hours.'

That was it.

He climbed the metal stairway eager for fresh air but the Scottish weather had changed, loch and mountains hidden in mist. They boarded the small chopper gratefully, glad the sergeant they knew was in charge.

As they flew south the mist turned into light rain and once across the border into Cumbria, the downpour increased, making him sigh with frustration. He had hoped the good weather indicated a general improvement. But when the chopper landed he dropped into the same muddy quagmire he'd left. His heart sank. He trudged across the field in drizzle, carrying Hayley to keep her clear of the mud. She clung to him again, reluctant to let go. He stopped once to look back and raised a hand to the sergeant watching them, strangely heartened when he waved in return. He stood in the rain as the helicopter disappeared, desperately lonely in the depression of anticlimax. Hayley said: 'He was a kind man.' He saw her tears, knowing she was equally despondent.

The sight of his home appalled him, untidy and packed with a gawping crowd. He knew more had arrived but wasn't prepared for the impact on the place. After the near sterile surroundings of the bunker the smell assailed him. He felt almost sick and disappeared upstairs, thankful for the bedroom as a sanctuary. Hayley tried to follow but the eager boys waylaid her.

He lay down to wait, wanting Sally to come; he'd glimpsed her through the kitchen door, surrounded by people and crockery. But it was Ben who came. 'Are you hungry, Dad?'

He shook his head. 'Not really, where's your mum?'

'Feeding time!'

'Ask her to come.' Torn between longing to see her and an odd reluctance, his mind was back at Ettrick with Kirstie. The memory shamed him. When Sally came he was shocked to see her, a tired woman with untidy hair in a stained T-shirt, making comparison unavoidable.

She closed the door but stayed back from him, feeling grubby when he looked clean and untouchable. This wasn't the way it should be after so much fear. Unwilling to face him she stared at the floor until he said: 'Sally.'

She peered up into his searching eyes as he said: 'Come here.'

She knelt beside him, head in his lap while he wiped a mark from her cheek.

She sobbed: 'I didn't want it to be like this.' He pulled her up and held her, rocked in his arms while she cried.

When she had to go he stayed sprawled there, staring at the ceiling. Later she brought the last of the whisky and they drank it together but when she tried to question him he shut down. 'I can't talk about it, not yet.'

She felt excluded and was silent until he asked: 'Is John still here?'

'Of course, he's kept everything going.'

'I want him gone. I don't want to see him.'

She resented that and spoke harshly. 'That's not fair. These last few days have been awful. I couldn't have coped without either of them and she's done nothing wrong, you can't come back here and kick them out. They must stay at least until things get back to something like normal.'

She waited for an answer but he said nothing, until at last: 'Do you think life will ever be normal again?'

He didn't see anything of the boys until the morning when Tom appeared, diffident and embarrassed. 'How are you dad?'

'I'm okay.'

'Was it bad?'

'Bad enough.'

Tom studied his father on the bed. 'Are you going stay up here?'

'For a bit, I'll have to face it soon.'

The boy had hoped for a more enthusiastic greeting. 'You haven't seen John then?' he asked.

'No, he's kept out of my way.'

Tom brought a chair over and sat by Adam. 'Look dad, you don't have to worry. Mum told me what you thought about John and me. But there's nothing at all like that. He's a great guy but I always thought he was a bit that way.'

Adam was surprised. 'Really?'

'I know all about that stuff, plenty of it at school.' He grinned. 'But I'm straight, I like girls, Abi and me are an item, we're close, y'know.'

'You haven't been —' Adam said sharply.

'Hell no, fat chance of that, not in this place, no privacy anywhere.'

'She seems a nice girl,' Adam muttered. 'I don't really know her.'

'No, you don't .You're so bogged down with everything but if we get out of this and it's anything like normal, I want to keep on seeing her. We're good together, dad.'

Then, as if it explained everything, he said proudly: 'I'm almost fifteen.'

He thought he hadn't been seen, drawn to the barn by a morbid need to inspect the bodies. With a hand over his face he gazed sadly at the body bags, the bulky bundle that was Philip with the child beside him. Their silent presence reproached him: 'I'm so sorry, Philip,' he whispered in the fetid air. 'There must've been something we could've done.'

'There wasn't!' He turned to face John who'd followed him.

'You.'

'Yes, you did all you could. Pre-existing medical conditions, just bad luck they were with us.'

'I feel so guilty.'

'Don't, forget the dead. There's enough to do with the living.'

John looked sideways at him. 'I suppose you want me to leave.'

'I do, yes. But Sally says we need you. And I won't upset her by making you go.'

'There's a lot more people here now,' John said. 'It's hard to deal with, the girls are exhausted.'

Adam was silent so John went on. 'I like your sons, especially Tom but that's all. I never had any designs on them. I thought we were friends.'

'So did I. But you lied from the start.'

'I didn't think -- ' he began but Adam burst out: 'Why weren't you honest about it? You lied about why you left teaching. I hate deceit.'

'I should've told you the truth but I was scared to. I've tried to make up for it in all this.'

'Maybe,' Adam shrugged. 'But things'll never be the same.'

'I realise that.' John sighed miserably. 'Let's get out of here. I'll give you an update.'

They stood together in the drizzle while he listened to a list of problems.

Each day's worst task was fetching water from the old brick well, the only source of drinkable water. The new pipeline had failed after just two days, probably an airlock, but it couldn't be fixed. So now a team of men had to lug heavy containers across the fields. For any sort of washing it was rain water.

Heating water, even for drinks was difficult. The last gas cylinder ran out the day after he left for Scotland and the only alternative was the wood burner. But without dry wood it was torture to light. The log stack was wet and even the small amount in the barn was damp.

Worst of all they were short of food again. The last drop had brought less than expected and more stragglers had arrived since.

'Good to be back!' He said with a hollow laugh.

'We're hoping for a drop any time but Ron doesn't say much.'

'They promised me you'd be looked after if I helped them.' It seemed like betrayal. 'Is there any good news?'

John raised a hand and said: 'We're getting more of this.'

'What?'

'Drizzle. It hasn't rained heavily for nearly five days. It's been like this.'

'That's not much comfort,' Adam was dismissive.

'It's something, it could mean the weather's starting to change.'

'Let's hope you're right.'

Being with John inflamed his temper and he left abruptly. The house stank and in growing fury he began flinging windows open. He wedged both doors wide to let air blow through, ignoring the protests and laughing as they shivered.

'Didn't any of you think to open a window?' he roared.

He felt guilty closeted upstairs but couldn't bear to face the horde of people, gripped by a lethargy he couldn't shrug off. He roused himself enough to remember his blog, annoyed by the lack of electricity.

But he began scribbling his thoughts on paper. He couldn't tell the world what happened, even if the net came back, it was all classified information but putting it down might clarify his feelings, mostly of guilt and frustration.

I can't get rid of the image, Tim falling from the helicopter, it haunts me. I keep wondering what I could've done to avoid it. The way his body crumpled when he hit the ground was horrible. And I still don't know how he is. I can't get hold of anybody, Harrison or Ron. I think they've forgotten all about me, now I've done what they wanted.

And this isn't my home any more, with ninety plus lodgers hanging around everywhere, I'm beginning to hate it. As for John, well, I won't go against Sally on that.

The worst thing is this guilt about her. When we're together I feel ashamed and she shies away from me at night and I have no urge to remedy that. I didn't do anything with Kirstie but I was unfaithful just the same, in my head. Because I did want Kirstie, wanted her very much. I would've done it but something held me back. Perhaps I should have had her. Sally keeps asking what she's done wrong and I tell her nothing, that I love her. And I do but when I get near her I imagine the other one. God only knows if it'll go away.

The phone roused him and he swore as it fell on the floor when he grabbed for it. 'Who is it?'

'Ron, what's wrong?'

'What's right?'

'I knew you were back, a major coup, well done.'

'Is that it? I've heard nothing from anyone. I can't get any answers. I don't even know if Tim Rogers is alive or dead. I thought you at least might have called me.'

'I would've but it's frantic keeping track of everything.'

'You said they'd look after this place but we're desperate for food.'

'I've done my best, that's why I've rung. There'll be a drop tomorrow.'

John was right about the weather, it was improving. The drizzle became a heavy mist which hung around until driven away by a warm breeze from the south, revealing the hills and trees on the skyline.

Hayley had missed him when he shut himself away. But he took her each day to the spot where the boys had built their cairn of stones. They strolled down the lane as a ghost of the sun struggled in an overcast sky. The drizzle was easing again and the sun broke through. At the water's edge their toes were lapped by the flood.

Hayley looked across the water and pointed: 'Look — the rainbow! There's two of them.'

The upper arc was bright against the pallid sky, the other a faint image, fading fast. But something else made her much more excited. 'I can see the stones,' she shouted.

The top of the cairn was visible a few metres out and Adam squatted beside her to look. The little girl asked: 'Does it mean the water's going down?'

'Looks that way.'

'So everything will be all right?'

He hugged her, realising much how he would miss her about the place. 'It looks promising,' he said.

'Come on,' Hayley pulled hard at him to get up. 'We must tell them.'

'No, not yet,' he said quietly, smiling at her eagerness. 'We mustn't raise their hopes.'

'But it's going down.'

'Yes, but it might rain again. Better not to tell till we're sure.'

Her face puckered for tears but he said: 'It's our secret, right. We'll come every day and check and when we're sure, we'll tell them. You can tell them, okay?'

'It'll be me that tells them all?' He anxious eyes peered up at him.

'Yes but not yet.'

At last he heard from the colonel with an attempt at an apology. 'I know you feel abandoned but there's been so much to deal with.'

'I can't get any information, especially about Tim Rogers.'

'I'm sorry but we are grateful for what you did. You may not think it was much but your presence at the farm made all the difference. There'll be some kind of official recognition eventually, a gong maybe or an honour for you and Mrs Lomax and the captain.'

'Thank God he's all right,' Adam exclaimed.

'I wouldn't say that. The sad truth is his back was broken in the fall. They've tried everything, they flew him to the States but the spinal cord was severed. It's unlikely he'll ever walk again.'

The improving weather encouraged most of them to get outside, increasingly keen to help.

Hayley always raced ahead of him on their mission to the flood line, impatient to gauge any change. Came the day he heard her happy shout and found her by the cairn, a good metre from the water.

'It's really going, I told you.'

The water line along the valley sides was definitely lower. Marker points such as trees and building tops were visible. 'Can we tell them now?' she pleaded.

He grinned at her. 'All right, you can tell them. Shall we have a meeting or just let you run about shouting?'

The boys were jubilant that their marker cairn had worked so well but they let Hayley make the most of her role in telling everyone. People trooped down the lane to stare at the gently lapping water steadily ebbing further from the pile of stones.

He regretted taking the boys. The road below Banks Bottom was strewn with the corpses of small mammals, including rabbits, rats and squirrels, mixed with dead leaves and branches in a stinking tangle of slime where the retreating flood had left them.

They saw several dead badgers and a couple of foxes before they reached the village and the boys, chatting eagerly on this first outing for months, were stunned into silence.

The pretty village was desolate, its stone smothered green. Some windows gaped empty, others still held glass, opaque with dirt and algae. Open doors and ruined gardens bore witness to the months of filthy water. Awed by the eerie stillness they entered the church to find tumbled chaos. In the nave precious ornaments lay jumbled together with the cross, while the ancient frescoes decorating the apse were mired in slime.

Behind the altar a tree branch had smashed through the lower section of the medieval stained glass. Only the arched tips on the angels' golden wings and an upraised hand remained of the two figures at the feet of Christ. His ruby-red raiment with the dove of peace above still sparkled as the brilliance of the reborn sun shone through. Along the aisle, many of the ancient ceramic tiles were smashed and detritus trailed from the brass chandeliers.

Tom whispered in the silence: 'Can it ever be like before?'

Adam hugged him for the first time since his return. 'It'll take a long time to put right. But listen.'

They became aware of the loud harsh cries of birds and out-side looked up to see hundreds of wings soaring above the fields, an agitated black flock of crows, rooks and jackdaws, squealing in angry competition. Buzzards and kites too and gulls, all following the ebbing flood and its harvest of death.

The trees were skeletal, bearing horrors instead of leaves. Dead cattle lay in the fields and a few horses. Rotting sheep lay in drifts like dirty snow against fences where the receding water had left them stranded, pathetic heaps of muddy fleece to be consumed by the scavenging birds.

Torn between revulsion and fascination, the boys watched several black-backed gulls tearing savagely at the bloated carcass of a horse.

266

'Those filthy birds!' Ben cried but Adam said: 'It's horrible to see, but they're actually doing a good job.'

Tom thought about that. 'You're right, that's their role on the earth, isn't it? They've begun the clean up.'

Gradually the water slid away, revealing more victims. He was caught off guard by Ron's call, hoping it was news about moving people. 'You'll have to keep them for a while yet. I've got bad news for your little girl, sorry. They've found her granny.'

'Dead?'

'Yes, she must've got a taxi that day. It was stuck under a bridge twenty miles down river, four people in it. Must've been swept away and into the river as the water rose.'

'You're sure it's her?'

'Driving licence ID.'

Adam didn't answer. 'You still there?' Ron asked.

'Poor kid won't be surprised,' he murmured.

He followed reluctantly when John marshalled helpers for another delivery. This time they waited in sunshine as the small helicopter flew in.

'You're a welcome sight,' he greeted the young lieutenant.

The officer smiled bleakly: 'First decent load we've had for weeks.'

Adam nodded. 'We'll be glad of it. I've got a very hungry bunch here.'

The young man looked clean and handsome in his fatigues. He hesitated before asking: 'Any news of Captain Rogers?'

The bleak expression came back. 'He's still in a bad way.' He paused: 'Might've been better if he'd been killed outright.'

'Don't say that!' He knew that voice and felt a faint tremor in his heart as the lieutenant helped her forward. She rounded on the soldier: 'It's early days, they said there could be more improvement. He's alive, that's what matters.'

'If you say so, ma'am but given the choice, I think the captain would've had it different.'

Kirstie's angry look focused on him. 'Adam, good to see you. Get me off this thing.'

He hurried to help and half-lifted her from the chopper, overwhelmed by the sensation of touching her again. With an arm still in plaster and a sling she was mobile with the aid of a stick.

She was thinner but still beautiful and he said: 'You're looking good.'

'No, I look bloody awful -- but I'm getting there.'

A small figure darted from the crowd to clutch her mother round the legs so fiercely that he grabbed her but Kirstie laughed: 'It's okay, I can stand a hug from my daughter.'

She bent to kiss the sobbing child. 'Don't cry, sweetheart. I'm here now.'

'You won't go away again?'

'No, I'll stay here till we have a new home of our own.'

'You won't find it very homely,' he said. 'The house is packed, bodies everywhere, I don't know where we'll put you.'

'I'll just doss down with Hayley.'

'She's in our room, along with the boys.'

'I don't mind, as long as I can get my leg comfortable.'

An awkward silence developed as they walked slowly to the house, eased only by Hayley's chatter. The prospect of having Kirstie in the same room was unsettling. But it was the only sensible option, the only place with space. She wasn't family but she was Hayley's mum.

The landing, corridor and the hall downstairs were all sleeping space for the flood victims. Some even slept in the kitchen, with Jock and Amy, in there to stop anyone stealing food.

September brought incredible contrasts, sunshine, blue heaven and achingly beautiful sunsets. The sun drew them all out like a magnet, the morning light dazzled, glinting on dew-bright grass, turning the gossamer wisps of spider webs to a silver path.

He could almost believe none of it had happened, that it was all a bad dream. But he missed the birds. Most of the songbirds which usually flocked round the farm were gone and the swallows had vanished weeks before. The tiny travellers who had returned so eagerly in April, to nests in barn and stables, had long ago flown home, driven away by hunger and cold in the lost summer.

The weary group were treated to an Indian summer, most appreciating for the first time the glorious landscape around them. Spectacular light shows entertained them as the sun sank at evening, clouds laced with a chain of crimson, or gold-tinted cumulus against a pastel sky.

Adam, content on his own, sat on the wall watching the sun, with Polly close by. The sound of footsteps made him turn as Jane Bryston approached. 'May I join you?' she asked gently.

'Of course.' She'd aged since Philip died. Deeper lines etched her face, the hair was a whiter grey but she smiled and touched his arm.

'How are you? We don't see much of you. So much to cope with and it's not over yet.'

'I wonder if it ever will be.'

'What's troubling you?'

He shook his head.

'Tell me.'

'I should have done more in all this.'

'But you've done so much.'

'It's not just here,' he said. 'It's Tim, you remember, the young captain. I can't get it out of my mind, when he fell. It seemed to take for ever before he hit the ground.'

She squeezed his hand. 'It's shock, a thing like that takes time to go but it will fade. You shouldn't feel guilty, after what you've done. You saved all these people.'

'I had no choice. But what about you? You must miss Philip.'

'Of course I do. I'd like him to be properly at rest.'

'I know, it's so undignified, I'm sorry.'

'It doesn't matter. When the light left his eyes, that was him, gone. You were so kind.'

'You take it very calmly.'

'What else can I do? Death comes to us all, but for him sooner than we'd hoped.'

He met her kind eyes saying: 'I liked Philip, he'd be alive if we'd got the drugs.'

'But you couldn't get them, it wasn't your fault.'

'But the army thing and the ark nonsense got in the way of what I should've been doing.'

'But you helped stop a vicious plot. You did your bit. I told you before, your ark is real.' She gestured around the farm, to people strolling and chatting. 'You saved these people. They'd probably be dead if you hadn't taken them in.'

'I had no choice,' he repeated.

'Those people on Ruttock Common wouldn't have survived but for you, and all the rest. But look, your ark even has ravens.'

He heard the beat of their wings in the still air. Ravens had nested in the Scots pines nearby for nearly thirty years but their trees had vanished in the flood, only the tops were clear. The huge black birds had gone away. Maybe this was them, back to reclaim their home and perhaps in the spring there would be a new nest in the treetop.

The cooling air sent Jane indoors but he remained, happy in the clean air of twilight. Over the silent landscape the moon was rising, huge and luminous, a harvest moon, its ancient face peering at the earth like a blessing. Polly spotted the unfamiliar sight and dashed barking across the field. 'Barking at the moon, Polly!' he laughed. 'It's a long time since we saw one like that.' She trotted back, tail wagging in pleasure.

With Polly barking he didn't hear Kirstie come up behind him. But he sensed her presence and said without turning: 'Why have you come?'

'We never have a chance to talk.'

'Do we need to talk?'

'You obviously find it difficult having me around,' she said softly.

He faced her then. 'Yes and not just me, it's awkward for Sally, having you in our room. I think she feels somehow diminished, second best in your company. It's as if she knows something.'

'There's nothing to know.'

'No,' he sounded wistful. 'But there might as well have been.'

'Does that mean you regret the night we never had?'

'I can't answer that.' He moved closer, cupping her chin to tilt her face towards him, wanting so much to kiss her. 'But I tell you, when this is all over you and I must never meet again.'

'That's very final.'

'It has to be. I'll be glad when you go, though I'll miss Hayley. She's a great kid.'

'Don't worry, the colonel's finding somewhere for us. It shouldn't be long.'

'Kirstie, I --' Swiftly she reached up, their mouths met and the familiar thrill surged through him before he pulled away.

She gave him a strange smile and sighed. 'Glad I met you, Adam, in another life maybe -- who knows?'

He watched her walk away in the half light.

Each day he searched for signs of change and renewal, studying the stricken land, leached and drained of colour, soured by long weeks under water. A silage crop still lay ribbed in rotting rows, hedgerow trees were bare, their autumn branches stripped long ago and patches of dried mud showed where new seed would never germinate this season. Dead grass made a brown shroud for the fields.

Across the valley a farmer ploughed resolutely, burying under each furrow the soggy remnants of his spring wheat, only fit as manure for a future yield.

The harvest was totally lost and he wondered how many farmers could hang on. His sombre thoughts were disturbed by the throaty cooing of two pigeons, oblivious of his presence, sidling along the roof ridge in a late mating tryst.

271

Afterword

On a bright spring morning he left the house for his usual walk, the sun shining above Rueberry Down. He couldn't yet fully reclaim his home but the numbers were dwindling as people were rehoused and the power and water were back. He stayed away when he could, walking with Polly or just sitting.

On the opposite slope a wild May breeze was shaking the barley, running through the young green corn like ripples on water. Rabbits basked in the sun near burrows in the bank and overhead he saw the ravens harassing a pair of buzzards too near their nest in the pines.

He had come to inspect the sheep his neighbour had brought yesterday, ewes and lambs purchased in the north to join what was left of his original flock. They picked eagerly at the lush new grass.

Polly startled them and they ran a short distance on bouncing hooves before they turned to study man and dog and stamp a warning foot. Enchanted he watched them prance in excitement, butting heads together before dashing to their mothers to suckle. His heart lifted as the ewes' heads tipped either side to nuzzle each wagging rump

What did you think of Adam's Ark?

Thank you for buying it when there are so many to choose from.

I hope you found some meaning and enjoyment in its pages, depicting a scenario which could so easily become reality if we don't tackle the creeping threat of climate change which is destroying our beautiful planet.

Perhaps you could share the book with your friends and family by posting on social media.

If you enjoyed it maybe you could spare the time to write a review, because your opinion is important.

About the author

Frances Brand lives in Shropshire, in the west of England among the glorious countryside of the Marches where a raven can fly quickly over the border into Wales. She left a career in journalism to open her hilltop home as a bed and breakfast and gain more time to write.

Her last job was editing a farming newspaper, working closely with farmers and others involved in agriculture which revealed the problems and vicissitudes of 21st-century farming.

She spends a great deal of time outdoors, watching wildlife and in tune with nature around the Shropshire Hills and the seasonal rhythms which can often reveal changing aspects of the climate. Her passion for nature, the local landscape and the power of the elements is often reflected in her writing.

At one time she and her husband stood a stallion at stud and for several years she evented successfully with a home-bred horse.

She finds running a guest house often gives a fascinating insight into human behaviour and sparks many trains of thought. Some guests inspire immediate empathy while others can sometimes seem alien.

Life is also kept busy caring for her dogs and elderly horses.

Printed in Great Britain
by Amazon